The
Temple
House
Vanishing

The
Temple
House
Vanishing

Rachel Donohue

CORVUS

Published in Great Britain in 2020 by Corvus, an imprint of
Atlantic Books Ltd.

10 9 8 7 6 5 4 3 2 1

A CIP catalogue record for this book is available from the
British Library.

Hardback ISBN: 978 1 78649 938 7
Trade paperback ISBN: 978 1 83895 024 8
E-book ISBN: 978 1 78649 940 0

Printed and bound by CPI Group (UK) Ltd, Croydon, CR0 4YY

Corvus
An imprint of Atlantic Books Ltd
Ormond House
26–27 Boswell Street
London
WC1N 3JZ

www.corvus-books.co.uk

To Ger, Ava and Charlotte.

We had fed the heart on fantasies,
The heart's grown brutal from the fare;
More substance in our enmities
Than in our love…

W.B. Yeats, 'The Stare's Nest by my Window'

Because strait is the gate, and narrow is the way,
which leadeth unto life, and few there be that find it.

Matthew 7:14

Prologue

The Journalist

I picture Victoria standing at the window of her office high above the city that morning. The face that must have once been lovely reflected in the dark glass, tired and wasted now. She holds the phone out from her, like it is a tasteless thing. My voice at the other end echoes into the bare room. The boxes stacked; shelves cleared.

I know there is a newspaper on her desk. They are delivered early to her floor. And that he, Mr Lavelle, is staring at her from the corner of page five, with my words underneath. He is like a spectre from the past, leaning against the bonnet of a car, his fair head looking slightly away from the camera, eyebrows raised. He looks dishevelled for a teacher, the collar of his tweed coat tilted up, the face unshaven. But beautiful, there is no doubting that. It's there in the symmetry of the bones and the evenness of the gaze. A sort of luminous quality to him. A face you would stop to look at, remember.

I think about how long she must have spent staring at the picture. And what it meant.

But Victoria didn't want to talk to me any more about him, or Louisa. She said nothing mattered much now. Her voice flat and listless. And this, in a strange way, was true. It was the end, not the beginning. The future, like the past, was already set. She hung up the phone then. She had no need for my intrusions any more.

I sat for a while on the edge of my bed. The early-morning light leaking in under the curtains. A weary, sleepless, draining night just gone. Victoria was leaving it all up to me. The responsibility of telling another's story. And it didn't surprise me.

It was reported afterwards that she cancelled her meetings for the rest of the week. She also deleted files and ordered flowers for her mother. No one, however, noticed anything particularly odd about her behaviour. She passed through the beige rituals of that day as she did every other.

A colleague was quoted as saying she ate lunch alone at her desk, and that this was not unusual.

Another said that Victoria had looked like she was bored or distracted at their last meeting. The sky outside of the window that evening seemed to catch her attention more than the conversation within. Several times she apologized for having lost her way in the discussion and checked her mobile.

But this was not an ordinary day. It had not been an ordinary life.

When the office emptied that evening, Victoria climbed the narrow stairs to the roof garden ten storeys high.

The garden where clients were entertained in the summer and junior associates were plied with free drink and promised opportunities for greatness.

A place where in the past I'm sure she had stood silently in the evening sun, waiting for the appropriate moment to leave.

The roof garden where you might walk to the edge of the building and pit the force of your life and all its glassy achievements against the strength of your desire to experience a fall.

The place where Victoria chose to take off her shoes, climb over the low, neat, box hedge that served as a barrier and then jump, unseen into the dark night.

A silent, resolute descent.

I imagine she thought about Louisa. But then, I will never know.

She remained conscious of reputation to the end. She fell not to the front, where she might have crashed through the shiny white atrium and on to the expensive Italian marble tiles, but to the back of the building, where there are bike racks, and the ground is littered with cigarette butts. Where Security wouldn't find her until the morning.

I know this because I went to see it for myself, the place where she fell. I stood behind the police line and looked up at the grey sky.

And I thought of Mr Lavelle and how once, when Louisa and Victoria were young, he had told them the fates might choose to come to the rescue of a hero.

But he had been wrong. I should have told her that.

There are no heroes in this story.

Louisa

Chapter One

I dream of it still, the school by the sea. It's always that first September day that returns. My legs warm and sticking to the plastic seats of the car. The radio drifting in and out of coverage. My parents awkward in their Sunday best. The half-opened map lying on the dashboard, slipping off every now and then. No one speaking.

Finally, the black sign for Temple House hanging off a crumbling granite pillar. My father turning slowly through the rusting, wrought-iron gates and up the winding, gravel driveway. The light more green than gold now, soft and low under the tall trees. The sense of hush as we finally emerge from shade to the edge of the cliffs, the sky stretching in front of us. The drive is narrow and sandy here, a sense of journey's end. I press my head to the cool glass, my curiosity like a fever. My suitcase and all that it signifies beside me on the seat. I open the window, strain my neck but can't see below to the waves, only sky and white birds. The air cool on my face.

Am I happy? I can't remember now.

A thin film of dust or sand is thrown up and smears the windscreen. The drive swerves away from the coast, the path is more uneven. We pass between tall, thick yew trees, a last gateway, before a green lawn opens in front of us. The cliffs fenced off with a small warning sign. There is a large pond, leaves and dirt gathering in the corners of the pale water, and beyond this, net-less tennis courts locked up since summer term ended.

In my dream, Temple House, in all its Victorian, turreted austerity, emerges from a mist but this must surely be a trick of memory. Though in truth, that winter of 1990, it did have its own climate. Even the sunniest of days elsewhere could be grey and dull there due to its exposed position high above the sea. There are girls, certainly, standing on the wide granite steps waiting to greet the new students. The prefects. Their long hair and black cloaks flapping in the wind as they wait to welcome us. There is a nun behind them in the deep, arched porch. She is ticking off the list of new students. The fourth-year scholarship girls arriving the Sunday after term begins.

I step from the car to the smell of seaweed that blows in from the beach. The air salty and colder, suddenly it seems, than September should allow. The car door is whipped from my hand and slams. The house looms over us. It is red brick, three storeys tall, with large windows, their frames painted a deep green. Thick ivy reaches up to touch the lower sills. One side of the house is shaped like a tower and protrudes forcefully from the rest of the building. The windows look dark in the early-evening light, shades pulled low, giving it a subdued, half-eyed gaze.

As we ascend the steps I look upwards. There are three girls watching us arrive from a large, arched window on the second floor. They are framed in an edging of stained glass and are standing in what I would come to understand was the Maiden's Chamber. The turn in the stairs.

The dream always ends here.

I know we, the scholarship girls, were greeted by the nun with the list, Sister Ignatius. She was a small, dainty woman, dressed in the navy and black habit of the order. Quietly spoken, she shook my parents' hands, directing us through the porch to a sitting room on the left of the hall where there were refreshments. There was an air of curt efficiency about her. Nothing wasted in her movements. As I walked past I glanced at her profile, she looked like a silent bird of prey. It might have been her nose, which was slightly beaked, and the way she had of turning her head very slowly. Her face was white, chalk white, and fine boned. I understood when you became a nun you took a different name. I wondered did any of them mind doing this, or were they just like the other women, like my mother who took my father's name when she married and pretended to be happy. All their old selves forgotten, packed away along with their records and books.

We entered a hallway, dark wood panelling on the walls and polished orange and black tiles on the floor, the pattern in the shape of a spiral. There was a smell of pine and lemon and behind that, very faintly, meat. A room off the hall had a sign on the door: 'Visitors'. We entered and one of the prefects, without speaking, poured tea into china cups. She had long, fair hair and around her neck there was a small silver cross on a chain. It dangled down as she leaned over the teapot. After pouring it she left the cups on the table and sat by the window, her head turned from us.

The room itself was large, brighter than the hall, with a high ceiling and the walls were painted a pale green. They were bare except for a large portrait of a nun and a crucifix. The floor was covered with linoleum, also green, and in places there were slight rips.

The prefect said nothing and stared out to the sea.

Eventually, the two other scholarship girls and their families joined us, along with Sister Ignatius. We stared silently and morosely at each other across the table. One of the girls kept biting her nails. The other hunched her shoulders in the chair and looked like she might cry. After a summer of shorts and T-shirts, my uniform felt itchy and constrictive. Sister Ignatius spoke a few words of welcome but so quietly and with such economy it was nearly impossible to hear. She barely opened her mouth, her lips were thin, tight.

My father almost slipped off the couch in his attempts to lean in and listen. My mother looked dazed and slightly confused as to how we had ended up here. She had also worn too much make-up and looked out of place, desperate somehow. Not that the other mothers looked much better; one woman wore a white tracksuit top. We looked cheap and our insecurities made us act as if we were suspicious of each other. Furtive. After some moments of awkward silence, Sister Ignatius clapped her hands gently, like an emperor whose quiet but insistent whims must be met. The prefect jumped to her feet. Awake again.

I don't remember if I hugged my parents as we said goodbye, but I imagine not. It wasn't our thing.

It has stayed with me for another reason too. That day. It was the first time I saw a dead body. After our parents left, the prefects led us to a small cloakroom off the hall where we dropped our bags. One of the girls addressed the group, telling us a nun, Sister Josephine, had died the night before and was laid out in the school's small church. The girl who spoke had dark red hair caught in a bun, and pale skin. Her eyes were grey and large. Her name was Helen. We walked behind her, down a long corridor with a polished parquet floor. The walls were lined with framed photographs – the hockey team of 1962, the debating team of 1979, the graduation ball of 1985. All of the faces frozen in time, with awkward smiles and bad hairstyles.

The church was accessed through a heavy door, which I would later learn led to the nuns' quarters. It was dark after the fluorescent lights of the hallway and it took a second for my eyes to get used to the gloom. It was tiny, like a church designed for a doll's house. It was lit by tall, white candles, laid out all around the altar, and the whole space smelt strongly of the same lemon polish of the other rooms. There were only eight pews in total. The altar, carved out of white marble with a vein of dark pink running through it, seemed too large.

The nun was laid out in an open coffin with thick cream satin lining the inside. The prefects led us to the front row and indicated that we should kneel. I was last into the pew and so my head was level with the dead nun. I could feel her pale, silent presence out of the corner of my eye. We all went on our knees, heads bowed. What prayer might I have said? 'Oh Lord, don't forsake me' possibly. Is that even a prayer? I find all the words and incantations that we repeated are gone now. Dissolved.

We stayed there in silence for what seemed like an age but was probably only five minutes. I was to get used to the sense of time suspended when you entered the church. The girls around me shifted uncomfortably. One stuck her fingernail into the centre of her palm and was slowly twisting it deeper into the skin, another was breathing quickly, short, tight breaths. Like her heart was shuddering.

As we got up to leave, I looked at the deceased nun full-on. Her hands were clasped together on her chest. She was holding a large wooden rosary, the crucifix intertwined between her wrinkled fingers. Her face, unlike her hands, was mostly unlined, taut, and a few strands of grey hair were visible under the wimple. She didn't look asleep, as I thought dead people might, but empty, like a hollow doll. It was the gap the soul left when it transcended to God. You weren't really a person any more. Just a vessel, vacated. I had read about this.

One of the other new girls said she felt unwell and two of the prefects led her out. There was always one. The prefects put their arms around her shoulders, smiles of satisfaction on their faces, as if this had been the appropriate response and the plan had worked. Find the hysteric. The rest of us trailed out behind them, tracing our steps back along the corridor. The girls staring out at us in the photos on the walls seemed more sympathetic to me now, like we had shared in some initiation.

Afterwards, we were brought to our rooms. We dragged our bags up the stairs, passing under the large window above the stairwell where the three girls had watched our arrival, panels of blue and red light reflected on the floor. The wallpaper was salmon-coloured and textured but in places mottled and peeling, as if the sea air was seeping through. The stairs to the third floor were narrow, less grand. My room was spacious, with a window that overlooked the forest that lay at the edge of the school grounds. I would learn later that the rooms with sea views went to the girls whose parents made donations to the school. There was a small bookcase and a desk beside my bed. The walls were white and empty, bar a crucifix that hung above the door and a large photograph of a nun holding a chalice. It was one of those pictures that was originally black and white but looked like it had been coloured in by crayon. The chalice was a gleaming yellow and her eyes an unnatural blue.

I was to share with a girl from the year ahead of me, Alice. As I unpacked my case she entered the room and sat on her bed. She was tall and broad, fresh-faced, her hair fair and curly. She immediately asked me what subjects I was taking and had I ever boarded before. I asked her where the other students were; the house was eerily quiet. She seemed not to hear me and began brushing her hair. I thought we might be due back downstairs that evening for a talk with Sister Ignatius and a chance to meet others from my class. Alice indicated no, we were to stay in our room and she would help me get settled. After all, I must be tired.

She told me then that the 'drama' girl in the chapel had apparently thought she saw the eyelids of the nun quiver as she lay in her coffin. I hung up my few clothes and laughed along with her at the girl's stupidity. We didn't speak much after this. But later that night, when the lights went out and Alice was asleep, I lay there thinking about resurrection and how it might be the worst thing ever. You don't want to see the dead rise, no matter how much you might miss them. That first night in the hard, narrow bed was long. By midnight all I could think of was the nun climbing out of her coffin and walking the corridors in search of her missing soul. Her rosary beads dragging along the floor behind her.

It began with death, my time in Temple House.

Chapter Two

Of course we were all bored. Bored and in search of meaning.

I have tried to remember who I was that autumn and winter of 1990, what was my defining feature. Maybe there was nothing that distinguished me, and that in itself could possibly be the answer. I do know I wanted to be seen as different, special. But then, doesn't everyone?

I try not to analyse my past. I mostly choose to actively fake my existence. To reinvent it as something different, something I have only a casual interest in. It is how I cope. On my last day at the school, lying in the grass, with the sea below me, I stitched the undamaged bits back together and then covered over the rest with new material. I created a new philosophy for existing that has guided me these past twenty-five years. I never attempt to understand anyone; I just observe them. They are truly the other. You can never know anyone. There are no soulmates, man or woman, just other minds and other histories. Intimacy is a kind of dream.

This approach has served me well and I only changed, thought differently about it, after Victoria jumped from the roof of her offices.

At Victoria's funeral I had a sudden vision of her. Her divorce had just been finalized and she was in overbearing mode, ordering wine and insisting people try the shellfish. Control was her way of handling failure, which divorce is, I suppose. She was talking about taking a leave of absence from work and going travelling. As I remembered her, I thought about how she had become an idea to me long before she died. We had no way of listening to each other any more. A kind of nervous anxiety took hold of her when I was there. Her head would turn sharply as if I was judging her, or she would fold her arms in a hunted, defensive manner. Our attempts to connect with one another were invariably unsuccessful. We were never able to recapture what had once been. There were too many barriers now.

It was only as she was standing alone under the neon light of the sign outside the door of the restaurant that she talked about it. A journalist had been in touch. A woman who was writing a story about Temple House and wanted Victoria to contribute and if possible to suggest other people she might talk to. Suddenly, all sense of her as an ordinary woman with a neatly packaged life and tidily referenced history fell away. As it always did. She could only ever play at normal for a while.

She was twitchy and nervous, fumbling for a cigarette. She looked frail and thin. She wasn't eating, wasn't sleeping. I felt like holding her. But I couldn't; that was not who we were any more. So I walked away, turning back only once to see if she had left. She hadn't, she was standing on the edge of the pavement, staring into space as the taxis drove past. And I thought that maybe this time, this time, she would speak and tell of all that we had been and how it had ended. Because she can never forget, no matter how much she tries.

And I can never let her go.

Her funeral was well-attended and elaborate, with an opera singer in an evening dress and a musician playing Handel on the organ. The people were the smart set, the ones she had known in tennis clubs. Their black coats were expensive, as were their bags. Victoria's father had been a judge and she grew up in a large house with granite steps that led up to the front door. I had visited once for a cocktail party. She was raised to be part of this world.

There was an awkwardness in the congregation. People avoided each other's gaze. The manner of her death was too open, too honest. It made them think of the stories they had heard, the reports that had appeared in the paper that week, the things that might have happened and what she might have known. There were journalists and a photographer at the gates to the church. If Victoria had taken a pile of pills it would have been easier for everyone to handle. Dark things should happen behind closed doors. Her fall through the air was too public.

I could make out Helen in the pews near the front. I had not seen her since that last day at school, in the summer house. Her red hair was still long but copper-coloured now, her back was straight and unflinching. I thought perhaps life had not broken her. She would not recognize me now.

The priest spoke of Victoria's sense of duty and work ethic. She was an admired colleague, a much-loved daughter and sister: platitudes that accompany the eulogy for a lapsed Catholic by a priest that has never met the person who has died. One of the lost sheep the shepherd tries to retrieve, even though it's too late and everyone knows it. She's already dead on the dark hillside.

It was warm in the church. I could see people stirring and shifting in their seats, touching their collars or their hair. Everyone vaguely agitated, listening to words of forgiveness. I found myself drifting off until the end, when he said we must remember that nothing human can ever be alien to us. It was then and only then that I felt like crying.

I left the church before the coffin came down the aisle. I have lost all care for ritual. Like understanding the past and saying prayers, the capacity for ritual is also gone and with it, I believe, the last of my humanity.

I am the alien now.

Chapter Three

I was to be a weekly boarder at Temple House, home on Friday nights and back to school Sunday evenings for supper and prayers. An embarrassment of high grades in the State Exams I took when I was sixteen secured my place. It hadn't been my first choice – indeed, boarding of any kind had not been on the agenda – but when the letter arrived in a heavy cream envelope with an actual wax seal, I was intrigued. There was an air of Malory Towers to the whole thing. The charm of running away, of being removed. Dedicating myself to higher things. I also liked tennis and the photos of the tennis courts perched on the edge of a cliff in the brochure were appealing.

I had another reason for taking the offer. My mother was leaving my father for a man she worked with. A man whose name and various deeds we had listened to her talking about innocuously enough for the last year as she prepared dinner. We had even met him once, at the cinema. He was standing in the queue ahead of us with his own three sons, when my mother called out his name. It was a faux jovial encounter with lots of

21

'Isn't this nice' and 'Imagine meeting here' and so on. He dressed better than Dad did and when he shook my hand he said: 'So I hear you are the bright one; have to watch ourselves around you.' He laughed then and his teeth were unusually small. One of his children made bunny ears over the head of a younger one. Thankfully, we didn't sit with them. My mother had some sense of decorum.

I wrote in my diary later, when I knew more, that the experience had been 'alienating'. This was a favourite word at that time.

Since she broke the news of her leaving, there had been a kind of entente cordiale at home. My father looked like he had expected it and was being weirdly gracious around her. She looked exhausted and left the house most nights to meet friends to talk about all that was not being said at our house. It was the summer before I would leave for the new school, I had nothing to do, everyone was away. I spent most of the time alone, unseen, listening to Depeche Mode on my Walkman and lying under the apple tree at the end of the garden reading, or just looking at the sky.

Conversation was predictable most days:

'You should go out more, Louisa,' says my mother.

'I don't have any money,' my response.

'You could look for a job. All you do is read,' says Mother.

'I like reading and it happens to be free,' I answer.

'Has your father fixed the light over your bed? Don't read at night if he hasn't done it,' she says, ploughing ahead.

'He hasn't fixed it yet,' I say.

'What is wrong with him. . .' She is speaking to herself now.

'I don't know, what is wrong with him?' I reply.

Silence.

It was a rare hot summer, the kind of summer you remember. The one that over time becomes the template for all the summers of the past.

The backdoor to the house open, the vague sound of tennis on the TV in the distance, flies trapped in the house at night and a strained silence over dinner. Sometimes the phone would ring in the late afternoon and I would traipse into the house, cursing, and answer it. Usually, no one would speak and I could hear heavy breathing and then laughter in the background. I used to hold my breath for a minute before hanging up, willing them to speak, to tell me who they were. But they never did. Something about the weird pointlessness of those calls became a strange metaphor for that summer.

In the evenings when my mother was out and my father had gone to bed, I would open the drinks cabinet and take some sherry from the heavy glass decanter that was covered in dust. It was thick and sweet and made me want to vomit, which was just what I wanted it to do, but I could never drink enough and so just fell into bed hot and vaguely nauseous. My dreams were the ones I had used to have as a child where there are two sets of my parents, the good ones and the evil ones. In the dream I am always standing behind a closed door, knowing they are inside but afraid to enter because I don't know which version of them will be waiting for me. I woke in the mornings with my sheets all astray and the pillows halfway down the bed. The sun would be coming through the thin material of the curtains and I would lie there trying to guess the time. If I guessed right, I would reward myself with an extra bowl of cereal at breakfast.

My exam results, the ones that would decide whether I could escape to a better school to finish my education, had been the most important thing all that year but were now fading into oblivion. The day they were due to come out was circled in red on the calendar that hung on the back of the kitchen door. The paintings for each month were by someone who was deaf or blind or who had used their foot to paint instead of their hand. The picture for August had a child with no face in a blue raincoat standing on the edge of a dark forest. I thought the images were depressing and freaky, like badly drawn omens for the months ahead.

Of course no one talked about my exams that much anyway. It was all about whether to sell the house or not. She was going to move with the 'new man' into what was being referred to as a town house in the centre of the city. She always hated the suburbs, she said. There was going to be a small room for me. She kept saying we would decorate it together, as if this was some kind of a bonus feature. I felt like telling her I had a room, here in this house, which we had also decorated together.

I had never really thought of them as unhappy. They seemed just like everyone else's parents. Occasionally silently resentful;

mostly tired from their jobs. I only ever remembered them fighting while in the car, for some reason. Possibly the enclosed space added to the tension. Also on holidays; those fights had usually involved small spaces and maps. And now, since the end had come, they were both being polite and respectful. What a fuck-up, really.

It was a new way to be marked out. To have parents that were separating. It used to be my IQ that people had heard of. But now it was this. Pity was the abiding emotion as they watched us come and go from behind net curtains on our narrow road. There was only one other girl in my year whose parents had split up. She had a set of house keys and every afternoon when we were packing up to head home, she would take them out and lay them on her desk. I guessed she didn't want to be locked out.

My parents offered no explanations, other than it was best for all concerned if they went their separate ways. I would understand; I was, after all, a bright child. They also assured me their love for me was never in question. They talked about this a lot. And I knew they were telling the truth so let it wash over me. The tendency to not judge was in me from the start. They both looked like they had aged ten years and it made me question if it was possible to build future happiness on the back of causing pain to others. I thought possibly not and that people tricked themselves into thinking this.

The day of the results came late that August and my mother made pancakes. She had taken the day off work and was all set to walk me to my school to collect them. She had plans for a day of mother and daughter togetherness. We would go and have cake in a coffee shop near her office, where the 'new man' might pop his head in and say hello. As she talked on, I watched the TV news. There was a giant number in the top corner of the screen telling how many days of fighting there had been in a far-off war. It was day 15. I thought it seemed kind of incongruous to have a number there, like it was a gameshow set in the desert.

As my mother did the dishes, I left the house quietly, picked up my bike which leaned against the front wall, and set off on my own. I felt she had forsaken any rights to gloat over me, to show me off to him.

The school was a crappy glass and plywood mess about five minutes from where we lived. I walked into the hallway where the teachers were giving out the envelopes. I remember feeling like the crowds parted; I was the best and everyone knew it. They had been waiting for me. The gifted kid. The one who would prove that great talent can come from a modest home and parents who can't stand each other. Ms O'Malley was smiling at me, envelope in hand. She whispered, 'It's just as we planned it,' and squeezed my arm.

Somebody took my photo for the local paper.

And I felt sure then that something was ending, and something else was beginning.

Chapter Four

Mr Lavelle, my favourite teacher at Temple House, once said there is something inherently dark and powerful at play in adolescence. A kind of alchemy that takes place underneath the surface of everything, including your skin. It bursts out in different ways and, depending on the era in which you live through, it will be met with hysterical fear and damnation or just attempts at coercive control. It's the necessary thwarting of an emergent power.

I told him that's why they tell us fairy tales when you're young. They tell you that you are powerless so as to make you less powerful. Don't go to the woods, for if you wander you will get lost and there is darkness everywhere. Wolves in the undergrowth. And be warned, only the pure and the lucky will be rescued.

He laughed at this and said of course we were the perfect fairy tale. The girls in the Victorian mansion on the hill, surrounded by fields, trees and the sea. A world of lemon polish and silence, incense and martyrs. The black wrought-iron gates locked to keep out the world and the changes he said were coming.

It was a life where in the last class on a Tuesday we typed job application letters to fictitious companies on large computers. Phones were attached by thick black cords to walls in draughty corridors and every few weeks we would kneel in the dark before a man to tell him our sins. It was a hermetically sealed universe of tradition and ritual, prayers and devotions, where the individual was born into Original Sin and required to examine their conscience and seek forgiveness. Endlessly. And we as teenage girls had much to make amends for. As Mr Lavelle said, alchemy was everywhere.

Those first few days, of course, I had no idea of the extent of this. As I dressed that first morning after my sleepless night thinking about the dead nun, I became convinced I needed a backstory, one that would be unusual. I couldn't fake being rich. Instead I thought I would go the bohemian route and claim my father was a writer and my mother a painter. We would be unusual. I would reinvent myself.

The first full day began with breakfast in the long hall, followed by a short assembly at eight fifteen that was led by Sister Frances, the Deputy Principal. We stood in lines in front of the stage. I accidentally joined the third years before hissing from several of the girls indicated I had made a major error. I briefly saw one of the other new girls who I had met the afternoon before. Her eyes looked huge and uncertain. I found my place at the back of the correct line. The girl in front of me smelled of sweat and her hair was greasy, tied up in a limp ponytail. The back of the line was clearly for the losers. The girl in front of her had spots on the back of her neck that every now and then she would pick at.

The prefects stood at the top of the Hall and for about three minutes they pointed and directed us until the lines were perfectly straight. All the while, Sister Frances stood on the stage, her head nodding up and down with each direction given. Her face was almost completely round and shiny, like a kind of ruddy apple.

When the lines were deemed appropriately straight, the prefects took their places and we waited for Sister Frances to speak. I expected the kind of sentimental speech that my old school principal would give, one where she told us we each had a talent that they, the teachers, would endeavour to excavate over the next year, while also warning us not to smoke or take drugs. But it was not to be.

Sister Frances spoke a prayer in Latin for a few minutes. I was oblivious to its meaning though charmed by the enigma of the words. Then she went silent and bowed her head. A strategic pause that lasted for two minutes. I knew this because I kept watching the clock on the wall in the corner. No one moved or even took a breath, it seemed. Finally, she raised her head and led us in a decade of the rosary. The hum of the voices in unison was vaguely comforting though the words over time became mangled and indistinguishable and every now and then I would lose my place. When it was finished she made a sign of the cross that we copied. She then left the stage, disappearing behind the dusty red velvet curtain that had framed her.

It was a dispiriting end. We didn't even get a timetable.

We were divided up into small classes that switched between subjects every forty-five minutes. Anyone who did make eye contact looked away quickly enough. I felt like a ghost. With each ring of the bell, I had to try and find my way down back stairs and corridors. The house had clearly never really been adapted to be a school. Some of the classrooms had fireplaces in the corners and cornicing, or a lone chaise longue under a window. French class was on the first floor in what must have been a drawing room at one time. Mustard-coloured curtains framed the large windows that faced the sea and a chandelier with some of its crystals missing hung at an awkward angle in the centre of the room.

The teacher of that class was somewhat glamorous and very thin. She had short blonde hair and was tanned. She was also French, which the teacher in my last school had not been. She was not friendly in any way and when she asked me to describe my summer holidays she winced openly at my accent. A few people laughed and the teacher frowned at them. She disliked us all equally, which was some consolation.

As the day wore on I did get some sense of who was in my class and what they were like. The few conversations I overheard offered fleeting glimpses of boats moored on rugged coastlines and hotels with terraces that hung over lakes. I also began to get some idea as to who was who. There was a group of three girls who moved as one in the corridors. They were leisurely and commanding in their ease, with the dull, listless expressions of those who know too early they are beautiful. They all had fair hair and wore small pearl earrings and the same brown brogues, their white socks perfectly straight. The others always left three empty seats for them at the back of each class. Then there were the duds, the ones who had stood at the back of the line with me. They had spots and cold sores and hair that seemed less shiny. And in between was everyone else, the blurred masses of the average.

The final class of the day was art. By then I was exhausted and presumed I could just sleep through it as I had done in my previous school. To reach the art room we had to leave the building and walk through a walled vegetable garden at the back of the house. Unlike the gravel drive and manicured lawn at the front of the building, this seemed surprisingly unkempt and scruffy. We followed the path through the garden and out of a gate in the wall that led to the edge of the woods to a small summer house. A thick vine grew over the door which was open, and a man stood, smiling and waiting for us. He was tall and lean, with fair hair. He looked young. The air was filled with the smell of wood and peat burning. A kettle was whistling in the gloom behind him.

It was here I met Victoria. And Mr Lavelle.

After that, everything changed.

Chapter Five

I imagine it is the same feeling one has when falling in love. Though I wouldn't have known about that then.

Victoria was sitting on a wing chair by the stove. She had a notepad in her hand and was sketching a stuffed parrot that was perched in a birdcage on the table beside her. One leg was tucked under her and a cigarette lay burning in an ashtray on the arm of her chair. There was also a mug on the table with a black Siamese cat on it and the words 'I hate you'. She looked up as we entered and her eyes were large and light blue, set wide apart in what was a small, delicate face. Her skin was tanned lightly and her hair was a golden brown. She looked vaguely surprised to see us all enter, raising one eyebrow. We were interrupting her.

I had a premonition of her importance in that moment and this is probably why I associate it with love. A recognition of sorts.

The room was bigger than it looked from the outside. The floor was stone, paint-spattered but covered with oriental rugs; there was a couch that was draped with some silk scarves and a few beanbags with colourful blankets thrown over them. There were easels standing against the walls and a shelf of paint tubes. In one corner was a large glass antique cabinet that looked to be filled with bones and animal heads. The vine that framed the front door was also growing inside and reached over our heads and across the ceiling. The overall experience of the space after the puritanism of the school building was one of a sensory assault.

Mr Lavelle welcomed us and made tea, pouring it from an old brown-coloured teapot with a striped tea cosy. He handed the mugs out, taking a moment to smile at the six of us there as he did so. One of the girls looked at Victoria before turning to the girl beside her and throwing her eyes up to heaven. They both smiled. Victoria didn't notice and continued drawing on her notepad.

Mr Lavelle's movements were measured and slow. He stooped slightly and the cuffs of his light blue shirt were frayed. It didn't make him look poor, though, as it would have in my last school. Instead, he looked like he was above caring about his appearance. He was handsome in the way of movie stars. He also sounded vaguely foreign, though I could not make out from where he might have come. It was hard to guess his age, maybe twenty-five or twenty-six. When he finished serving the tea he took a seat beside Victoria. As he went to sit, I saw her look up and they stared at each other for a second longer than they might have. She looked away first.

Mr Lavelle said we wouldn't be working on anything curriculum-related that day, instead we would be discussing art and what it means to us. He felt this was a useful way to get to know us. I thought this sounded like the best way to launch my fake, bohemian life and readied myself to discuss my obsession with Dalí and the fictitious summer my parents and I had spent travelling Catalonia in a van.

He spoke first.

'I would like to tell you about an artist that I recently came across. I feel like her life will have something to add to our discussion here.'

He leaned back in his chair and cupped his hands behind his neck.

'After the outbreak of the Second World War, this artist, Friedl Dicker-Brandeis, was sent to the Terezin concentration camp. This was a camp where the Nazis would try and pretend they treated the Jews well, so although a harsh and no doubt frightening place, it did allow for some small freedoms. It was here that this artist decided to use her talents to teach art classes to the some six hundred children who were there.'

His voice was clear but low.

'She encouraged them to draw what they felt, not what they could see. So it wasn't barbed wire and mud that emerged from the drawings but flowers and butterflies and gardens with children playing. They painted their lives, but as they were before, or as they would like to imagine them. Art as a sort of therapy, I suppose. She would hold these classes most days, even grading their drawings.

'After class she would pick a child to help her tidy up all the work. To secure this job was considered a real prize, for the chosen one would get to go to her room, where the walls were covered in her drawings of flowers. A place of colour and light, amid the grey and the miserable.'

He stopped here and lit another one of his cigarettes, Camel Lights, before continuing. He took a deep drag on it. The nuns must have allowed him to smoke around the students. I was glad, I liked the smell. I noticed Victoria lean her head back and close her eyes briefly as if to inhale in unison with him.

'Eventually, though, things would change for this teacher and her class. The camp was to close and most of those in it were to be sent to other, darker places. Our teacher was sent to Auschwitz.'

He moved in his seat and for a second he looked at the fire. Victoria opened her eyes and caught my gaze. It felt like a question. I looked down at my hands.

'Before she left, though, she handed one of the other women in the camp a suitcase. A suitcase with over four thousand pictures drawn by the children,' he said quietly. 'I think about what made her do this.' He got up from his chair at this point and moved to the window, his back to us.

'It is to me the most compelling of all her decisions. It is the action that turns, in a way, what was a distraction and simple activity into something more, into something great, something meaningful. Art, essentially,' he said.

He turned back and reached down to the ashtray beside Victoria, stamping out his cigarette. She looked at his arm reaching across her as he did so.

'You may guess how this ends. The suitcase and the pictures survived the war, but she and almost all of the children did not.'

He stayed silent for a moment and rubbed his forehead. The fire spat and crackled in the corner. I felt hot. The silence in the room was suddenly oppressive. My eyes were drawn back to Victoria. She was staring into the grate now, biting her lip as she looked at the flames.

'I tell you this so you can have some understanding of what art means to me,' he said finally. 'It is a parable about how art gives us all the ability to transform and transcend, to create something unreal, from what's around us. To create art is to go on a journey inwards. You each have the potential to find and express what you discover on this journey, regardless of the external circumstances in which you may find yourself.' He gestured subtly with his head towards the big house, our school.

He spoke the way I wanted to someday. Lyrical and knowing, rich and inspiring.

'It's not about exams or assignments and who is best at drawing; we are engaged in something else when we create art, we are revealing ourselves in the truest fashion. My role is not to teach; you rather must show me, tell me who you are through your work. Authenticity, truth, will be our only measure.'

He sat down again and exhaled loudly, as if there had been effort in telling us this story and now he needed to rest, to be idle for a moment to recover from the depth of his insights. There was a majesty now to the silence in the room, like something had been accomplished, we had crossed over. The light was beginning to fade outside. And for a second I felt like crying. The idea of the teacher with her students, getting them ready for their early death by painting blue skies and flowers. It was the most beautiful thing I had ever heard and the saddest. He seemed like a poet.

Victoria moved then, as if awaking from a long, intense slumber. She unfurled her leg from under her and stretched out, her arms over her head. Mr Lavelle shifted slightly in his seat to watch her.

'Creating art is about trying to get close to someone else,' she said. 'It is the attempt of each of us to connect with another.'

Victoria's voice was sleepy and rich. I thought of my parents reading the *TV Guide* and watching soap operas. I wanted to be close to her, to her world, and leaned forward in my seat, as if her words might be precious.

'It fails, of course,' she went on. 'We end up just staring at other people's psychodramas in art galleries and museums, not really closer to anyone, if anything just further apart.'

After she finished speaking she picked up a chess piece on the table beside her chair. She twirled it in her fingers. Mr

Lavelle smiled at her. His eyes shone, as if she was a thing of magnificence. One of the other girls coughed.

'She is my outlier, the student provocateur,' he said, turning briefly and poking at the fire. 'That is her role here and don't ever feel the need to agree with her, or pay her any attention.'

They looked at each other as he spoke those last words. She touched the collar of her shirt. There was a strange calm between them that made me feel excluded, an outsider.

One of the other girls said there is no difference in art, books, music – it is all the same expression. She was struggling for depth in her thoughts, anxious to impress. Mr Lavelle was kind but bored at her efforts. Another said that after the Second World War there had been a big question as to whether art had any meaning any more. Art since then was kind of frivolous, and that's why someone like Andy Warhol had just painted cans of soup. It all meant nothing.

Victoria liked this and nodded enthusiastically.

Finally it was my turn.

'I think it's mostly about loneliness, like when Ian Curtis sings "Love Will Tear Us Apart". It's about trying to make up for all the gaps in us. That's what I feel, when I look at or hear something someone has created.'

I couldn't think of anything else to add to this so decided to just stare at the fire in the stove, meaningfully. My voice had sounded thin, unusually high. I could feel Victoria's gaze on me but I could not look at her.

Mr Lavelle said, 'So you agree with Victoria: it is the drive to reach out and connect with others that makes us decide to create an artwork, but you believe it helps us to do this, while she thinks we are doomed to isolation.'

Thank God he had read something into it.

'Yes,' I said, emboldened by his words. I looked her straight in the eye. Excitement rose in my chest, an expectation of something. Victoria looked vaguely amused. A slight spark of interest in her direct, blue stare.

'You are a woman of few words, Louisa, but we are okay with that, here.' He drank from his mug after he said this. 'It means you are thinking.'

Victoria looked at him briefly as he spoke to me. Then went back to caressing the chess piece.

Mr Lavelle thanked us for our contributions. He said we must understand the source of what we are doing in this class and that this is a useful approach to all lessons. One should think first, about the why, before rushing to engage in the detail and the how. I liked the sound of this.

He then walked over to the cabinet that stood behind the couch and, taking a small key from his belt, he asked each of us to select one item. We would study the object and write a short essay on it that we would then have to read out in front of the class that Friday, an essay describing what it represented to us. After this, we would begin sketching it. He gestured to me to come and pick first.

I squeezed through the girls sitting on the beanbags and stood beside him in front of the cabinet. It was a warm rosewood colour, engraved with flowers and berries and heavy branches. The glass was curved and protruded from the wood surrounds, creating the sense of three distinct sections. It was tall too; I was not able to see what was on the top shelves. It was at odds with the shabby thrown-togetherness of the rest of the room. He told me the cabinet had been in the old house, had belonged to the family that lived there before the nuns moved in. One of them had been a collector, travelling Europe in the 1920s and 1930s.

'You know the church?' he said, watching me closely. He smelled of smoke and earth.

I nodded.

'It was actually the billiards room of the old house,' he said. 'People drank whiskey and played cards there before the nuns took over.'

He turned to face the rest of the class.

'I think it's important to remember that, here, nothing is ever as it seems.'

There was a light in him as he spoke. A hunger for something. I smiled, not quite fully understanding what he meant or why he seemed quite so interested in me and my opinion. Then I gazed back at the wondrous array of strange objects in the cabinet.

'Choose, choose something that will matter to you,' he said, almost under his breath. He had turned back to me. I could sense the closeness of him and I had the distinct feeling that he wanted to impress me. That he needed this from me.

The cabinet was filled with curious and bizarre items. There was a jar with a dead tarantula in it, a case of butterflies and one with insects, a chain made of teeth; there were stamps, an ivory horn, a photo of a two-headed calf, an old jewellery box, some gemstones, a miniature violin and other jars filled with liquid which was too murky to see what was inside. I chose a skull. It was small, like that of a child. Mr Lavelle nodded as he handed it to me. And for what would not be the first time, I felt like he was a seer and that everything that would come to happen he had already foreseen. I held the skull in my hands. I imagined, for a moment, I could squeeze it and it would shatter.

I have not thought about this for many years, but now I wonder if I should not have chosen the skull. That perhaps if I had just picked a gemstone, things would have been different. I would not have become what I did. But then I remember the way I felt as they both, he and Victoria, looked at me, and I think perhaps not.

It was all inevitable.

Chapter Six

Victoria said that moments of happiness are always followed by a fall that is in direct proportion to the previous high. Nothing good lasts.

Within a day of my first art class, I became a target for the pack of Rottweilers also known as the prefects. It began innocently enough with my failure to wear indoor shoes. My mother and I had read the direction about the shoes in the uniform section of my letter of acceptance but had presumed it was some kind of a mistake. It was also an added expense so we conveniently chose to ignore it. But apparently there were shoes for indoors. I hadn't noticed anyone changing theirs before leaving for art class but it seemed they had. There was also a correct side of the corridors of the school to walk on. I had been witnessed ignoring this rule also.

The red-headed girl, Helen, from the first night in the chapel, was the head prefect. She called me to the empty sixth years' common room which was on the second floor of the house. It was a dismal space and smelled vaguely of wet sports clothes. There were a few chairs around the edges of the room and a large green couch in the centre. A sink in the corner had unwashed cups in it and a kettle. Some of the students' paintings and sketches were Blu-Tacked to the wall. One was of a man in profile; it looked like Mr Lavelle.

Helen sat on the couch and I pulled up one of the chairs. Looking at her closely she appeared to be made from alabaster, like one of the statues that lined the hallways. All she was missing was the halo. Her skin was pale. Her shirt looked crisply ironed and fresh. Everything about her seemed upright and unrepentant, including her collar. She held a pen in her hand and kept flicking the lid up and down as she spoke.

'Louisa,' she said. Her eyes were cold and she enunciated my name almost too clearly. It made me think for an instant that maybe she too had something to prove. She certainly wanted to seem older than her age, which could only have been eighteen at the most.

As she was about to speak, one of the other students walked into the room. Helen responded swiftly with a turn of the head and a raised eyebrow. The student left abruptly without saying a word.

'We know this is your first week and that Temple House is a new experience for you, but these rules are important to us.'

I blinked at her, uncertain as to where this was going.

'We have expensive parquet floors on the corridors. They are about a hundred years old and we need to protect them. That is why we have indoor shoes for wearing,' she paused, 'indoors.'

That's not the reason, I thought to myself, it's because you live for rules. They make you feel like there is meaning in the world. It also makes it easier for you to spot the people who don't fit in.

I could feel myself hunching in my chair and so made an effort to sit up.

Life is a performance.

'You will have to make a phone call home this evening and you need to ask to get an extra pair of shoes sent to the school. If you can't afford this or any other parts of the uniform there is a hardship fund that your parents can apply to or they can buy things in the second-hand uniform sale which we run twice a year – I see you got your jumper from there. We also have some old shoes in Lost and Found that you can wear in the meantime.'

'My jumper isn't second-hand,' I said.

'Oh, really. I thought the green was slightly a shade off, like the one we used to have a few years ago,' she replied.

She smiled at me like I had some kind of a problem, which I suppose in her eyes I did. A deficiency. A lack of status.

'Anyway, I just wanted to remind you we have standards here; it's what sets us and the school apart. And I'd hate for you to feel like you don't meet them. It's happened before: girls who join at this late stage sometimes struggle. It's not enough to be good at exams.'

I wanted to answer back, to be ironic and amusing. But I didn't have the shoes.

She looked at me for another few seconds, as if she expected me to respond with something, anything. Instead I just stared at her, in what I hoped was a cold and dismissive manner. Then I checked my watch. And looked at her again.

'I know you might think this isn't a big deal, but it actually is. It has been noted by Sister Ignatius. She keeps a list,' she said.

She was irritated with me now. And I felt sort of glad, as well as uneasy.

'Yes, I understand. We just forgot to pack them,' I replied finally, shrugging my shoulders.

I wanted her to feel as if she had overreacted and, as a result, was vaguely ridiculous. Like her stridency had been wasted on me.

'You know in Japan,' I said, leaning forward in my seat, 'they take their shoes off before entering a building. Maybe that's something we could think of instead? Not only would we be creating less clutter by having to store more and more shoes, we would be reducing the chance of infection and the spread of bacteria.'

I noticed an ugly, creeping redness on her white neck. And I felt guilty and unsure then.

'Do you expect us to walk around barefoot?' she said, her voice now raised. 'We reduce dirt by having shoes that are not worn outside, that's the whole point of indoor shoes.'

'I still think there might be some merit in the thought. I know there is a student council, I might propose it as an idea. I really do want to get involved in the school. We also can learn so much from other cultures, don't you think?'

She abruptly got up from her seat then and indicated that I do the same. We walked to the door where she turned towards me.

'You know, it's like a family here. We all know each other; our mothers, aunts, sisters were at school here too. We have a way of doing things.'

I looked at her but there was nothing more to say, so I began to walk through the door.

The harsh, shrill sound of the bell rang above my head.

'Louisa,' she called after me.

I turned back.

'We see everything, we know everything,' she said.

Her eyes were pale now, like pebbles bleached on a white shore. I felt suddenly cold.

We looked at each other in silence for a second before a river of girls poured out of the room beside us and carried me off in their noisy midst towards the stairs.

I descended into a fog of unease. I perhaps should not have answered back as I did. I felt her judgement, her pity of me. But the need to defend myself, to be ready to be hostile, ran close to the surface. I was as good as them; I had proved that in getting the scholarship. Or so I thought.

I sensed a sharp pain behind my eyes, a headache brewing. I didn't notice Victoria, who stood on the last step. I hadn't seen her since the art class the afternoon before. Her arms were folded across her chest, her books forming some kind of a bodily defence. She touched my arm as I passed her. I jumped slightly in surprise.

'You look like you've seen a ghost,' she said, before adding quickly, and taking her hand away, 'Do you know what time you have Library at?'

I briefly looked down at my arm, where her hand had been.

'I think it's Thursday at four; I haven't had it this week so far, why?' I answered, still distracted by the conversation with Helen.

'Oh, I just wondered if you were in mine or theirs,' she said vaguely, squinting slightly.

I wanted to ask who was she referring to but figured if I paused for long enough she would answer it herself. I noticed the marks of three piercings in one of her ears, the holes almost closed up. Her hands were covered in ink, words I couldn't read properly. She was even more beautiful close up, her face elfin-like, the dark eyebrows slanting upwards. The sense of a question again.

'You'll have Ignatius on duty; enjoy that, she sees everything. Though I did manage to slip a Virginia Woolf book into my bag last year.'

I wondered if I made her nervous. She fiddled with her books and then her hair as she spoke. I would have been nervous too, but the misery of my encounter with Helen had left me deflated, which perhaps mistakenly led me to appear numb and cool. It was the only positive I could take from the last ten minutes.

'Which one?' I said.

'*To the Lighthouse*. I checked the lending slip at the front and since 1975 only two people have taken it out. Can you believe that? It's a hardback and all. A bunch of cretins really.'

She was willing me to smile. It felt like a favour she asked of me. I wasn't ready, though. I trusted no one.

'Couldn't you just have borrowed it? Been the official third person with taste to take it out?' I asked.

I could hear myself adapting my voice to hers. The archness of it.

'Yes, I suppose,' she said, 'but I felt like it needed rescuing, not just reading. I am obsessed with the Bloomsbury set at the moment. I want to wear more tweed, or a kimono possibly, and smoke very thin cigarettes. I am going to be a writer, or failing that, a muse.'

Her problems were different to mine.

'Where are you headed now?' she asked

'I have to borrow some indoor shoes from Lost and Found,' I responded. 'I forgot mine.'

She ignored my answer completely.

'What do you like to read?' she asked, leaning towards me.

There was the sound of a nun clapping her hands together somewhere in the house and then the voices of the choir. Followed by the sound of a badly tuned violin.

Her question seemed strangely childlike and innocent. Like when you were little and someone would ask you your favourite colour.

'Beckett,' I said, unable to remember a single one of his plays or books in that instant.

She looked thoughtful then, her head tilted upwards slightly.

'I thought it might be something like that,' she said. 'I can always tell. I thought it could be Jane Austen, but when you chose the skull I knew it wasn't. I'm glad it's not. I have a stash of books under my bed, you can borrow some. I have *Malone Dies*, I have underlined all the parts I like.'

'Don't you like Jane Austen?' I asked.

'Oh I do, it's just they are all into her,' she rolled her eyes, 'and I wouldn't mind but it's for the wrong reasons, like the romance. They don't even see how black her humour is. She is dark and angry. As dark as the Brontës and not as mad, though none of them notice.'

She spoke to me as if she had never before met anyone as interesting, as if this conversation could only be had by us. Her eyes light and inviting.

I had to smile then. The charm of her was seductive.

'Anyway, you will be with the Maidens in Library, not me. Pity,' she said finally, starting to walk by me up the stairs.

'Who are the Maidens?' I asked.

She turned back and smiled.

'The princesses, the Vestal Virgins, the paragons of virtue and all things ideal.' Then she added, 'By the way, if you have time on Friday, after art class, Mr Lavelle lets some of us stay on later.'

She looked sharp and mischievous.

My heart rose. The air lighter, brighter suddenly.

'You chose the skull,' she said as she continued walking slowly up the stairs.

'Yes,' I said, willing her to be impressed with me.

'I am writing about the heart; I am determined to avoid all clichés,' she replied, disappearing into the coloured light of the Maiden's Chamber.

I had to know her. It was fate, I decided.

We had prayers that night in the Hall before supper. All the teachers sat on the stage and Sister Ignatius and Sister Frances led us in another decade of the rosary. After this was completed, there was a further set of prayers for the repose of the soul of Sister Josephine, the dead nun. Her funeral was to be the next day down the country, in the town she had left when she was eighteen. The prayers were followed by a short speech of gratitude to the parents of one of the first years who had donated money to the school. The girl in question went up on the stage and shook hands and did a sort of bow in front of the rest of us. I suspected she had a room with sea views. And a pony.

From where I was standing I could see Mr Lavelle. I noticed he had chosen to sit beside our French teacher. He had his arm stretched out behind her, along the length of her chair. She looked cool and elegant and I thought that maybe they were a couple and that their future children would be attractive and artistic.

Helen got up to speak then. She flicked her long hair behind her shoulders, smiled at Sister Ignatius and then turned to her audience.

'Temple House is a school of great honour,' she began, then paused, 'with a long history of charitable works.

'Tonight we welcome those students who are here at the gift and bequest of our kind donors and the board of governors. We speak honestly when we say, you have been given an opportunity that many would envy.' She paused again and looked around the room as if searching for the handful of lucky, marked-out scholarship kids.

'And we hope that very soon you will also come to feel as we do about the school. It is truly a great privilege for me to be your head girl this year, something I am not embarrassed to say I have long aspired to be.'

I smiled at this.

'Please know I am here as a friend, to help you make the transition to this, our world,' she put her hand up to her heart as she said this.

She flushed then and Sister Ignatius stood up and gripped her arm. She descended the steps at the side of the stage and the blonde prefects walked over to her. With their arms around her, they escorted her back to the rest of us. As if she had achieved something special and needed care and reverence. I looked at Mr Lavelle, suspecting he too might sense the ridiculous in it, but he was staring at Helen as she retreated back into the crowd. And he looked serious.

There were two long tables laid out at the end of the Hall and after prayers we sat down for a meal. The food was served by three women dressed in lime-green housecoats, with white hats and hair nets. No one thanked them as they filled the plates, so I didn't when they served me. Invisibility is repaid with invisibility. Everyone was still ignoring me, except Helen, who I could see whispering to the prefect beside her, after which they both stared at me.

Victoria was on the opposite side of the table, a few seats down. She held her chin in one hand, wasn't eating much or talking to anyone either. With her other hand she was building a mountain with her potatoes and then dragging her fork through it to make a pattern. Someone passed her a note and for a second she looked up from her plate, read it, and then caught my eye. We stared at each other, not smiling. An acknowledgement. As we did so I noticed she crumpled the note in her hand and shoved it into her pocket.

My indoor shoes were pinching me, and I kept thinking that the person who had them before me might have had some kind of a skin disease which was silently being transmitted to me. The other girls at the table talked about a skirt Miss Clement was wearing that they were sure came from Paris. I asked if anyone knew how I could get involved in the school newspaper. They acted like they didn't hear me.

When dinner finally ended we were directed down the long, dimly lit corridor to the church. A strong, thick smell of incense hit me as we stood in line outside, waiting for the younger classes to come out through the heavy door. Victoria squeezed in beside me. Tapping me on the shoulder and without speaking, she handed me the crumpled-up note. It read, 'Louisa is a cheap SLUT.' We didn't speak for a second but looked at each other and I felt gratitude towards her. Like the heavy sense of unease was lifting or being shared. It was always better to know, rather than just suspect, what others thought of you.

'Why?' I said, looking into her eyes.

She shook her head before responding, 'Why not? Think of it as the welcome Helen spoke about.'

Her words did not contain pity, but a challenge. As if Helen, the school, life even, all were things to vanquish. And we might do this together.

The heavy door of the church creaked open and we walked into the shadows.

Chapter Seven

I didn't see Victoria the next day, Wednesday. We had no classes together. I worked that evening on my skull essay, determined to try and impress her and Mr Lavelle with my nascent nihilism. I wrote until it was dark, all manner of disgust at vanity, at flesh and blood, seeping on to the pages. I was making a case for the soul. The only thing that lasted. The thing that was eternal. The words in the secret note Victoria had shown me were the rhythm I wrote to.

Body. Slut.

We fill our lives with trinkets, thoughts, lovers, art to distract us from the reality that lies underneath. The end that waits for us all. The skull is the manifestation not just of death, but the illusions we create around it. Our lives.

Alice didn't mind me working late; she had a torch and was reading a biology textbook in bed. She wanted to be a doctor. It runs in the family, she had said to me. And I thought, what runs in mine?

My mother had written a letter. I was only gone two days and would be home on Friday but this hadn't put her off. She said everyone on the road was asking after me. One neighbour was praying things would work out for me. I should have seen it as kindness but didn't. She then wrote about the move; the van would be coming early on Saturday morning. She was going. I tore the letter up into small pieces after I finished reading and dropped it in the bin. It was my old life; I didn't belong there any more. They had dismantled it anyway.

I stayed sitting at the desk, doodling on the page. I couldn't be homesick, there was no home to miss. I thought of my earliest memory. I was standing in our small garden and saying over and over, 'I am Louisa.' Twirling and twirling, the tall concrete walls closing in, until I fell over. Repeating it again, and again, as if there was a danger that I might forget.

A soft knock on the door broke my thoughts. It was Sister Ignatius. She looked like a phantom in the dim light of the hall, even more powdered and white than in daylight.

'Your light,' she said. 'Off.'

She turned away before I could answer and disappeared into the gloom. Alice shook her head at me, like I was an amateur, and put her torch down.

I got into bed but couldn't sleep. There was a strong wind outside and if I held my breath I could almost hear the waves against the cliffs. Alice began to snore lightly. The sash windows didn't close properly and every now and then there was a whistling sound through the gaps. I got up to see if I could close them more fully, pulling the curtains aside. As I looked out the window I saw Mr Lavelle was walking through the kitchen garden, a long coat pulled around him. A cigarette glowing in his hand and sparking in the breeze. He must have been working late in the summer house. He looked up briefly and for an instant I thought maybe I should wave but then he was gone.

The next morning we had choir practice before breakfast. I saw Victoria sitting alone on a low bench at the side of the stage. She smiled at me and I felt relief. She moved over and I sat beside her. We said nothing for a minute. The nun who led the choir hadn't arrived yet and the students were talking loudly, standing around. One girl was doing another's hair. Their friends had gathered together and gave shrieks of approval when it was finished. Someone else played a slow and stuttering version of 'Chopsticks' on the piano that had been dragged into the middle of the Hall.

'Sometimes I think I despise everyone and everything,' Victoria said suddenly.

I turned to stare at her profile. She was biting her lip again, her chin resting on her hands.

I wanted to say something profound, moving. Tell her I felt the same.

But the words wouldn't come.

'I prefer *Mrs Dalloway*,' I said, thinking about our conversation on the stairs, and wanting to reach out to her in the only way I knew.

'Me too,' she replied, slowly turning to look at me.

She didn't smile, but her face was open. A stray hint of light in her eyes.

I had that sense of recognition, again, like when I first saw her in the summer house. An unfurling inside of me.

And very imperceptibly, something changed between us.

After art class on that first Friday, Mr Lavelle asked if Victoria and I would help him. I blushed when he said my name as I was gathering my things together. I could feel the others staring. Victoria looked triumphant and was smiling at Mr Lavelle. He wanted us to see the swimming hole as he planned for the class to do some landscape painting before winter set in and he thought it would make a good venue, though he needed to check first if we could make it there in one piece. And also how we might carry our art supplies.

The light was low as he led us through the trees. I vaguely heard Victoria somewhere behind me say that it was like the perfect autumn afternoon one reads of in a poem, where the trees are laden with ripe fruit and you catch the smell of leaves burning in a bonfire in the next field. Mr Lavelle laughed when she said this. But she was right. The ground beneath our feet was like a carpet, soft and springy, with pine needles, ferns and even some fallen chestnuts. I felt like collecting them in my pocket but decided against it. That was something the old me would have done. Leaving them to dry on the kitchen windowsill at home. I felt like home was very far away now, and I was only five days in.

We were walking to the swimming hole, an abandoned outdoor pool that had been cut into the side of the cliff. To reach it we had to go through the small forest at the back of the summer house, the one Alice and I could see from our room. As we made our way through the woods, every now and then we would pass a tree that had fallen over and was leaning somewhat companionably on another. We had to bend and climb through or over them. I remember thinking it was like a kind of paradise, so full and abundant with sounds and smells. The enchanted wood. Even though the leaves were starting to yellow and curl on some of the trees. And we walked on decay and were breathing in the slow rot of summer's once dense foliage.

Mr Lavelle walked ahead of me. He was wearing the same light blue shirt from the other day, but before we left the summer house when art class finished, he had pulled on a navy jumper with brown suede patches on the elbows. His neck was tanned and when the wind blew his hair I noticed that it was much darker underneath.

He stopped and turned to me as we left the woods. We were standing on the cliff, high above the sea. There was scrub grass and yellow gorse bushes all around us, bees and wasps hovering above them. I could smell seaweed.

'We have decided to christen you the Thinker, Louisa. Everyone in our class has a pet name and this is yours. Victoria, as you know, is the Outlier.'

He was slightly out of breath and his shirt was open at the top and there was a small bead of sweat in the hollow at the base of his neck. I focused on it as he spoke because looking at him straight in the eye was almost impossible.

'What is yours?' I asked.

He looked at me with amusement.

'Shaman, perhaps, or Alchemist. Victoria, what do you think?' he asked.

Victoria had emerged from the woods into the clearing where we stood. She had put on large heart-shaped red sunglasses. She had also removed her jumper and tied it around her waist. Her arms were brown. She looked the epitome of Eurotrash cool.

'I think Shaman. He is trying to help us break on through to the other side. He also takes drugs. He really is our very own Jim Morrison.' She ducked her head as he gently swung for her.

'That is a ridiculous and completely unfounded rumour, Victoria. I inhale nicotine only, now. And that is less an addiction and more of a long suicide note to myself.'

They were sophisticated and other-worldly.

As they bantered, I felt like an outsider, as usual. The girl who experienced life as if she were behind a thin pane of clear glass. Near but far, seen but out of reach. I had been the bright one in my other school, the one with the library card and the good marks. I was the one who walked on, head down, past the other girls as they stood in groups outside the fast-food shop down the road from our house. And now here, I could not decide who I was. My personality, my character, was not yet set, it was fluid. I was a shape-shifter. I would be studious if everyone else didn't give a shit; I desired to be idle and rebellious, if all around me followed the rules. Was I particularly contrary or just without a backbone? The only thing that tied all the elements together was some need for recognition. I seemed to carry that with me, regardless of circumstance. It made me nervous, this need to be seen, because behind it, I knew, lay something else. A sense of shame.

I was looking for someone to absolve me of this.

And now with Victoria and Mr Lavelle I wanted to be part of their world, creative and bohemian but also uncaring. Despite my glee, the sense of excitement, I knew deep down, even then, that there was something cruel about them. An unthinking playfulness that might lead to hurt.

Mr Lavelle pushed through some of the gorse bushes and another path, even more overgrown, emerged and we were winding our way down some broken and uneven steps that had been cut into the side of the cliff. The sea was calm and inviting in the light of late afternoon and we could hear only the gently rhythmic sound of the waves against the rocks below. Seagulls flew over our heads; they were nesting in the craggy rocks above us. The path was narrow and you had to concentrate on not slipping so we were silent for a while. An old sign indicating the area was prone to rock falls lay half hidden and rusting on the ground.

'This is a feat of engineering. Built in 1925 by the son of the house, our collector, he travelled all over Europe and took a liking to the French Riviera, where cliff-side villas and pools were de rigueur. He was also into young pool boys, so the story goes,' said Mr Lavelle.

He pulled his jumper off and tied it around his shoulders as he spoke. His shirt raised up as he did so and I noticed his back was lean and tanned. I wondered again what age he was. And imagined him for a second naked with Miss Clement, the French teacher. I shook my head to try and remove the unwanted image. It made me embarrassed.

'Isn't there some kind of a ghost story about him? Like he killed himself in the house or something?' asked Victoria who was behind me.

'Not in the house, in the woods. He hung himself. He had run up debts and was about to lose the house. That's when the nuns bought it, in the 1940s. And dear, dramatic Victoria, no he does not walk the corridors at night. That's Sister Ignatius.'

'I haven't been able to sleep properly since getting here,' I offered.

Victoria laughed behind me.

'Oh, that's mandatory. You don't sleep for ten days. I think they have it written somewhere in the student information booklet,' she said.

We had to climb down the last section as the steps had given way completely. Mr Lavelle held my hand. Then he did the same with Victoria.

The swimming hole was grim. It was a small rectangular structure, built into one of the narrow ledges that formed part of the cliff. It must at one point have been painted white but was now covered with green and brown moss. The short ladder into it was rusted and broken in parts. It was less a pool and more a very large outdoor bath. There was some graffiti on the side.

'It's ages since I've been here, I forgot how unimpressive it is,' said Victoria, 'almost not worth the trek.'

She sat down on the section of long grass that ran on one side of it and took out a bottle of water from the small bag she had carried on her back. She offered me some but I refused.

'Can I have a cigarette now?' she asked. 'We are far enough away from the school.'

Mr Lavelle handed her the packet and his lighter. I pretended not to be surprised.

'You just aren't seeing the potential. Think of it painted pale blue or green on the inside, or even better with some Roman mosaic on the bottom and you floating, with this view out of the corner of your eye. Not that we are here to plan a renovation. Anyway, I just love that he had the idea for it; sometimes that is enough,' and he sounded slightly disappointed that she hadn't been impressed enough with the site. He sat down beside Victoria and lit a cigarette, looking around the scrubland that surrounded the pool.

'I think we can sit six or seven of us here easily in the grass. The school has insurance anyway, in case of any casualties on the walk.' He shielded his eyes against the sun with his hand and looked up at me. 'I liked what you wrote about the skull in class today.'

I noticed Victoria's knee was touching his, they sat so close together.

'I expected you to give me death, but you chose vanity instead. Unusual. I don't think in my year here anyone has suggested it as a symbol for that. But then I'm not sure if anyone has chosen the skull before.'

I shrugged my shoulders.

'I think anything to do with the face or head is vanity, really. Whether it be beauty or brains. The fact that it's a skull just shows the pointlessness of everything,' I answered.

'Can you quote some lines for my pleasure again?' he said.

Victoria raised her eyebrows as he spoke. She stared out to sea.

'I can't really remember it now,' I said, acting like it was all nothing.

He sat forward suddenly.

'I remember some of it: *Often placed in still-life settings with rotting fruit and wilting flowers, skulls are a physical demonstration that beauty disintegrates.* So visceral.

'Well, I hope your drawing next week captures this underlying sense of futility in the human condition,' he said, sitting back again, 'and the vanities we distract ourselves with.'

64

'You know, when I think of myself, I only ever think of my head. As if everything about me ends here.' I gestured to my neck.

'A disembodied consciousness,' said Victoria.

'You think therefore you are. A Cartesian,' said Mr Lavelle. 'The skull will be your emblem this year.'

He took his hand down and put his face up to the sun.

They were closer to the truth than they knew. I mostly felt like I was barely there. My body only an idea, something that could not be seen or trusted fully.

'I'd like to do some philosophy classes here, actually. I think it would really benefit everyone, teach you to think more clearly. You know, in France it is compulsory in all schools. I studied philosophy for a bit, back in the day,' he said, 'though it's not for everyone. Some people can't handle the blankness. The reality that one is alone in all this.' He pointed to the sea and the sky.

I looked up and I thought that refuge, if there was any, was up there, in the sky. A world of illusion and dreams. The heaven the nuns talked about.

'They can go to religion class then, while we are with you,' Victoria replied.

He smiled at her.

'Your essay on the heart was interesting, Victoria,' he said. 'It did feel more, how would I say, Catholic, all that intense suffering. Maybe you can stay with religion and Louisa can join me and the existentialists.'

Victoria stood up suddenly. I watched her walk to the edge of the cliff and for an instant I thought she was going to get angry with him.

'I could just about make out the words between the smudges. Were they teardrops?' he said.

Crying. It was like a flicker of something. Like when in the Hall she had said she despised everything.

'I spilled my drink. It was late by the time I started writing. I was tired,' she said.

She stayed standing on the edge of the cliff, staring out to sea.

'Well, you each have your emblems now. It will be interesting to see what you make of them,' he said.

Silence for a second.

'Where did you teach before here?' I asked, sitting down on a rock across from him, seeking to change the subject and entice Victoria back.

'I was in college before I came here. Then I travelled for a few years in Europe. Temple House is my first official teaching post. I have done some private tutoring.'

He didn't bother to look at me as he answered, and I felt strangely put out by his lack of attention. But he was watching Victoria.

'What did you study and where?' I asked.

He didn't seem to hear me.

Victoria threw her cigarette over the edge of the cliff.

'He really is the most favourite teacher by far, among the

students and teachers, especially Helen, and Mademoiselle Clement,' she said, turning around, all sense of her annoyance now gone.

He laughed at this.

'Though not our religious brethren. There have been murmurings and complaints,' he answered.

I wondered what about but didn't have the nerve to ask.

'Oh, they love you really,' said Victoria, staring at him. 'It's all about new thinking these days, a fresh perspective. They let *him* do what he wants.'

'How do you like it here so far?' Mr Lavelle asked me, ignoring Victoria.

'It's different. A whole new set of rules to get used to,' I answered.

'Oh don't get too used to them, you will bore us,' Victoria said, kicking the dirt with her shoe.

'I doubt that, I have already pissed off Helen. She pretty much told me I am destined to fail here, or something similar. She seems especially unpleasant.'

I could hear my voice changing again, the language more elaborate.

I smiled as I spoke and Victoria responded, interested again.

'Helen is just madly uptight and jealous,' she said. 'Her father was in the papers the other week, he seems to have misplaced some cash. A scandal brewing, by all accounts, which should be amusing. He's the head of a bank, you know, and they say he's very religious. Apparently he hits himself with a leather strap in the evenings.'

I laughed and so did Mr Lavelle.

'No, I am serious, he is like a monk, or not a monk but some kind of a priest, lay priest type thing.' She stumbled over the words. 'It's like a secret society of some kind.'

'I have clearly failed the secret handshake test,' I answered.

Mr Lavelle laughed once more.

Victoria walked over to me and put her hands on my shoulders in a kind of mock-serious manner. I could see myself reflected in her sunglasses. And for an instant I felt like I was wavering, distorted like my reflection and not real any more.

'You are a big deal when it comes to exams. I overheard Sister Ignatius talking about you in her office. You apparently have a withering intellect, which will reduce us all to putty. They didn't, of course, say that you are also very pretty, in a kind of unconventional way, which for Helen and her like is the ultimate sin and therefore you must be denounced publicly.'

I had never thought of myself as pretty, my face a riddle to me. Something undecided about it, like it hadn't found its place in the world yet. It wasn't ready to be categorized. I felt myself blush.

'Beauty, they say, is the highest form of genius', said Mr Lavelle, checking his watch. 'I think it's time we headed back. It's going to be tricky enough to convince Sister Ignatius of this visit here. I will need to use all my powers of persuasion.'

'Or you could just lie to her?' said Victoria.

He stared at her briefly, a quizzical look on his face, as if she was constantly surprising.

'Helen told me everyone is, like, related to someone else who went here. Is that true?' I asked.

I could sense tension between them.

'Oh yes, I am the last in a long line of Temple House girls. We are born, not bred,' Victoria said with a laugh, starting to put her jumper on. 'It's tradition.'

'It's like inbreeding', said Mr Lavelle, 'they need some new blood. They are starting to grow three heads and get hunched backs.'

He looked at me calmly as he spoke, no smile this time, and he didn't need to shade his eyes with his hand. It was then I noticed the sun had gone in, the glare off the white rocks had faded. Victoria looked at me and I shivered. It would be evening soon. In that moment, it seemed very clear to me that they were both going to feature strongly in my life over the next few months. And that nothing would be the same after.

I could hardly wait.

'I think we better plan to bring food with us next time,' said Victoria. 'You don't want people complaining or passing out.'

'Noted,' said Mr Lavelle.

We started to make our way back, only speaking occasionally. Mr Lavelle whistled for a bit. Victoria, who was at the front, had picked up a large stick and trailed it along the gravel and dust path. Every now and then she would throw a question over her shoulder at me, like what was the last film I had seen, and whether I considered Morrissey's solo career a failure. There were blackberry bushes along the way. I thought maybe we could come back and pick them together, have a picnic and smoke. I decided I was going to start smoking. And maybe wear tweed.

As we reached the woods, she picked up the pace and moved further ahead. I watched as her back slowly retreated into the gloom, her uniform disappearing into the shadows of the trees. I had a vague sense of fear, as if I would not see her again, that the afternoon had been a dream and nothing would ever match up to it. I regretted that it was Friday and my parents would be collecting me in an hour and I wouldn't see Victoria until Sunday evening and she might have forgotten me by then. I distrusted happiness. I walked quicker to try and catch up with her.

I heard Mr Lavelle call out after me. I turned back and gestured at my wristwatch so he would know that I rushed, not away from him, but rather to something else. That time was against us. There was a shaft of light coming through the trees overhead and he stood under it. His hair was golden and shiny. Celestial, I thought, and it seemed like everything was exactly as it should be.

He didn't respond to me or smile and for a second we just looked at each other.

And I sensed the same unease as I had standing beside him in front of the cabinet of curiosities on that first day.

He is hungry and restless.

Chapter Eight

The lives of the saints.

I was sitting beside the window. There was a gardener kneeling and digging in the vegetable patch. Victoria sat behind me. Every now and then she kicked my chair with her foot. I turned once or twice, thinking she wanted me, but each time she just stared blankly back. The late September sun reflected on the blackboard and we had to pull the blinds down. Someone in the class had a cold and kept sneezing. Their desk was covered in balled-up used tissues.

The clock over Sister Frances's head ticked on. She was red-faced and gesticulating with her hands. Every now and then the black cross around her neck would swing with her movements. She started to walk back and forth at the front of the class.

When she was facing away from us, Victoria leaned forward and whispered in my ear, 'She is lost in the majesty of suffering.'

Her breath was hot on my neck.

Sister Frances went on.

Saints were grilled on red-hot stones and pierced with arrows.

They were pressed to death, the weight of a door on frail bodies.

Their skin was removed.

One was hacked to death by his own pagan students.

Victoria laughed then. And I did too.

We were sent from the room.

In the corridor outside the classroom, she leaned against the door and I slid down the wall and sat on the floor.

'Can you believe this?' she said, pretending to knock her head against the door.

'Yes,' I said, closing my eyes briefly.

And I did believe it. The shaming of the body, the sacrifice of the flesh.

But I couldn't tell her that.

'I might get a tattoo,' I said.

Victoria sat down beside me, interested.

'Of what?' she asked, her eyebrows raised.

'Sister Frances's weirdly round head,' I said, 'right here.'

I pulled my sleeve up and pointed to where the tattoo would be. My arm looked frail and thin, pale.

She laughed and lightly traced the spot where it would go.

'I'll get one too,' she said, 'of Mr Lavelle.'

This didn't surprise me.

'Or I could get a full list of the school rules branded on to my arm,' I said, sitting forward and looking at her.

'No make-up, no painted nails, no jewellery, socks to just below the knee, skirt to just under the knee, hair to be tied back if long, hair to be behind ears if short, no fringes, whether long or short. And no hair dye. No looking at watches in class, no yawning, stand up when the teacher comes into the classroom, stand again when they leave the classroom. Only walk on the right side of the corridors, do not make eye contact with teachers outside of class, wait to be spoken to. Bring your lab coat to science and if you forget it go to the office and see Sister Frances who will give you a menial task to complete, like cleaning the blinds of the office with a toothbrush.'

We were laughing loudly then. A classroom door further down the corridor opened and Helen stuck her head out. She was wearing her black cloak and frowning. She gestured that we stand up. We didn't move. I expected her to march towards us but she didn't, she just stayed staring at us and put her finger to her lips.

Victoria jumped up then and gave her a mock Nazi salute.

And I thought, thank God you are here, with me.

By October we were inseparable. Twin flames.

Time moved too quickly when we were together and too slowly when apart. I didn't have many classes with her, except for art in the summer house, and those others we did share were a relief, an oasis of bounty in the otherwise long, withered day. I had them highlighted in red on my timetable, then outlined again in gold. I stuck it on the wall beside my bed. And we would pass the time in these classes whispering, or if sitting apart, passing notes with amusing comments about someone's hair or another's misreading of an important theme in the book we were studying. We were never caught. The universe conspired on our behalf.

I remember it felt as if we had a secret, something unique between us that we kept concealed but that lit us from within. At other times I thought it was an armour, a shield, and I wore it so that, even when without her, it protected me from the rest of the world. It was something to cherish, that set me apart from them. We took to calling the others in our class 'the atoms'. I could stand silent and ignored in the line outside a classroom and not care. I could face the cold dislike of Helen in the corridor and be unmoved. Victoria helped me withstand the side glances. I felt my shame fade, for a while anyway.

Victoria was popular with most of the teachers, which surprised me a little at first as she was not a conventionally exceptional student and spoke out of turn. Her family lived in a large house in a smart part of town and a ridiculous amount of people she was related to had become someone important. Public figures who were referenced in obscure law books and had footnotes dedicated to them in the story of the State. She wore it lightly, the deferential respect. She would talk little in class and only ever offered something of insight just as were packing up our books. Only I knew she had barely been listening and had spent most of the time doodling quotes from the Smiths on her jotter. Or asking me whether Jim Morrison would have been better off sticking to life as a poet and avoiding rock and roll. Or why it was that the muses of artists nearly always seemed so lame. She would be different, she said, if she ever became a muse.

I envied her a bit, the ease with which she could unleash her mind and how she only did it when it suited her. She did not feel any need to prove anything, unlike me. My intellect was my badge of honour, the sword I prodded the world with so that people could see, understand that I had power, value. Her decision to upend our entire class discussion on the rules of tragedy by quoting directly from Aristotle, or to suggest that Heathcliff represented a god of fertility, was part amusement and part actual belief. She was comedy; I was tragedy. She was irony brought to life, if irony was a girl.

I had seen that first afternoon in the summer house that she wasn't liked by many of the other girls. They looked at her with a sort of unease. Like she might say something that would embarrass them or damage their sense of self. She told me she had had a best friend last year, but that girl had been forced to leave the school. Victoria had tried to see her over the summer holidays, but for some reason, never explained, it was not allowed. She would look sad and faraway when she spoke about her.

'How is it possible to once feel love for someone, for that's what true friendship is,' she said, looking at me as we sat on the front steps of the school, 'and for it then to disappear?' She clicked her fingers.

I felt uncomfortable when she talked of her, this nameless friend from before. A shadow crossing us.

'I don't understand how people change. I see it as a moral failure,' she said in conclusion, her head bowed.

I thought of my parents and their wedding picture on the mantelpiece. Things end, I felt like saying, and there is no reason, except a change of heart. But I didn't. I had a need to agree with her.

Sometimes I wondered why she had chosen me. For I did feel like I had been chosen. But I didn't dwell on it. It appealed to my ego. She and Mr Lavelle had seen me. My essence. I stared at myself in the mirror a lot. I wondered if my eyes were too far apart or whether my lips should have been fuller. Then sometimes I would see only mystery or melancholy in my face. Like it was a portrait from long ago, dark and stern. And not me at all.

Victoria told me we needed a philosophy to live by. Like the Bloomsbury set. And so irony became all that we were about that autumn. A form of quiet rebellion that allowed us to obey but gave us breathing space. It seemed the most appropriate response to the rigid and farcical rules of the school where at times it felt as if the walls were closing in and your mind was being requested to shut down rather than open up. Irony became a reflex, accompanied by rolling eyes and sighs. Irony infected our thoughts. It was a way of being that we didn't give up, until the very end.

The rules we applied our ironic response to included –

– *Stand in straight lines.*
– *Pray. Often.*
– *The soul is transcendent. The body is not of the same value.*
– *Examine your conscience.*
– *Recognize you are inherently sinful.*
– *Think about Eve and what she did to Utopia.*
– *Everything pleasurable is followed by a fall into darkness.*
– *Hell is a place of fire.*
– *Purgatory a place of mist.*
– *Heaven is glorious.*
– *God sees everything.*
– *He knows your thoughts before you express them.*
– *Though you do have free will, hence God is blameless for all that goes wrong in the world.*
– *Never express an original thought.*
– *Unless your family is particularly rich and influential whereby we will listen respectfully, for a time.*
– *Upon this foundation we have built the education of many a young woman, just like you.*
– *You are not unique.*
– *Go bury your gifts in the ground.*

So irony became our companion, our weapon. It felt like an action. I left behind bits and pieces of myself as a result. But I thought it a form of sophistication, so didn't ever question it.

Or wonder if it might be worth the sacrifice of other things, other parts of me.

Chapter Nine

My mother had moved out. The house was quiet most weekends. My father had taken up fishing.

It should have been the defining feature of those months, my mother leaving us, but somehow it wasn't. I would sleep in late, read for a bit and watch old black-and-white films on the TV in the afternoon, sometimes while ironing a school blouse. My father would bring a takeaway home in the evening and we would watch a quiz show. I would usually get the answers right and he would say I should apply to go on. We'd laugh then. No one rang, not even Victoria, though I had given her my number. She kept forgetting to write it down and would be filled with heartfelt, dramatic apologies every Sunday evening. And I always forgave her.

I lived instead for the summer house. This became my new home, my refuge. The lamps lit as the afternoons faded earlier and earlier, the stove hot, the vine growing like a thick cover of protection over our heads, keeping the school out. Here the stray and orphaned bits of myself were connecting. I felt safe and accepted.

Mr Lavelle would be smoking, drawing sometimes, but often just looking at the flames in the stove, describing worlds for us to explore.

'I need you to free your minds,' he said, looking at me.

'The route to happiness is not with striving to be the same as others. Whose life are you living? The real purpose is to find your quest, your path to truth. If there is a God, if he does exist, he will not ask if you have sinned. He will ask, did you love?'

His voice loud now in the room. Some of the girls looked uncomfortable. Notebooks closed tightly on their knees. Nothing he said was on the curriculum.

'Don't you want to be remembered, to fight the drive to conform?' he asked. 'It's the lovers who are remembered, the ones who gave themselves to their passions, whether it be art, literature, nature, life.'

His blue eyes darker now, pleading.

Listen.

And I did.

Victoria would be languid, lying on the couch, much to the annoyance of the others in the class.

'I was here first' was her only explanation when there were complaints from people looking to sit down. They had to make do with the beanbags.

Mr Lavelle loved her wildness. The way she didn't care if they hated her. It was true freedom. He and I both recognized it, for we were not as brave.

She had taken to trying to complete a Rubik's cube and would fiddle with it as Mr Lavelle spoke, never managing to get the colours together on one side.

Mr Lavelle would laugh at her failure.

'I know what to do with it,' she said suddenly one day, holding the cube up to the light. 'I will peel the stickers off and rearrange them according to colour. Then it will be completed, but just in a different way.' There was delight in her voice.

'My outlier,' Mr Lavelle said, shaking his head. He knelt down beside her and took the cube, holding it with reverence in both of his hands. 'When you do complete it, I will put it in the cabinet,' he said, bowing his head to her.

They were glorious together.

Mr Lavelle spoke with irony too. He also could throw words up into the air, turn them inside out. He could set them on fire, then blow out the flames, hide them in hats, then pull out roses. They disappeared and reappeared.

And Victoria and I were not alone in our admiration. He was the favoured among the other girls. They liked his hair, they liked his smile, they liked the way he smelled of the outside. Grass and woods. They liked the way he made them feel like they had something inside of them, undiscovered. They liked his car, the Citroën Dyane and its folding window, and the way he would speed away in it in the evenings out the black gates, gravel flying.

Or the way sometimes he would hold your arm for a second when he spoke to you. As if the words were spilling out into the physical world, could not be contained in something as narrow and constricting as a sentence. You, and only you, had jolted them out of him which meant there was something special about you.

Victoria liked the way he would stand on the steps of the house in the morning before classes began and just stare out to the sea. A mug of coffee in his hand, sometimes a cigarette, and always giving the impression that much was on his mind. As if something or someone was calling him. Sirens, perhaps, Victoria said.

Helen said his family were very wealthy and had a yacht and a castle and a house in France. The blonde prefects claimed that he was in love with Miss Clement, the French teacher, or she was in love with him. They were seen together going for walks.

Some thought he was ancient, at least thirty.

Victoria said he was not that old, only twenty-five. And that he swam naked at night off the cliff rocks.

I imagined him backpacking across Europe and reciting poetry on the sun-drenched terraces of cafes in return for food and a bed for the night. He was surely going to do something great, become a painter, or a sculptor of note. Maybe write a book. One that would change the way everyone thinks. An instant classic.

Victoria said he was guardian of the cabinet of curiosities and he would show you things, pick an item especially for you and tell you its story. And this story would be about you, it would become the emblem for who you are. The hidden depths uncovered. The thing that marked you out. My skull and her heart.

He understood you. He could see you. And he might draw you. In charcoal.

And everyone knew Victoria and I were special to him.

It was there in the sideways look, the exclusion zone that sprang up around us. It was there in the language we spoke. Our words weaving together in a complex and intricate pattern, taking the thoughts we expressed in class higher, and further away from reality. The way we brought our best game to the table, the wits sharpened, the gun of our intellect loaded and ready to fire. Follow us, if you can.

In being the beneficiaries of his gaze.

In being the ones he asked to stay late after class.

The woods dark outside.

The Journalist

Chapter Ten

Monday. Everyone was tired, hugging their coffee cup, phones on their laps.

The room was glass. Windows on one side out to the street and glass partitions on the other, overlooking the open-plan office. It was cold outside, February weather, but in here it was already warm, the early-morning sun striking the whiteboard making the words on it illegible. You had to squint to read it which made you feel slightly angry, even though the day had barely begun.

The intern, always covered in layers of clothes, removed her cardigan while stirring what looked to be a homemade green smoothie. I could feel a headache starting over my left eye.

'It's the twenty-fifth anniversary this year. It's one of those stories people remember – the boarding school, the student and the teacher who vanished,' my editor said.

Mr Edward Lavelle and Louisa.

A truck was reversing on the street down below, a loud beeping sound coming through the open window. Every now and then others in the room would turn to look at where the sound was coming from but chose not to do anything about it. I got up to close the window, taking a last, deep breath of the cold outside air. In the building opposite a man in a suit was standing at a desk staring back at me.

'Yes,' I said as I turned back to the room.

We had already spoken about it. I had an interest in this story.

'Women and true crime. . .' my colleague said behind me.

He was rolling a water bottle over one eye as he spoke. A headache too, I imagined.

'The fear of imminent death haunts us more,' said the intern.

A few people laughed but in a depressed way.

'You knew her, didn't you?' my editor asked.

'I didn't *know her* know her. I just lived on the same road. We knew the family,' I said, sitting back down again.

People looked at me.

Louisa: she was the reason I never got to go anywhere on my own as a child.

I was too young to remember when it happened. But the story was very familiar. Louisa, the missing student, had lived in the house opposite mine. I had no real memories of her, just a few scraps of images. A bike thrown against the front wall, music coming from a bedroom window of a summer's night.

She and I had gone to the same primary school. There they offered a spelling-bee prize in her honour. A cup on which my name had been engraved one year, exactly ten names after hers. Louisa's mother had even come to the school once to present it. She was painfully thin and grey-haired. She had moved away from the road by then so was not a familiar face. I remember feeling not so much sorry for her, as embarrassed. She sat on the stage with her head down. When she did speak, it was to warn us of strangers in cars, people who pretend there are puppies in the back seat. Everyone was awkward around her, even the teachers.

The conversation about missing women continued.

'Well, you can take it in two ways: either it's a retaking of this dark space by women and an overcoming of the fear, or really it is a fetishizing of victimhood,' someone commented.

'What?' the intern said, putting down the smoothie.

'It started with *Twin Peaks*. . .' he said.

'Let's leave it,' said my editor.

'Wrapped in plastic,' I said.

Everyone turned.

'Laura Palmer,' I answered quickly.

'Via Marilyn Manson,' said water-bottle man.

'Quite,' said my editor.

'It's the opposite of romance; that's why women read it, listen to the podcasts,' I said. 'It teaches us not to trust anyone.'

I shrugged my shoulders. It all seemed obvious to me.

The intern smiled.

'There is a man missing too,' my editor said, eyebrows raised.

No one reacted.

The meeting moved on.

Someone was going to do a quiz on the world's favourite fictional dogs.

I returned to my desk. It was my third month in the office. I needed things to go well.

The story of Louisa and the art teacher, Edward Lavelle, was already very familiar to readers. It appeared, in a bid for new leads, in the paper and on some websites every two years or so, around the anniversary of the disappearance. It was like a mark in the calendar.

Louisa's father stayed living across from us until his death a few years ago. He rarely left the house, and I remembered that as a child my mother had explained to me he was a recluse and an alcoholic. I hadn't known what that meant but she said it was a sickness, brought on by sadness. She warned me not to throw things over his front wall or ring the doorbell as some of the others kids did. I had a phase of being afraid of him; he looked messy, unkempt. And the house with its curtains drawn was so uninviting. I would never walk past it, always crossed to the other side of the street.

At my computer I opened an article about Louisa and Lavelle from two years earlier and studied their photos. They were beautiful and young. You treated people like that differently, even when they were no longer there. Like a dead celebrity. Louisa was dark, and in the photo most often reprinted she was thin, boyish almost, and wearing a Depeche Mode T-shirt. It said:

'Enjoy the Silence'. Lavelle was fair and foppish. He looked both entitled and lost at the same time, his round, china-blue eyes almost childlike in their open gaze. Together they were emblems of youth, from a time and a place that was recognizable but also vanished.

'It was mentioned in a documentary that was on a few weeks back. A repeat. Check it out. There was a detective, retired, interviewed on it. He might talk to you,' my editor said, standing at my desk.

The intern came over.

'Can I do anything for you on it?' she said.

I tried to like her but always failed. It required time to actually make any use of her and I couldn't be bothered. I liked working alone.

'Maybe later, not yet,' I said.

She looked pissed off and left.

That afternoon, as research, I watched back the programme my boss had referred to. It was a late-night show dedicated to unsolved crimes, hosted by an earnest-looking lady with bobbed blonde hair and an air of professional compassion. She wore a bright red dress and had a charm bracelet on her wrist that moved a lot when she gestured with her hands. She spoke to the retired detective; he was grey and dishevelled in appearance. It all looked vaguely incongruous.

The last shot of the TV programme was of the locked black gates of the school. A light mist enveloped the screen as the camera panned out. The house was scheduled for demolition, text across the bottom of the screen read. A telephone number and an email address flashed up after this, as it always did. But for more than twenty years, no one offered to provide anything useful or new to the police. The anonymous crime hotline lay silent. The pair stayed missing. Only the ghoulish liked to remember. The ones whose lives had some kind of a vacuum that they filled with stories of serial killers and abducted children.

I stayed late in the office. The blue screen of my phone delivered more information. I browsed old articles about the disappearance and watched video clips on YouTube. There were reports on how people had closed ranks after it. There were old news clips of girls scurrying up the steps of the school, avoiding eye contact and covering their faces from journalists. A woman in a red Mercedes and wearing a camel-coloured coat and sunglasses poked an umbrella at a photographer before claiming things of this sort didn't happen in a school like this. It was darkly comical.

There were interviews with Louisa's mother as she sat red-eyed in what must have been their living room. She failed to make much sense and was strangely unsympathetic. She had held up the girl's report card at one point, instead of her photo. There was old footage of police scouring fields in the sleet and rain, and standing at the side of a beach. Vaguely confused-looking people stood in the background, and one even waved at the camera. Perhaps they thought the student and teacher had sailed away in a rowing boat together and it was something to celebrate. Like the owl and the pussycat. She was sixteen and he was twenty-five; it was not unheard of. Perhaps they were now living in the south of France. Far away from the street we grew up on.

I felt tired, my eyes hot from all the screen time, but then a Wikipedia page popped up so I kept going. The entry took the conspiracy slant in its retelling, claiming the nuns in the school had something to hide. There were rumours of complaints made about the teacher; he had been seen as being a little too friendly with some of the students. It was said he had also been a fantasist, with a pretend foreign accent and a fake degree in art. But he was very good-looking, with exciting new ideas on how to teach, and he looked well-off so no one checked anything out about him. A more innocent time.

The question it posed was, had the nuns been aware of any of this; how culpable were they, if at all? Less than a year later they had closed the school, selling it to a property developer who had never been able to get planning permission. Hence the broken, decrepit state of the house. The nuns too had disappeared, it seemed.

I showed the Wikipedia page to my editor at his desk.

'This might work, looking into the nuns. I mean, some of them must still be alive. Maybe they would talk now?' I said.

It was dark outside. The man I had seen in the building opposite earlier was still there in his office. All lit up. His back to the window now.

My editor looked at me blankly.

'I think we might stick more with the underage sex with a teacher angle, if you don't mind,' he said. 'Find her classmates, that's what we want.'

Of course.

'Don't you have another article to finish, for tomorrow?' he called after me.

I went back to my desk. It was after seven.

I watched a short interview from the news at the time with the head girl of the school. She looked like a Pre-Raphaelite, with white skin and red hair. A nun stood behind her, with her head down, threading rosary beads methodically through her fingers. The student held a piece of paper in her hand and said Louisa hadn't been in the school very long and had been somewhat troubled. It was difficult sometimes to adjust, she said. She looked up as she said this and stared directly at the camera. There was a slight, almost imperceptible pause, before she finished. They were all most concerned for Louisa's welfare.

The Wikipedia article also mentioned the missing student's best friend, Victoria, and included a link to more information about her. They had been inseparable, an intense and much speculated-about relationship. Afterwards, it was said she had some kind of a breakdown and refused to speak. Supposedly, she had spent some time in a hospital. It noted her family had a tendency to sue newspapers. They were important people.

A few clicks more and Victoria peered out of the screen, as she was today. Airbrushed and well-coiffed. She was standing on what might be the roof garden of an office, or perhaps on a balcony, in a black trouser suit. Lots of sky and clouds behind her. She looked like the kind of woman the publication I wrote for would interview as their business person of the month.

One of the links beside the article led to a random piece about teenage friends in the US who had murdered one of their teachers. They claimed a man in the woods had made them do it. Another article referenced teenagers who said the Virgin Mary was appearing to them in a local shrine, telling them secrets about death and the possibility of miracles. I was Alice falling down the rabbit hole of alternative youth. A channel dedicated to the weird and the excluded and their hidden, ritualized worlds. A tribe of outsiders, who were no longer stoned by the villagers but just ridiculed and judged.

My editor was leaving for the evening and as he passed my desk I showed him the screen.

'I've heard of that, the Slender-Man. They think he's real,' he said, shaking his head.

I nodded and smiled.

'Who's she?' he said, pointing to a picture of Victoria.

'The best friend,' I said.

'Make sure to get her photo in,' he said, walking towards the door. 'And, I need that other piece, tomorrow. . . '

There was something alluring about Victoria, a wildness or defiance that had been tamed by a black suit, but might escape again at some point. Her eyes were alive and intense.

I made more coffee, a giant stewed cup. I spent the rest of the evening on the internet tracing Victoria's life, chapter after chapter of it opening up with each new random link. Events she was photographed at, conferences where she delivered a paper of note, her professional profile information all unfolding before me. She would age and then become younger in front of my eyes. A life in reverse. It was strangely mesmerizing.

I had googled my own life before. One is only ever pictured when one has done something notable. Make-up on, hair done. Your story compressed into one small achievement after another. Bits left out, gaps. Like where you grew up.

There was one photo of Victoria in her school uniform; she had won a debate. I wished there had been videophones in those days. I was missing gestures, quirks, a sense of character: the things that give you away. Standing beside her was a nun and Louisa, the missing student.

I clicked in and out of the trail, scrolling through sidebars and links to nowhere. So much had been written, but none of it added up to anything. A scholarship student goes missing with her art teacher a few months after starting at a prestigious school in the middle of nowhere. No trace ever found of either.

I spent a short time finishing the other article. It was already half written. A woman who once had everything no longer did, due to her own stupidity and bad choices. But she had survived, come through it. Was not a victim.

The stories we told were ancient. But we acted like they were new.

I left to catch the nine o'clock bus home. There was no one else at the stop. It was a new part of the city, reclaimed from the sea and reshaped for capitalism. All shiny glass buildings and steel coffee shops. It buzzed in the day but emptied quickly at night. I pulled the collar of my coat up and took my headphones out of my ears.

Uneasy under yellow street lights.

Louisa, Louisa. Always the whisper and warning on the side of my narrow, suburban life. The girl who got above herself and came to a bad end. What lessons did we take from this?

All of us, the bright girls, who followed in her footsteps.

I couldn't sleep when I finally got home. I was trying to remember anything I could about Louisa, anecdotes my mother might have told me, gossip about the family, something, anything that could add colour and create more interest to the piece. I would need to talk to her about it, and some of the neighbours. I heard my flatmate come in around 2 a.m. In the distance there was the vague sound of cars from the motorway that encircled the city. I could only hear it if the wind blew a certain way.

I thought about my childhood home on the other side of the city, my mother alone now and asleep in the house that faced Louisa's. Her slippers resting at the side of the narrow bed. The tiny garden out her back window, mostly concreted over so she wouldn't have to cut any grass. How long would she have searched for me? Would she have walked the streets at night looking for me, scoured the beaches and the woods, chased the nuns down? Would she have handed out the perpetual spelling-bee trophy in my name?

As the dawn began to creep through the gap in the curtains, I knew what I had to do. I would start by putting out a small advert, like the kind people use to announce engagements and births. I conjured up the words as the first of the cars drove out of the underground car park beneath me. The advert would be discreet and suggestive of privacy and some kind of a faded sense of preppy elitism. Very nineties analogue with a PO Box number that would redirect post to my apartment and an email address.

I would get in to work early.

Chapter Eleven

It was like turning over a rock.

First came the emails.

Conspiracy theorists with claims of pacdophile rings, and stories of priests visiting the school in the middle of the night and choosing their prey; a clairvoyant who said she could see the girl, she was buried on her side, and there were yellow flowers all around her. A man who said he was Mr Lavelle's half-brother and that he had only been trying to help the girl, but something had gone wrong in the escape and she had drowned. He was now living in Africa, he said, with a new name.

An amateur historian who claimed Temple House was of architectural interest and should not be demolished. A petition had been signed. A great collector had lived there once.

A woman who said she had also been taught by Mr Lavelle and had borne his child. He had been fragile, she wrote, and she never felt the situation was abusive. She remembered him fondly, and her child, a son, had his blue eyes. They were the colour of the sky on the most perfect of cloud-free, summer days. His hair was yellow, like a cornfield. She included a picture of him. It was an image of Kurt Cobain. She asked me to pass on her email to Mr Lavelle, if I was successful in my endeavour.

I encountered many links to lesbian porn involving teenage girls in school uniforms.

Some prayers and several pictures of the Sacred Heart. His skin fair, his light brown hair flowing over his shoulders and his burning red heart. Underneath one of the images was the line, 'My love is unfathomable.'

A link to a short, poor-quality video of a priest standing in a circle of girls giving some kind of a talk. The image kept shuddering and the sound was distorted and patchy. His audience looked vacant and in a trance of boredom. At one point he raised his hands and said, looking up to the ceiling, 'We are born in sin and die in sin.' I was about to delete when something about the uniform made me look again. It was that of Temple House. I paused the video anytime it landed on one of the girls, to see if one of them might be Victoria or Louisa. But I didn't recognize any of the faces.

I also received several images of the Slender-Man, a faceless, dark figure who looked like a stick-man drawing that had been stretched. His limbs an exaggeration. In most of the pictures he was standing on the edge of a forest, while children played in the foreground, happily unaware of the spectre behind them. The Pied Piper.

I had stepped through a crooked mirror in a fairground and things were jumbled up and fractured.

Feeling like I needed to look beyond the reach of the advert, I called up a favour from a college mate and did an interview with a late-night radio show where I talked about the case. The producer said any messages that had come in were from the usual crackpots and nothing she would even pass on to me. The intern told me my voice sounded very different on the radio, high-pitched.

The next night I was invited to talk to a psychic live on air who might be able to help. I declined the offer.

My mother asked me if I knew what I was doing. She looked concerned. A few days into my research and I wasn't sleeping, had dark circles under my eyes. When I closed them I could almost feel the outline of the sockets, like the skin was stretching thinner and thinner.

I told her I was fine and not to worry. All part of the job.

She was making tea in the kitchen when she turned to me and said, 'You know, sometimes there are no reasons. Things just happen and they have no meaning, really.'

I was surprised by her nihilism.

'I don't expect to solve the case, it's not about that,' I answered, laughing in an attempt to lighten the mood. 'I'm just writing about it.'

She was drying a cup before putting the teabag in.

'And it's not stressful, it's interesting, which makes a change from what I have been writing,' I said. 'You know I can do more and my editor is really supportive. . .'

She must be shrinking, I thought, standing beside her. She had always been taller than me but she no longer was.

'I know, of course you can do more,' she said.

I stirred the tea.

She looked weary of me. I had that effect on people.

I sat down at the table.

'You know she minded you once,' she said, 'Louisa.'

'Really?' I replied.

This had never been said before. I felt the pull of a connection again.

'I had to go to your grandmother's, she'd had a fall. Louisa was tying her bike up in her front garden so I just ran across the road and asked her. It was just for half an hour or so,' she said.

'When was this? What age was she?' I asked.

She looked at me with surprise; my words were rushed, agitated.

'You were about four or five so she must have been fifteen, I suppose,' she said. 'It was before her parents split up. I remember her mother came out of the house as I was talking to her. She said she would keep an eye on you too.'

'And what did Louisa do with me?' I said.

'She minded you, of course, read you some stories. I can't remember exactly but you seemed happy when I got home,' she said.

She left the room then. As if I had insulted her approach to child-rearing.

It was eerie, disconcerting somehow, to think of Louisa here in the house.

Just as well no one can see the future. It was a thought I always had whenever I saw pictures of people who had died young or suddenly. Best not to know what lies ahead.

I opened the laptop.

I started to describe the street Louisa and I had lived on. And it felt urgent and real.

The narrow houses; the grey rippled concrete on the road; the uneven kerbs; the bins standing at the corner of the street so the bin truck didn't have to reverse down the road; the way the trees were planted too close together outside Louisa's house and had started to unearth the low stone wall in front of her front door; how a lone plastic bag was trapped in the branch of one of the trees outside their house. And how it must have been there for years, because it was tattered and frayed; how it must have got caught in a random gust of wind before being trapped in the branch that tapped on the window that might have been her room. The room that had been empty for so long.

I wrote until it was dark.

I wanted to make people feel as though it could have been them.

Your ordinary, average life could be interrupted.

Wasn't that what we had all learned? Don't stray beyond the corner of the road.

Make sure your ambition isn't too big. It could lead you elsewhere.

It was late when I finished. My mother had already gone to bed. I turned off the lights in the kitchen and walked to the hall door. I thought about Louisa, sitting on the floor of our sitting room reading me stories. And for a second I felt like maybe I did remember it. Maybe I had remembered it, all along.

I took the bus across town. When I opened the door to my apartment, there was a letter lying on the hall floor.

Chapter Twelve

She was sitting on a couch in front of the fireplace. The grate was empty and in place of a lit fire there was a large arrangement of dried flowers. The hotel was plush, with thick carpets and heavy curtains on the windows. Staff in waistcoats, with their hair pulled back in tight buns, stood behind doors and carried silver trays noiselessly between the overstuffed chairs and couches. A group of Asian businessmen were crowded around one low table in the corner.

She was pale. Her hair was still noticeably red but must have faded a bit and was now gold in tone. Her nails were the same colour. A large diamond flashed on her hand and she was clothed almost entirely in shades of cream and fawn. Everything about her was coordinated and expensive. She stood up as I approached and shook my hand, gesturing for me to sit down. With a single nod of the head she summoned a waitress.

'Ms O'Neill, Helen, thank you for agreeing to meet, for responding to the advert,' I said and took my notebook out and put it on the small marble table between us. It knocked against the sugar bowl as I laid it down and some cubes tumbled out. She raised her eyebrows slightly as I attempted to pick them up and leave them on the edge of the coffee tray.

She flicked something off her scarf.

'We have had every kind of person contact us over the years. As I am sure you can imagine.' Her voice was slow and measured.

'Yes, it must have been so difficult at times. I am trying to do something quite different, though; I am really trying to understand the impact it had on all of you, the trauma it must have been to lose a friend and a teacher in such mysterious circumstances,' I replied.

Was that it? Their trauma. Or more my own sense of danger. The phantom child we never knew but who was mentioned every year when the nights got dark and the Christmas lights were put on.

She raised her eyebrows very slightly again as I spoke.

'Much as I would love to get any new information on the case from you that might help, I just really want to try and understand what it must have been like, being there, the impact it had,' I said once more.

She sat a fraction more upright in her chair.

'I feel like it's this moment in time, this huge loss, and you have all been sort of frozen in it and I wonder what that has been like. . .' my voice trailed off.

I was talking too much and possibly stretching empathy too far.

'Are you a therapist or a journalist?' she answered, taking a sip of coffee from her cup.

So she wasn't dumb.

She set her cup down gently on the table between us and folded her arms. Her eyes were grey, not just a pale blue, but actually grey.

We sat in silence for a few seconds.

'I'm sorry,' I said, 'and thank you for meeting me. I thought...'

The waitress arrived with my coffee.

'I am in touch with many of my class and those in Louisa's too. We face this kind of tabloid interrogation every year or so. Our lives get hijacked, letters in the post, pictures in the paper and that kind of thing.'

The coffee was good, proper, not like the rubbish I drank in the office.

I took another sip and thought about saying to her, *I know it's such a drag, isn't it, living in a democracy, with a free press.*

'I know there was a lot of rumour, insinuation about the school, your relationships with your teachers, with him. It's been a feeding frenzy for a very long time. I have read a lot of the reports from the past; they can be lurid and not helpful,' I said.

'Yes, not helpful. That's one way of putting it,' she said, looking not quite at me but over my shoulder. 'They all wanted to know about us, the girls on the hill. I believe that was one of the headlines. One of the less offensive ones.'

And would I be adding to this tally of sensationalist press? No, however tempting. Louisa alone deserved better.

Helen looked around as she finished speaking. A man sitting nearest us did not stir behind a copy of the *Financial Times*.

'What do you think happened?' I asked, leaning forward in my chair. My best expression of earnest interest painted on. She sighed heavily and shook her head.

'My name better not appear anywhere,' she said.

'Okay,' I said.

'They ran away together. Everybody knows, or at least presumes that. They were always together, everyone knew it would end in some kind of a mess. They were obsessed with him. . .' Her voice quietened and she looked down at her hands.

Her face was so white. There were cracks where the make-up was sitting in the lines around her eyes. Powdered and dry. It was the only evidence of decay, of imperfection.

'They?' I said.

'Louisa, I mean,' she answered.

'I don't think most people think Louisa ran away. They think something happened, he abducted, murdered her,' I said.

She didn't respond.

'People don't just vanish, when they have no money or passport or anything,' I continued.

'Don't they? If they want to?' she answered, shrugging her shoulders slightly.

'I am sorry for bringing it all up, I really am, but surely you must know that this kind of a case, it resonates with people, it's a mystery they want to solve, and you were all there with her, you knew him. I don't think it's ever going to end for you until people find out what happened,' I said.

More silence. Helen was staring at the dead flowers in the grate.

'People don't just vanish into thin air. Part of the interest all these years later is the silence from those who must have known more. Maybe I can help start the process of closing it down now, help get closer to the truth, explain more about what might have occurred or at least why and how it affected you,' I said.

She reached under the table to retrieve something from her bag. She was bored. I hadn't even managed to irritate her.

'Truth. Like that is ever a motivation. What even is the truth at this stage?' she asked me, checking her phone in a distracted manner.

'Well, the truth is finding out what happened, not just that but also finding a way to explain what it's like to be defined by something that you couldn't control,' I replied.

'I was never defined by this, why would I be?' she answered, looking straight at me.

'No, I'm sorry, of course not. I just mean, it's like seeing an accident happen or something, or getting sick; you were this person before, and after you are something different,' I said.

I felt my throat drying. I got the attention of a waitress, who went to get me water. Helen made me slightly nervous. A depth of coldness to her.

She looked at me as if I was ill. I was losing her, had never had her, really. She didn't seem to have been changed by the tragedy of a lost classmate. I would try a new track.

'Edward Lavelle, did you sense that he was not what he seemed in any way; he must have appeared charismatic, unusual?'

She took a deep breath.

'I don't remember much about him, he was nothing special anyway. . . Charisma,' she spoke the word as if it was poison, 'what even is that? We were sixteen, seventeen; even the gardener seemed of interest, to some of us anyway.'

That's a good way of putting it, I thought to myself.

The waitress returned, laying a small white doily on the table before putting the glass down. It was filled with ice and lemon with a sprig of something green in it.

'It was a great school, you know, and he played no part in that history. It educated women who went on to make a difference in this world. Do you know that? No, of course not. No one cared about what had been ruined or the way it had been before. We became these grotesque headlines. It broke the nuns; everything they had worked for was gone, covered in shame. They came out of it as evil and he. . .' She didn't finish the sentence.

It was the first time she had seemed authentic throughout. A slight red glow on her neck and cheeks. The nuns and their world had meant something to her, Louisa had not.

'They are all gone now, the nuns. I mean passed away?' I said.

'Really, I must ask you to leave it now and let it go. There is nothing to be gained by going back and dredging it all up for the sake of some article filled with your perhaps well-intentioned but amateur psychological insights.'

'Why did you agree to meet me?' I asked.

She didn't answer but stood up then.

'Are you still in touch with Victoria?' I pressed.

She stopped, just for a moment, and I watched her stare at her face in the gilt-framed mirror above the fireplace. For a minute it seemed like the hard, brittle energy had drained away.

She turned back to me then, fixing her bag on her shoulder.

'Of course,' she answered. 'Victoria and I were always very close. She feels the same about this endless game of cat and mouse that people like you play.'

Outsiders. Onlookers.

She, by contrast, was an insider. Smug but in an elegant, dismissive way. And strong as a result.

I told her I had emailed Victoria directly and was looking forward to hearing from her.

'I know she was closest to Louisa,' I said, hoping that I would be able to get Helen to stay or at least give me more of her story.

'I think you'll find that was much exaggerated in the media coverage,' she replied.

'Really?' I said.

She didn't respond.

'Well, I will ask her that myself,' I said.

'She won't speak to you,' she said finally. 'None of us will.'

She was still head girl, the guardian of reputation. That was why she'd met me.

'I'm sorry again for bringing it all up,' I continued. 'But about Louisa – can you tell me who she was really, what she was like? I grew up opposite her, she used to babysit me. I mean, I didn't know her but I went to the same school as she did. She is this tragic, lost figure to me.'

I was grasping for something, anything. One last shot at empathy.

She looked at me and I saw contempt pass over her face.

'Louisa didn't fit in. She misunderstood everything,' she said, walking to the door.

I called after her, the silence of the hushed and expensive room broken by my voice.

She turned, her eyebrows raised, eyes darting from one side of the room to the other, checking if anyone had noticed.

'I meant to ask you, when was the last time you saw Louisa alive?' I asked.

Her face went red and she strode out of the lounge then. Her heels were sharp, pointed and loud on the floor beyond.

I rang my editor on my way back to the office.

'Well?' he said.

'Not good,' I said. 'I don't know why she met me. I think maybe to warn me off a bit.'

'Look, it's something, keep going,' he said.

It was starting to rain.

'I will,' I said.

'There is a touch of the pioneer about you,' he said.

'You mean desperate,' I said.

'We got a response from the mother. She doesn't want to do an interview.'

'Shit,' I said.

'We can print the response, though,' he said.

'What does she say?' I asked.

The rain was getting heavier. I took shelter in the porch of a church.

An elderly man was sitting behind a small desk; there were magazines on the table in front of him and a collection box. He smiled at me, his anorak too big for him and damp in places.

'Well, the most interesting part is. . .' my editor said.

I could hear him fumbling with paper on the desk.

'My daughter was let down by her school and the authorities. In those first few hours of her disappearance, no call was made to the police or to us, her parents. This made all the difference. . .'

'That's not news, really; she has said that before,' I said.

'It's something,' he said. 'Write to her again, you should be able to coax her out. She hasn't spoken in a few years to anyone about it.'

'Maybe she has finally given up,' I said, ending the call.

I smiled at the old man and dropped a coin into the box and picked up a copy of the magazine; it was called *The Good News*. He gestured to the doors of the church.

I pulled open the heavy door. It was semi-dark within and almost completely empty. A few elderly people, their backs to me, sat in the pews ahead, heads bowed. The candles wavered and danced in the gloom.

The nuns and their world. It had vanished too, and that's what Helen mourned.

Beside me there was a small side altar, with purple tea-light candles on it.

I thought about Louisa and how possibly you need to ask permission to tell someone's story, and so I lit one.

Chapter Thirteen

'You won't have enough for a series. Maybe a long read at the most,' the intern said.

She was sorting through photo files beside me.

I drank some coffee and kept typing.

'I think they ran away,' she said, holding one of the images up to the window behind us.

'Based on what?' I said, turning to her.

'Well, everyone says they were really close and he is kind of attractive. Like it could have been a crush that went too far,' she said.

I pulled up the picture of them on to my screen. They did look good. If they had been less attractive would anyone have thought this a likely explanation? Or if she had been from a better place, a richer family?

'People don't usually run away with their teachers,' I said.

'It happens, you hear it in the news from time to time. . . all that repressed emotion in the classroom,' she said.

'I wouldn't know,' I responded.

She raised her eyebrows.

'Though, I mean, it would have been a total abuse of his position and all that.' She sounded embarrassed then.

We worked on together in silence.

'Are you coming to the drinks on Friday?' she asked.

'I doubt it, might have to go away this weekend,' I said.

'No one thinks you will come.'

'I am predictable.'

I stood up from my desk and grabbed my coat.

'Can you keep an eye on social media for me, see if anything is coming through that side?' I asked.

The first article had yet to run but already there had been some crossover from the advert, a few threads and conversations online. I recognized some of the names, people who had emailed me directly and were now sharing information. The advert too had been shared.

'Where are you going now?' she said.

'I'm meeting the detective who was on the case.'

'Can I come?'

I shook my head.

'They stuck together; that was the thing we all remember most from it.' He drank some tea from a large mug and as he did so he slurped slightly.

He looked as tired as he had on the TV show.

'Every case has some sort of a feature that stands out. In this one it was the communal silence, like they had a kind of lack of curiosity about what had happened. We felt we were intruders, rather than people there to solve something. There was no urgency, on their part, to get to the bottom of it all.'

'Even Victoria, her friend?' I asked, pushing one of the old press articles with her photo across the table to him.

'Yes, she was no different; if anything she was more closed off than the others,' he answered, holding the paper up and at a slight distance, as if he had trouble reading.

'She was odd, almost mute, in the first days of interviews, with her father beside her and a priest, if I remember rightly,' he said. 'All she would say was that they had been in the art room together cleaning up. She had then left for evening prayers and Louisa said she would follow her. The next thing she knew she was being woken up, it was close to midnight and the bell was ringing in the house. It had been discovered that Louisa was not in her room.'

He rubbed his eyes; they were red and watery. I took some notes.

'But people react in odd ways to a shock, they don't always say or behave as you imagine. I have learned over many years not to judge them on this alone. She was young too. They had obviously been involved with the teacher in some way that was outside of the norm and she knew it was all going to come out.

117

She wasn't going to talk and get herself into any more trouble. She just repeated the same line over and over.'

Victoria, I had to make her talk to me.

My phone beeped on the table in front of us.

'I knew she was lying, though,' he said. 'The last sighting of Louisa had been in the village; she never made it back to the school. The bike did, though; it was found at the side of the school and I always felt Victoria had been with her at his house in the village; she cycled back without Louisa, left her with Mr Lavelle.'

'Did Victoria seem devastated, shocked?' I asked.

'I think alarmed is the best way to describe her. Like a game had got out of control. She was in a kind of retreat when we interviewed her. Daddy was going to fix things as best he could.' He dipped a gingernut biscuit into his tea.

'Why do you say a game?' I asked, stirring my coffee.

'I don't know, really; it just didn't feel real. There was a sense of artifice in her, like she played roles, parts.'

'So you think she was complicit, helped Louisa to run away with him or to be with him that night?' I asked.

'Yes, Louisa was last seen near his cottage; she must have been meeting him, but I don't think she ran away with him,' he said, shaking his head.

He looked out the window then.

'There was a delay, wasn't there – the school, they didn't call the police until the next day?' I asked.

118

I thought of her mother's letter. The sense of her daughter lost and no one even knowing for almost twelve hours.

'They didn't raise any alarm until about twelve the next day,' he said, wiping some crumbs from his lap.

'Was that not really unusual?' I asked.

'The nuns must have known from early evening but I'm sure they figured they were just on a night out and would creep in by dawn. It had probably happened before,' he answered.

Nuns, who were they really? I had never been taught by them, our school was secular. We celebrated all religions. We were tolerant and welcoming, according to the sign over the principal's door. But the nuns were interesting in their own way. They were powerful businesswomen, educators, medics. Admired and ambitious, yet now viewed only as cruel fanatics.

'There was also a fete being set up in the school that day, Christmas celebrations and such; it seemed the usual strict rules and controls had been relaxed. An air of confusion. They presumed it would be a minor scandal, easily handled if she came back by midnight,' he said. 'They always maintained Louisa was troubled, had struggled to settle; they never moved from their view that she had run away.' He checked his watch as he finished speaking.

'Do you think they knew more than they let on?' I asked.

'Yes, I think so. But that doesn't mean they were complicit. However, they were masters at secrecy and it was a different time; maybe we didn't ask all the right questions. They gave you the sense that something might have been going on with her and the teacher but would never confirm it, just hinted.'

He paused and looked out of the window. He looked annoyed, tense. It had overtaken his tiredness.

'There was still a deference, some level of innocence maybe, on our part. And maybe theirs also. They just wanted to cover the whole thing up, if they could. There was little will to cooperate. They must have known, suspected he was. . .' he said, energy suddenly draining from him again. 'A strange one, a danger to the pupils in their care, and they should have acted sooner.'

Mr Lavelle, blond and charismatic. More fancied than the gardener.

The cafe was starting to empty and the staff were cleaning up loudly behind the counter. There was a large blackboard near the cash desk with a quote from Andy Warhol on it – 'Life is Pretty'. The staff eyed us impatiently. We were keeping them from their other lives.

'If they were willing to believe he ran away with her, they must have thought there was something going on between them,' he said. 'They failed in their duty of care, either way.'

'Was the fact that she was the scholarship girl a factor in all of this?' I asked.

He clenched his hands together and looked down at the table for a second. Like he might be praying for patience, guidance.

'I fear so; if it had been one of the other girls they might have moved quicker,' he said slowly, 'but then I don't know, I mean. . .'

That sense of lost worlds again. When the rules were different.

We didn't speak for a few seconds. I watched the waitress clean down the counters near the cash desk and thought about how hard it is to keep going sometimes, to create a life, to have dignity, to be someone.

'Who do you think he was, Lavelle?' I asked, turning back to face him.

'I think we would describe him now as a classic paedophile, attracted to vulnerable young women, targeting them. I think Louisa, she was an outsider in there, and he would have recognized that. When we looked into his background, his family, we discovered he was something of an outsider too. He was an only child, spoilt, kind of indulged by his mother who thought he was going to be the next Picasso or something,' he said. 'He was expelled from a number of schools before being privately tutored at home. He did get a place in art school but dropped out and travelled Europe for a year or so. Then he arrived in Temple House. There had been no convictions or indeed any violence or crime in his background but I don't think that anyone was terribly surprised he had ended up doing something, if not criminal, at least scandalous.'

'Wasn't he an unusual choice of teacher for the school?' I asked.

'I don't know really – maybe, yes. He must have been. But then he seemed to have been a bit of a fantasist, with extravagant tastes and a sense of himself as superior, special. He enjoyed the attention I'd say he got from the students, the access he had to them. He had. . .' He paused.

'Charm,' I said.

'Yes, yes, that was probably it,' he said.

'And where did he go, do you think?' I asked.

'If I knew that. . .' He smiled at me. 'He probably had it all planned. For him there would have been no rush, he had maybe six or seven hours to get on the road, jump on a boat, and disappear. It's possible to do.'

'You think he murdered her?' I said.

'Yes.' He spoke the word softly but firmly.

'How did you find her parents?' I asked.

'They were cowed, I think, by the school. The talk in the first few days was that she had run away, not been abducted. Of course we recognized something suspicious had happened, but somehow they'd had this bad start to the investigation and were never quite able to get back to the point of being parents of a victim, rather than some loose, wild teenager, who should have known better.

'It was sad, her father used to ring me every few months or so, for many years after. He would always be sort of apologetic, as if he was bothering us, then finally the calls stopped,' he said.

'He died,' I said.

I could see him, leaning against the low wall outside their house. His coat too large, and a bottle just visible in a side pocket.

'Yes, I know,' he said.

'Did you ever believe she might have run away, willingly, with Lavelle?' I asked.

'No, I never felt she was this troubled person they all claimed. It all felt concocted, a better story for them. She wasn't very popular and may have had a hard time but that is not the same thing as wanting to disappear,' he said.

The waitress began to clear the table around us. He held on to his cup and nodded to her.

'Can you tell me more about the search itself?' I asked.

'We concentrated mainly on the village and the surrounding fields. We searched the school grounds also, but there was nothing. Her room was untouched, nothing taken. She hadn't run away,' he said, shaking his head. 'His cottage had been emptied, though, and the summer house.'

'The summer house?' I said.

'Yes, at the school, where he held his art classes.'

I wrote 'summer house' down in my notebook. We said nothing for a minute.

'Why are you writing about it, can I ask?' he said.

'It's the twenty-fifth anniversary later this year, we are trying to jog some memory. It's going to be a series, if I can get enough together. But besides that it's a story that's kind of haunted me anyway,' I answered.

I had never really said that out loud. I wondered why.

He looked at me sadly.

'I can understand that,' he said. 'It's stayed with me, a case like this, it does. I was broken that we didn't get further than we did on it. You lose sleep. . .' His voice faded off slightly. 'You know, I used to think about those fields around the village, even after we had scaled back the search. It was there, she died there, near that village. I was sure of it. I'd dream of it sometimes, even years after.'

'It's like a fairy tale,' I said.

'More a nightmare; the school was a strange place. Cold, unyielding and not the kind of institution where I'd send my daughter. Harsh.'

'Black masses,' I said.

'What?' he asked.

'It's one of the theories, that it was this place of pagan ritual and sacrifice historically, like a hell-fire club before the nuns took over,' I said.

He laughed and said he doubted that.

I smiled.

He drank the last of his tea.

'I lived in the house opposite Louisa's.' I stared out the window. A homeless man with a small dog was laying out some cardboard on the ground.

'Yes, you said in your note,' he responded.

I noticed he had gently reached into his pocket for his keys. I hoped he didn't think I was a nut, like my new internet friends and their talk of pagan rituals and the killing of virgins.

'Well, at least I have the keyboard warriors, they have much to say on the case,' I joked.

'Ah yes, we didn't have them to contend with then. Though, you know, sometimes there is truth, buried in the madness,' he said.

He was looking at me intently now and I felt it was something he was probably good at, watching people, seeing things in them others didn't. Then making a measured and careful judgement.

For a second the image of the Slender-Man at the edge of the forest came into my head.

Who led Louisa away?

'I want to write something different, something more meaningful about it,' I said.

And I meant it.

He watched me for another second, then started to pull on his jacket.

'I think you shouldn't expect too much of them, any of them. They thought they were above the law, did not see themselves as tabloid fodder. It was about saving face,' he said.

I packed up my notebook and phone as he spoke.

'Keep in touch; if there is anything more I can help you with, I would be happy to meet up again. And if you do come across some new information let me know and I can link you with someone inside to talk to. You never know. The case remains open, though not active, to be honest,' he said.

'I'm going to see her, Victoria,' I said, almost as an afterthought, 'tonight.'

'Really?'

'Yes,' I said, gesturing to the offices across from the cafe.

'She is giving a lecture,' I said. 'I have a good feeling she will talk to me. I have been writing to her a lot, explaining why I am doing this.'

He paused a moment and frowned, like he was worried for me, then nodded politely and walked out.

I left the cafe and looked across the square to the building where Victoria worked. The last of the evening sunshine was reflected on its windows. Even though it was chilly and would be dark within an hour, it felt like spring was waiting quietly in the wings. There was a slight change in the light and an urgency in the air. People rushed past to catch buses and trains home to the suburbs or greeted friends outside smart bars, ready for a night of ease and glamour after their day at a desk.

I had taken to writing in the cafes near Victoria's office. In my head she would walk in one day and queue for a sandwich or something. But I had yet to catch sight of her. And she had still not responded to my emails.

Maybe my mother was right. I took things too far. Always had something to prove.

Dear Victoria,   February 2015

I am sorry you did not respond to my earlier email. I do
believe there is an angle and insight to this story that
you, and only you, can provide. Your memories could
really help people understand who Louisa was. Her short
life has been marred by rumour and innuendo. This is a
chance to set the record straight. . .

Dear Victoria,   February 2015

I am again sorry to not have heard from you. I
understand this is difficult. And if my last email in any
way suggested otherwise, or reopened the emotional
impact and loss you must feel, I apologize. I recently met
with Helen O'Neill. She was adamant that you would not
open up to me about Louisa, but I feel she is wrong. . .

Dear Victoria,   February 2015

It's been over a week since my last email. I am again very
disappointed not to have heard from you. I do sincerely
understand how difficult this is. I did want to let you
know, however, that I will be speaking to some college
friends of Mr Lavelle. They are very keen to talk about
him, even after all this time. They feel that only now, so

many years later, will they be able to open up about who he was and also discard some of the things that were written about him. They feel he was not a violent man. . .

I thought much about what I would say if she did respond.

I walked across the square and entered her office building. There was a security guard and a welcome desk in the glass-fronted lobby. The fading sunlight was coming through the clear roof high above my head and I could see small bits of dust floating in the air. I imagined them landing on the polished marble floor and forming a layer of dirt.

A large TV screen displayed revolving images of planes, high-rise offices and young smart people shaking hands. There was a photographer in the corner of the foyer lining people up for photographs against a large backdrop that had the name of the company in giant letters. A lady with a foreign accent in a black suit gave me a name badge and directed me to the room where the talk would take place. She said the event would be followed by drinks and food in the rooftop garden and she gave me a ticket for a free glass of something. I would need this, she warned me with an air of precision and efficiency.

The room was filling up when I entered; young, enthusiastic graduates chatted around me and drank white wine. I squeezed through the crowd and went to the refreshment stand where glasses of champagne were lined up, an army of them, with strawberries floating on top. I took a bottle of water and stood at the side of the room. There were no windows. The walls were pale grey and covered in a kind of thick, hairy fabric. There was a table at the front and it was laid out for three, with notepads and pens.

My bag was heavy. The leather strap cutting into my arm. The pain was dull and matched the one I could feel starting to grow behind my eyes. The chatter grew louder and the room felt airless. The light from the long tubes of fluorescence above was harsh on the exposed skin underneath. Everyone looked vaguely green or yellow. A long winter lay on us. I closed my eyes for a second and leaned my head against the wall.

A shadow passed over the red blurry haze behind my closed eyes and stopped. It didn't pass me by.

And somehow I knew, without opening my eyes, that it would be Victoria.

Louisa

Chapter Fourteen

Rumour. It speaks first in dull whispers.

And what does it speak of?

A plain and banal truth, with a covering of lies.

Like someone painting leaves on to a dead tree. A sparse, harsh, winter thing, cloaked in the pretence of abundance. Seductive and convincing but only at twilight.

I understand now, all these years later, you do inevitably become something of what others say of you. Rumour sharpens the mood, it is an expectation the audience has been primed for. And it shapes the outline, the scope of your performance. Your life. It is judgement, without any need for the gods.

That's what happened to him, and to me also.

The evenings drew in and became cooler but mostly we chose not to notice. Victoria and I played tennis in the late October afternoons after class, and sometimes for a few minutes before the bell rang, we would just collapse on the damp grass with our school jumpers for pillows. We would stare at the clouds going past and the leaves on the trees golden against the sky. There was always a cool, fresh breeze and the faint taste of salt in the air. I have that sense of Technicolor again when I think of it, those moments of heightened consciousness when you know that this, this moment right now, will be important to remember. Because it won't last.

The birds would soar high above our heads and we took to predicting the weather. If the seagulls came in droves off the cliffs it meant rain was on the way. And we were almost always right. The mist, though, was harder to foresee. A few wisps at first that you failed to register as anything much except the slight dying of the light. It was only as you stood up, brushing the grass from your jumper, that you would notice the creeping damp on your legs and in the air, wet socks and shoes. And the school would no longer be tall and all-seeing but blurred and ghostly, its edges rubbed out.

Some nights, when the fog was really thick, the fog-horn could be heard far off down the coast. A mournful cry, a warning let out into the waves and the night. I found it strangely comforting, like someone else was awake in the dark. Watchful and concerned. I slept very little. The room was cold and shadowy and when it was windy, the heavy, dusty curtains would blow slightly. The windows were old, with cracks in the glass and the wood splintered, with moss growing around the edges of the frame. In the mornings the entire pane would have condensation on it and each day I wiped it away with the sleeve of my uniform. It became a morning ritual.

Victoria believed in ghosts, and in communion with the dead. She told me once that after her favourite aunt had died she woke up one night and could smell her perfume in her bedroom. It was a particularly romantic and flowery smell, orange blossoms and hyacinth, and not something Victoria would ever wear. She dared not move in the bed. It happened three times and then nothing. She wondered had her aunt got bored and just left. She was sure the school was haunted. She thought it was by the dead, but I was more certain it was by the living. With their petty hatreds and awkward, mean desires. They were the shadow that lay on everything.

As we sat in the grass those afternoons, I remember telling Victoria about the strangely religious phase in my life as a child where I'd take the Illustrated Children's Bible out of the library on a regular basis. Jesus was blond and blue-eyed in it and always wearing white, glistening robes. He was taller than everyone too, like a giant Aryan beauty. I read it every night before bed, tracing the Hebrew names with my finger as if they contained magic within them. Exotic and elusive in equal measure. I had never told anyone about this. No one before would have been interested.

I also spoke of the small statue of Mary I had that glowed a light green colour in the dark. I made an altar for her in my room and picked daisies from the garden and put them in a glass as we didn't have any vases. She seemed benign by day and I felt that I had appeased her well enough with my morning prayers and wilting weeds. But by night she turned on me. Her glow was ethereal and terrifying. I was sure I had been singled out for a special fate. She would come calling, insisting I had a vocation, asking me to remove my eyeballs, or walk on hot coals in bare feet, just to prove my love. I had a strong sense that there was something I was going to be forced to do, and I would have no choice in the matter. I was the one.

'Maybe that's what brought you here,' Victoria said. 'You possibly do have a calling.'

'No, but the nuns are intriguing. Brides of Christ,' I said.

'Don't you think it's ghoulish the way they wear wedding rings?' she said, shaking her head.

'Not really,' I said. 'They have given themselves up for something greater, bigger than themselves. I admire that.'

What was I trying to tell her? That I believed in angels that floated above us and a fiery hell down below? I don't think so. It was something else.

'It's all about suffering,' said Victoria. 'It's not the romantics who invented that idea, it was Catholics. You can't have pleasure without pain. It's not real if your palms haven't been nailed to the cross.'

She had turned on her side now to face me and was leaning on her elbows. I could see Mr Lavelle over her head, standing at the steps to the entrance. He was talking to Helen. A committee to celebrate the fiftieth anniversary of the school had been recently set up and he was the nominated teacher. A popular choice.

Helen was more animated than usual, her arms gesturing, her cloak and red hair blowing in the breeze.

'I don't believe in God and I don't believe in love,' I said, lying back.

We were to have a week's holiday from school for Halloween. My mother had asked if I would come stay with her for a few days. A part of me wanted to go, the other part felt guilty. Dad would be alone. Left behind. I felt resentful at having to make the choice.

'Really?' said Victoria.

'No, they are both myths. They make people feel better about themselves for a while. It's that whole opium for the masses thing,' I answered, looking at the sky. 'I might become a socialist, actually.'

I said things then just to catch her attention.

Victoria laughed and, leaning over me, pulled my hair back from my face the way she sometimes did, like she had to see all of me. Nothing could be concealed. I held my breath at her touch and looked at her. Her eyes were large and darker, navy in the fading light.

'I could never be a socialist; it means you have to admit you are the same as everyone else. You couldn't do it either,' she said.

I felt like we had known each other all our lives. Time had distorted for us, was compressing the gaps and distance of the past. I dreaded the next week apart from her.

She pulled away and sat up, looking out to the coast.

Gone.

'And that's why it fails,' I said. 'Everyone wants to have something else, be something more than the person beside them. The curse of human nature.'

The need to be seen.

'Last year I asked if we could get a theologian to visit the school,' she said, 'to ask what happened to all the people who died before Jesus lived. They didn't know they were leading sinful lives, like he hadn't arrived on earth yet to tell them. So it seems to me they had an unfair disadvantage. They knew no better and where's the mercy in that?' she said.

Her voice was sad; melancholy rose in her.

I sat up. The wind had grown stronger, and large, thick, grey clouds were moving across the sky. Victoria's back looked thin and narrow. She pulled her jumper around her shoulders.

'Weren't there all those prophets, though, with burning bushes? Weren't they the ones spreading God's word before he came?' I said, trying to coax her back.

I could picture all those pre-Jesus sinners and Victoria inspecting them, pondering their lack of knowledge, the dark fate that awaited them. The fate that only she knew of. No mercy in the Old Testament.

'Oh, Moses, I forgot about him.' She paused for a second. 'Anyway the school sent a letter home – ". . . we feel it is our duty to inform you that your daughter has been disrupting the class, we welcome open debate but she is asking inappropriate questions. . ." Like curiosity is a disease.'

I laughed; she was making it up. They were far too diplomatic and clever to write that.

'I mean, at least have some intellectual might behind your teachings; like even one day a week, a theologian would be good, a part-time one, to take questions. . .' She had turned back to me as she said this and noticed Mr Lavelle and Helen.

'They are together a lot these days,' she said.

She was frowning as she spoke.

I pulled the sleeves of my jumper down slightly. They were already frayed and I wondered how I'd managed that only two months in. The clouds had thickened over our heads and it felt like it would rain this evening.

'He has to put up with her these days. He probably feels sorry for her; her father is all over the papers and the nuns are running around after her, worrying she will have some kind of a breakdown with the shame. Let's head in anyway,' I said.

But neither of us moved. We sat in silence for a moment, watching them.

'Why don't you believe in love?' she asked, still staring at them.

'I don't know,' I answered, 'maybe I can't believe in something I've never seen.'

An image of my parents sitting in silence at the kitchen table came into my head, suitcases in the hall. For a second I felt cold and fully believed what I was saying. Love seemed like a trick. You won or were outwitted by it. You thought it was there, and then it wasn't.

'Like doubting Thomas. . .' Victoria answered, her voice fainter. 'But you can't see it, you feel it.'

She put her hand over her heart.

I didn't respond, just lay down on my back again looking at the tops of the tallest trees and the leaves that were dying, falling back to the earth.

She spoke the truth. A part of me knew that, even then.

'Helen is in love with him, you know,' she said.

I waited for the ironic comment to follow. But it didn't come.

I stayed lying down but turned on my side to look at her.

'We did this séance thing with a Ouija board last year after the Christmas concert. A few of us stayed back behind the stage when all the parents had gone for drinks. Someone had stolen a bottle of wine and some brandy. We were all drinking. Anyway, you had to get the planchette to move with the power of your thoughts and spell out a name. For ages nothing happened, everyone was half-drunk anyway and overtired from the concert, kind of giddy and taking the piss out of it.'

As she spoke her gaze did not move from Helen and Mr Lavelle.

'Then a few of the lights in the Hall that had been left on started to flicker. Someone went to check and look around the curtain on the stage. We thought maybe one of the teachers had come back to start tidying up or switch things off. But the Hall was empty, with this light in the middle just going on and off. The mood of everyone changed after that. I think we all wanted to leave but no one wanted to be the big pussy and say it. We stopped laughing, closed our eyes and held hands in silence. It was Helen's turn next and when she did it, it spelled out his name. Clear as anything. She went all red. Like the colour of her appalling hair.' Victoria turned her head to me as she finished.

Mr Lavelle was holding Helen by the arm. The way he did.

'But that's how you communicate with the dead; if it spelled out his name it meant he was dead, or going to die or something. And not that it means that either, it's just like a joke,' I said.

Victoria looked tired, like her usual glow and energy had been diminished, weakened. I wanted to reach for her, protect her from her thoughts.

'No, it means that they have a connection, like the spirit world was trying to bring them together,' she said, 'and you weren't there, you didn't see her face. Like her biggest and darkest secret had just come out.'

'Did anyone say anything when it happened?' I asked.

'No, she is too powerful to make jokes about,' she said.

'They all love him,' I said, 'he's the most popular teacher here. It doesn't make any difference anyway what she feels. He just likes the attention; it doesn't mean anything.'

Victoria looked at me; she was flushed, irritated. I had said something that was not allowed.

'He sketched her, you know, just before we broke for summer,' she replied. 'He even told me about it.'

She looked at me intensely as she spoke, and I felt for the first time a defiance in her, of me and my disbelief.

'Have you seen it?' I asked.

'Yes,' she answered. 'She's lying on the couch in the summer house. . . naked.'

She spat out the last word.

I looked away to Mr Lavelle and Helen on the steps and let Victoria's words sink in for a moment. I did not know what to say. I felt a bit like I had the first day I met her, as if all my words carried weight and the future of our friendship would be determined by my answer. I felt my mind crawl inwards to excuse him and find justification, something, anything that would lessen her burden. And his.

'What did he say when he showed it to you?' I asked, turning back to her.

'He said he needed a model and she had helped him out, like it was nothing. He was all light and breezy, you know what he's like,' she said. 'And I believed him. I mean, why wouldn't I? He's an artist; the body is just something for a canvas, his work.'

She was watching them again. Helen was laughing like the greatest joke ever had just been shared.

'I didn't want to seem petty and bourgeois.'

She shook her head slightly as she spoke.

'Except lately. . . it just seems like it's all bullshit. He's with her all the time.'

Mr Lavelle had left Helen now and walked over to his car. He bent to touch something on the wheel and as he did so he noticed us and waved. He was wearing a tweed jacket that looked too large for him.

I responded with a wave but Victoria didn't; she just stared at him, motionless. He didn't open the car door and for a second I thought he looked nervous, even afraid.

'He won't dare come over,' she said, her face paler now and her voice flat.

He didn't walk over. Instead, he got into his car and we watched as he drove out through the gates.

'Where does he go in the evening, where does he live?' I asked, getting to my feet.

My skirt felt damp. These afternoons in the grass would be ending soon. Autumn was no longer a cautious visitor to the gardens.

'In the village. There is a lodge house on the corner, near the pub,' she answered.

She remained sitting cross-legged and in no hurry to join me. She played with a long piece of grass as she spoke.

'It's painted a very pale pink. There is honeysuckle growing around the door, and a small table and chairs on the path outside.

Sometimes there are flowers on the table, in a blue jug, and he leaves his boots outside the front door. It is how you know he's there. The sign that he's home.'

When she finished speaking she looked up, not at me, but at the cloud of dust left behind by his car.

And I felt cold, as if winter had arrived.

Chapter Fifteen

The committee meeting was in one of the attic rooms. I hadn't been to this level of the house before. A small rope usually hung across the narrow stairwell indicating it was off limits. I climbed the steps, the sounds of the school below becoming muffled and distant.

Mr Lavelle and Helen were already seated in one of the rooms off the hallway, as was one of the Vestal Virgins. Helen had a clipboard in front of her. The other girl was twirling her long fair hair and looked bored.

The space was empty of furniture except for a round table in the centre of the room and some decaying chests in the corner. A faded zebra skin hung on the wall. The windows were smaller than downstairs and it was warmer, stuffy compared to the chill of the rest of the house. The only light came from a small lamp on the floor under one of the eaves.

'Welcome, welcome,' Mr Lavelle said, smiling and pointing to a chair.

'Is anyone else coming?' I asked, standing at the entrance, unsure as to whether to close the door.

He didn't answer, just shook his head and shuffled some papers on the desk.

Helen barely looked up as I sat down. She was scribbling furiously.

'Nice pen, Helen,' I said, smiling at her.

Mr Lavelle moved his chair an inch further back from the table, put his hands behind his neck, spreading himself wide.

Helen lifted her head to me, ice in her grey, pale eyes.

'Well, Louisa, we know you have only been in Temple House for two months now but to celebrate the school's fiftieth anniversary, we are creating a book that will gather as many student experiences as possible,' he said, 'and we would like you, as one of our new scholarship students, to contribute.'

He looked at Helen as he finished. She nodded her head at him and smiled sweetly.

'I would be happy to do that,' I said.

He made you want to please him, even now when an air of fake cheeriness hung around his words.

A vague look of surprise crossed Helen's face. She thought I would say no.

The girl beside her leaned forward on to the table, putting her arms under her chin as if the whole conversation was exhausting.

'That is super news,' he said. 'I thought possibly you might write about our art classes, our new way of learning, experiencing art and how it is different from your last school, maybe something about the skull project we worked on? You could elaborate further on your essay. '

Helen breathed in sharply and laid her pen down.

Mr Lavelle gave her an anxious, sideways glance.

'If you are sure, I could, I could do that. . ' I said, looking from one to the other.

'It's up to you, Louisa, what subject you write about – within reason, obviously,' Helen said.

'We would, however, like to showcase how Temple House is moving with the times, opening its doors to. . .' she paused. 'New people. Like you.'

She spoke like I was diseased.

The other girl closed her eyes for a second.

'I am honoured to be singled out,' I said, and gave Mr Lavelle my biggest smile.

'Indeed,' Helen said, squeezing her pen and briefly looking at him to check his expression.

'It's settled then,' said Mr Lavelle, rubbing his hands together.

Helen flicked her hair over her shoulder, impatient for my departure.

'We are getting it professionally printed,' said the other girl, raising herself slowly from the table and then holding her nails out to the low light. Checking for any imperfections.

'Yes,' said Helen.

'Thrilling,' I responded.

'So there will be deadlines, which have to be met,' said Helen, her eyebrows raised.

'Yes, they have to be met,' said her sidekick, 'otherwise, it's really expensive.'

'I get that,' I said.

We all looked at each other in silence for a second.

'This Friday, Louisa, before we break for Halloween. If you could have it ready then that would be ideal,' Mr Lavelle said.

He got up then and walked me to the door.

'Mr Lavelle,' Helen said.

He turned back to her.

'There are some other things we need to discuss. We have lots to do,' she said, her pen tapping on the table.

'Yes, of course; just walking Louisa out,' he said.

He closed the door behind us and we stood in the hall. The roof was sloped and he had to stoop.

'I appreciate this, Louisa; it's really important to have new voices,' he said, looking at me.

I smiled at him. He didn't smell of grass and earth, more of dust. Like he had been locked in the attic. I again had the feeling that he needed something from me.

'It's no problem,' I said.

He put his hand to his forehead and rubbed it gently. As if he was in pain.

'Are you okay?' I said.

'Yes, yes, just, you know, lots to do, little time,' he said, raising his arm against the door frame beside my head and leaning forward towards me.

I felt small beside him.

'Victoria, is she. . .' His words hung there, his eyes locked on me.

I said nothing and looked at the wallpaper. There were brown stains in the places where the walls met the ceiling. I didn't want to talk about her. The knowledge that she had been to his house made me nervous.

'Oh, it doesn't matter.' He paused, looking down to the floor and kicking the rise in the carpet with his foot. 'Another time.'

He shrugged his shoulders and I felt like I had disappointed him. Like there was a part of me he couldn't reach, even if he wanted to.

There was laughter from Helen and the other girl to greet him when he re-entered the room, as if he had been gone months.

I walked down the narrow stairs. It was almost seven and I had a chemistry test the next morning that I needed to study for. Victoria was sitting in the half-light on the floor outside her room. She had laid out some playing cards in a semicircle around her.

'Where were you?' she said, looking up.

'The attic, weirdly, with Helen. I have been roped into writing for the anniversary book,' I said. 'Can you imagine?'

'Was he there?' she said; her eyes looked sharp and glassy.

'Yes, of course; he's on the committee,' I said.

She collected the cards and got to her feet, turning to push open her bedroom door.

I touched her shoulder. It felt brittle and fragile.

'There is nothing between them, him and Helen,' I said.

She turned back to face me. Her hair was wet and a tear rolled down her cheek.

'There can't be,' she said, leaning in and whispering in my ear, 'or I will rip her heart out.'

It felt like a slap.

Before I could answer, she was gone. The door slammed behind her.

The thin fluorescent light in the hallway switched on suddenly over my head. The signal that night-time was here and study and sleep was due.

I walked to my room, thinking of Victoria, feeling things for her I was not sure I fully understood.

Chapter Sixteen

The purpose of art class in Temple House is to expose us as students not to the surface, but to what lies beneath. We explore the motivations of not just the artist we are studying, but ourselves and our interpretations of their work. It is radical and exciting to uncover one's own deepest and often hidden fear and anxiety when observing an artwork. We are faced with ourselves and in this manner come closer to the truth. The truth of the artist and our own self.

In a recent project we were encouraged by our teacher Mr Lavelle to choose an artefact that we felt represented us, an emblem. I chose the skull and. . .

The words were stopping and starting as I tried to write. For some reason I found it hard to remember what Mr Lavelle had been teaching us over the past months. His words came back and they seemed almost meaningless, nothing connecting with anything else.

Beauty, truth, arouse, enthral, lustrous, taut, indecipherable, the void.

I could mouth the words but on paper they dissolved.

There were random phrases too and the feelings they had created in me as he spoke.

The artist can abuse us; the union of the pure and the vulgar; the exploration of the unconscious.

They returned, but little else. I searched in the cupboard beside my bed and dug out my art-history book; it hadn't been opened since I started in school. The pages shiny and unmarked.

I sat back in the hard chair and looked out the window. The sky was grey and it was getting dark. A wind was blowing the tall trees of the forest beyond the walled garden, the last of their brown leaves drifting to earth. The room was cold and in the corner of the window the small growth of moss at the edge of the frame looked damp and slimy. I picked at it aimlessly.

I wondered what they spent the school fees on. Everything was decrepit but no one ever mentioned it. Helen and the others talked of the school as if it were some majestic palace. I wondered could they not see it, was it just me? Like the boy observing the naked emperor. Even Victoria never spoke of it. The cold, the dust, and the patched-togetherness of everything. You could hear it, though, at night. The neglect. Someone was always coughing, the damp settling on their chest after dark and the sound of their struggle for air keeping you awake.

I breathed deeply on to my hands to warm them up and looked at myself in the mirror. My face was in shadow, the low lamp on my desk not reaching this far across the room; only my body was caught in the light. The Cartesian. Despite the cold I took off my jumper and started to unbutton my blouse. My body was pale, white and narrow. I was thinner than before, the tasteless, watery food pushed from one side of the plate to the other most nights. I turned to my side, my breasts a bare curve in the shadows, my stomach almost concave; it explained the way my uniform skirt had started to swivel on me. The label invariably found at the front now, rather than the back. I liked it, the sense of bones, angular and sharp. Hollow.

I remembered briefly the boy, hot and insistent last year, and how he had whispered into my neck, so quietly I had almost not heard it, *where did you buy your body?* It had struck me after as being the strangest thing to say. But then I thought maybe I had never heard it and had imagined everything about that unfamiliar night.

I looked different now, anyway, to that girl. I was disappearing. And it was a strangely enchanting idea, like something from a fairy tale. A metamorphosis that defied the short time I had been here. Victoria could put me in her pocket, carry me away. The old me was literally no more, unrecognizable.

There was a knock at the door.

I quickly pulled my shirt back on.

Mr Lavelle was smiling, his arms crossed. The hall light made his hair shine and it seemed like he glowed again. We said nothing for a second. Girls were shouting down the corridor and he watched them for a moment.

'Your essay,' he said, turning back to look at me, 'for the book, I will need it tomorrow, Friday.'

I saw him glance into the room behind me as he spoke, squinting almost into the dusk of it. I was curious to know if he had been in one of the students' rooms before and, if not, did they represent the forbidden to him. The off limits. The painting of Helen came into my mind.

I nodded to him.

His eyes were back to mine, then. And I wondered what it was he wanted to say to me? Why he, Victoria and I spent so much time theorizing about truth and yet never spoke a word of it? Irony cloaking everything. Yet there was always this feeling that each of us had something to say, if only we could find the words.

'Mr Lavelle.'

It was Victoria.

She had emerged up the stairs and from the Maiden's Chamber.

She stopped for a second at the top. Her eyes looked large, hunted, and they stared not at him, but me. Her gaze filled me up.

Mr Lavelle didn't move but he sighed quietly.

She walked over to my door.

He turned to her only as she reached his side.

'Yes, Victoria,' he said. 'What really can be so urgent?'

He put his hands behind his neck as he spoke, as if to stretch.

'I am leaving, my parents are here, we are leaving tonight and they wanted to ask you something. They are outside.' She sounded breathless, like she had run up the stairs.

Something I knew she would never do; it was part of our philosophy for living to move slowly. As though everyone would wait for us.

'And you know they can't be left waiting; I mean, what would be the outcome?' she said, trying to laugh, looking at us both.

She spoke fast, nervously. She fiddled with the strap of her watch, a kind of earnest desperation in her voice.

He didn't answer her but watched me and smiled. The wistful, melancholic smile, the one that hinted he had discovered the hidden mysteries of the world, solved them and been left wanting by it all. Jaded.

I could feel Victoria looking at him and then at me.

'Don't disappoint,' he said, his voice low, 'or Helen will be on your case. And me too possibly. Tomorrow.'

I nodded again.

He turned and walked to the stairs. Victoria hesitated for a second, her gaze briefly travelling up and down my body, distant, as if she had never seen me before. Like I was an intruder.

She was about to follow him, so I moved and took her arm as she started to walk away. Her eyes were very bright.

'I can't right now,' she said, shaking my hand off.

I felt discarded.

'See you after Halloween. . .' I said to her back.

She didn't answer. I could hear their footsteps on the stairs.

I closed the door of my room and leaned against it. As I did so I caught sight of myself in the mirror. I had buttoned my shirt wrong in the haste and it was uneven and gaping. I touched my neck and it was hot.

I should have felt embarrassed but I didn't.

Chapter Seventeen

I called Victoria once over the Halloween holiday but she had been distracted on the phone. Happy, laughing people in the background.

I was staying with my mother and her boyfriend. We did a day trip to a wet, deserted pier. The ice-cream and sweet shops closed for the season. Bad jokes repeated over dinner in the pub near their house, as if I hadn't got it the first time. Disagreements overheard downstairs after we got back. I woke to the sound of glass bottles being dropped in bins in the dark, early mornings.

I felt restless. Sullen. As if my life was improvised. Time, which accelerated when I was at the school, slowed again. I wrote a lot in my diary, copying out quotes from famous writers and then repeating them, but in my own words. I was trying to capture something. To tell of a feeling. But it never came out right. I thought perhaps when I had lived more it would be better. I would be better.

I could tell of everything then.

My father was at the window when they dropped me home. Waiting. He waved at the car. No one responded. He asked me how it had gone. There was nothing to say.

I was relieved to be back at school.

November. All Souls.

The dead among us.

The afternoons were dark by four now. The lights low over desks, hallways gloomy, wet leaves on the front steps. Exams looming. Judgements to be made. An air of purpose in the voices of the teachers.

The names of long-dead nuns were placed on gold and purple cards around the altar of the church. Candles lit.

Eternal rest grant to them, O Lord.

We prayed for them all, with words that promised salvation. Forgave them their sins.

An essay I wrote about Advent was read out at assembly one morning by Sister Ignatius.

'Advent is the season of being alert inside. The season of waiting. The soul patient, ready for the birth of its saviour.'

Her voice was reverential. She held my arm afterwards. She sensed the pilgrim in me. The quest. Helen was stern and white at her side.

They all watched my progress. Especially Mr Lavelle. He pursued my half-formed ideas in the summer house, chasing them down as the light died and the stove blazed. He knew I was searching but that I was too afraid to even name what it was I sought. Something was calling me, devouring me. It lay with me every night. It made this world as illusory as the next.

Victoria was mostly dreamy and idle. She didn't speak of Helen and Mr Lavelle or the anniversary celebrations to me again. In the evenings when I was doing my homework, she would sometimes put notes under my door, inviting me to meet her in the summer house, or at the back of the stage in the Hall.

My room-mate, Alice, was unimpressed.

'She was like this with the other girl, the one who had to leave,' she said one evening.

I shivered as I always did when she was mentioned, the enigmatic girl from before.

'Who was she?' I asked.

'No one knew, really. Her father was an ambassador, I think. Always moving around. She and Victoria were like this,' she said, crossing her fingers.

I didn't want to ask any more.

I went to the door and picked up the note.

Come this time. You're becoming very
dull. I will be in the Hall.

Victoria

I made my way down the stairs. One of the cleaning staff, head down, stood on the last step with a mop. Someone had been sick. I could smell it.

The Hall was lit only by moonlight. The large windows facing out to the coast. I walked quietly to the stage, climbed the steps and pulled back the heavy, velvet curtains. I thought about Ouija boards and flickering ghost lights. I called Victoria's name softly but there was no reply.

'She couldn't come.'

I jumped at his voice. Mr Lavelle.

I walked back to the steps and pulled the curtain aside. He was standing below me in the Hall, a shaft of light at his feet.

'She asked me to let you know,' he said, walking over to the steps.

She had sent him.

I descended slowly.

'I am leaving now, finished for the day,' he said and he brushed his hands on his trousers, as if cleaning them of dirt.

'Is she all right?' I asked.

I had stopped on the last step.

'Yes, yes,' he said.

We were at eye level. But there was no light to see his expression.

'She just had something to do,' he answered quietly; his voice was made of silver and shadows.

'You better go too,' he said, moving closer to me, 'lights out.'

I thought he might touch me. It seemed something that might happen, like in a dream.

'The nuns will be looking for you. I won't tell.' He laughed then.

It echoed around the Hall.

He turned and headed for the door, the lesson he had come to teach me, untaught.

I ran to Victoria's room on the second floor.

She opened, torch in hand, yawning. She was wearing her yellow dressing gown; it had small daisies embroidered on it.

'Why weren't you there?' I said.

My throat was dry. I could hear my heart. Awkward and out of time.

She just smiled and put her finger to her lips.

It reminded me of my pre-school teacher. She would make us line up and put our fingers on our lips before break time. The girl who sat beside me was a bit slow and could never seem to do it, and she would get into trouble for it every day and had to stand facing the wall on which the pictures we had drawn were hanging. The pictures were never hers because only the best got hung up on the wall. And one day, she just never came back to school and we all forgot that she had ever been there.

I put my arms around Victoria suddenly, and buried my head in her neck. She smelled like lemon, sharp and fresh. I thought she might pull away. But she didn't, she was still.

I wanted to stay there.

Unseen, buried in her.

I imagined she felt the same. That her inert body was complicit. And it wasn't a game we were playing but something real and alive between us.

A nun clapped her hands somewhere down the hall and lights turned off.

Chapter Eighteen

Victoria didn't send me any more notes after that night.

She was quieter, a part of her elsewhere. I sat on the floor of her room reading in the afternoons before study. She lay on her side in the bed. I would ask her things about her life. I wanted to know everything about the past, how it had made her. Sometimes she answered, and a glimpse of her childhood darted across the shadows. Sometimes not. I didn't mind. There was peace in just being near her, the lights on low.

And I didn't ask her about Mr Lavelle.

I was probably at my happiest in those dark December afternoons. A drowsy, dreamlike sense of complacency. I felt like there was time. That there was nothing to fear about myself or doubt. She accepted me at some essential level. I just needed to be brave. Her silence was an understanding.

Was I thinking of myself or her on those afternoons?

Myself, of course. Lovers are selfish. Obsessed not really with their love, but with themselves. It was what I wanted that kept me happy and awake. It haunted me and the phantoms were seductive. And I forgot to notice things. I saw the world through my own, unique reference points. All signs and symbols were pointed at me. I was happy.

I didn't recognize the melancholy that hung over her. I took it for contentment.

I was proud too. My academic results were still stellar. The nuns were watchful but they were giving me a chance in their own way. I was on the path to fulfilling my promise. The thing everyone had talked about in corridors and at parent–teacher meetings. The gift that I had been given. That would not allow my life to be like everyone else's.

I began to understand that things would work out. How could they not? I had Victoria.

I was wrong, of course. About almost everything.

A sad, stunted-looking Christmas tree was put up in the entrance hallway of the school. It was too short for the high ceilings. Thin silver streamers hung precariously off each branch. They would sway and blow every time the front door opened, some of them drifting to the floor. An empty crib sat on the ledge behind, a purple candle lit beside it.

There was going to be a Christmas concert and vintage fair as part of the anniversary celebrations. There were auditions and rehearsals in the Hall after class. A tone of ruthless ambition and mock humility characterized most conversations. Helen was in drill mode, surrounded by girls, looking concerned and saying she had taken on too much. We stayed out of her way.

Mr Lavelle was busy and distracted. A man in perpetual motion, always on the edge of our vision. Faint laughter on the front steps with the French teacher, cigarettes in hand. Framed in stained glass, dashing to his car as the moon rose and we climbed the stairs to bed.

We watched him. The show that never got boring.

Towards the middle of December, the weekend before school was to finish, Victoria invited me to a party at her house. It felt significant.

A man, possibly Victoria's father, opened the door; he displayed an air of vague indifference and called up the stairs before leaving me alone among the grandeur.

Somewhere at the back of the house came the sound of that Frank Sinatra song, 'I've Got You Under My Skin'.

And people were laughing. The kind of laughs reserved for cocktail parties, light and hollow. Not that I would know. We had barbecues.

Her home was just as I expected. It stood on a quiet, tree-lined street of large red-brick houses. The hallway where I was standing, waiting for her, had shiny black-and-white tiles on the floor and a marble fireplace with a fire burning. A towering Christmas tree, gold and green, flickered in the corner. Presents, the gift-wrapped kind, were piled up underneath.

Over the fireplace was a large painting of a woman and two young girls. The lady wore a white lace dress and a hat with a veil over her face. Something about her stare reminded me vaguely of Victoria. Like they both might have sipped iced tea and ruled colonies from a veranda. I wondered if I had worn the right dress. My coat was hanging over my arm and I didn't know what to do with it. The man who opened the door hadn't offered to take it from me. It did not seem the kind of place where you dumped it on a chair.

'It's going to be ghastly. I'm warning you,' Victoria said.

I looked up and she was standing at the top of the stairs. She was wearing jeans. I felt self-conscious in my dress. Then I thought, fuck it, I never get to go anywhere or dress up. This might be my only chance to shine at a cocktail party. She bounded down the stairs two at a time, grabbed my coat and threw it on the end of the banister. I gave her my present, a book of poetry. She left it under the tree.

'Come on, we need to show our face,' she said. 'You look nice.'

That made me happy.

'Do you ever slide down those?' I asked, gesturing to the banisters.

'I used to,' she said, 'before.'

She turned to me as she spoke, then took a deep breath, before opening the double doors into the room where the party was on.

Elegance, I thought, that's what's been missing from my life. And ease. For a second as I stood at the doorway, I was the scholarship girl with ambition again. But the good version of me. The one who had drive and worked hard. The one who was on a journey upwards. The one who was sure there was no God-given right to wealth and success; there was no plan laid down that said some people are eligible and some aren't. There was no fate, nothing divinely laid out. There were seats at the table for everyone. When you had talent. And were perhaps naive.

We moved slowly through the packed room, Victoria stopping every now and then to shake hands and occasionally hug someone. Most of the people seemed old to me, and not just parent-level old but grandparent old. It was a fragrant mass, of fur coats, powdered hair and pearls. Up-dos and expensive bags. And people smoking thin cigarettes and flicking the ashes into conveniently placed, heavy, crystal ashtrays. She didn't really introduce me to anyone but I didn't mind. I was like her shadow, head down, a few steps behind her. She spoke of tennis and a trip to Italy. Everyone agreed the holiday would be a marvellous experience for her. I wondered why she had not mentioned it to me.

There was a baby grand piano beside the French doors that led to the garden. We took refuge there and Victoria left to get plates of food for us. I looked down at the wide varnished floorboards. Everyone I knew had carpet in their good room. If they had a good room. I will have varnished floorboards with rugs, I thought to myself, when I am older and fabulous, and free. As I raised my head, I met the gaze of Helen. She was with her parents, or that's who I presumed they were. The woman beside her had faded copper hair and was waving an arm laden with gold jewellery at a piece of porcelain on a side table beside them. Helen looked sour as usual and pointedly looked me up and down before turning her head away from me.

'You didn't tell me she was coming,' I said to Victoria when she returned with plates laid high with potato salad and mushroom vol-au-vents.

'Oh yes, didn't I? Sorry. Our parents are the best of friends. I told you it would be dismal,' she responded.

We started eating.

'Mother's canapés,' said Victoria, sighing. 'She likes food that is bitesize and comes with a helpful stick in the middle of it.'

'You're good at this,' I said, nodding towards the crowd. 'All the small talk and stuff.'

'I was raised on it,' she said. 'It's all about appearances and maintaining them.'

'Kind of shallow,' I said.

'Well, yes, but it serves a purpose. You can get away with anything, if you just keep the outside shiny and perfect,' she said. 'See him,' she nodded in the direction of one man with a moustache. 'He's a politician, always does the readings in church on Sunday, fully paid-up member of the morality police, and you know what, he's screwing his au pair. Everyone knows but no one says anything. She's had to leave, gone back to Barcelona for a few months. . .' She raised her eyebrows.

The room filled up, and thankfully Helen disappeared from view. I thought the miniature food was delicious. Every now and then a waitress would walk past with a silver tray with wine on it and cheese cubes on sticks. We each took a glass of wine. It tasted sharp and bitter and I wondered why people drank it so enthusiastically. We took another two glasses without anyone noticing and soon I began to understand. I started not to care what I looked like, or who was watching. We observed the crowd around us and Victoria filled me in on their backstories, like who had affairs, had gone bankrupt, or had a drink problem.

Her uncle, a priest, talked to us at one point. He was quite young, an enthusiastic type who might hold youth clubs and take kids on hikes. He had a beard and glasses and looked to me like he was wearing one of those funny disguises that you buy in a joke shop. He asked us about the subjects we were taking and what college courses we were considering. For a laugh I said I was planning to study Russian and theology as I thought it would be interesting to combine the two opposing views of society. Victoria made faces behind his back and drank more wine. I attempted to keep my lies coherent but could feel my cheeks flushing and my head turning soft, fuzzy. I finally asked him if he thought priests should be allowed to marry, and not just nuns but normal women. Atheists even.

Maybe Russians. Then Victoria said didn't he think divorce should really be allowed and not just for rich people? He left soon after this.

'Job done,' said Victoria as he walked away. 'He is vaguely ridiculous. Actually, not vaguely. They all are. Charlatans. That's why I needed you. It was our destiny to meet.'

I turned to look at her.

She held her head high and was watching the room as if everyone around us had the plague. I was swaying slightly from the wine. I felt like I needed air or I would vomit on the perfect floor. I gestured to Victoria and we opened the French doors and went out into the garden.

It was damp and cold. The terrace was covered in fallen leaves and was slippery. We sat on black wrought-iron chairs that were rusting slightly. I thought it might mark my dress but then didn't care. Victoria had concealed a bottle of wine under her top and poured some more into my glass. We laughed as she did so. I had taken some mince pies and laid them out on a napkin on the table.

'I have something to tell you,' she said.

She looked hot and elated, despite the chill in the air.

'I'm planning – we, I mean, are going to go, to leave the school, here, everything.' She threw her arms out as she spoke.

'What are you talking about, are you moving?' I asked, though I knew before she answered that this was probably not what she meant.

'No.' She laughed excitedly. 'Me and Mr Lavelle. We're leaving, running away, after Christmas.'

I felt like falling backwards, like the earth was upending me.

'We have it all planned out: first France, then Spain and then on to Morocco,' she spoke triumphantly. 'But you can't breathe a word, obviously.' She laughed again.

'Aren't you so excited for me?' she asked, tilting her head back to look at the stars in the black sky.

My face betrayed me. I could hear her voice describing his house in the village.

I felt my hands start to tremble, and I put down my wine glass.

'But it's illegal, you can't run off with your teacher. I mean, the police, your parents – they will all come after you. And school, exams, you won't have any. . .' I said.

My voice didn't sound like me. There was something choking and uneven about it. Like I couldn't get the breaths right.

'Oh please,' she said. 'I couldn't care less. I am an artist, a writer. And anyway, we are in love. How does that even compare to some piece of paper?'

I felt less drunk now. The words 'we are in love' tumbled on to the wet ground at our feet. She had never said it before.

'Look, I don't mean to be totally boring, but it's just a really huge thing and you could get into a lot of trouble,' I said. 'I'm worried about you, that's all.'

I wanted to say, *But he painted Helen. And sometimes he looks at me. And you can't leave me alone. I need you.*

I didn't say any of that.

'When are you going?' I asked, trying to rearrange my face and my thoughts. The rule was to act casual and uncaring. She had taught me that.

'January, after the holidays. My parents are going to Rome then. I am going to claim illness and stay here. We are going to get the boat the day after they've gone,' she said.

So soon.

'And money and stuff, what are you going to live on?' I asked.

'Oh, that's all taken care of. I have been saving all my pocket money and he's going to teach along the way, and paint, of course,' she said.

I felt a weight settle on my shoulders. And in truth it has never really left me. It alighted on me that cold, damp night and I would carry a part of this despair for ever.

'But you and him, I didn't know you were. . .' I fell over my words, lying to her and myself.

'Louisa, you are so innocent sometimes. Didn't you guess?' she said. 'We've had this connection,' she leaned forward, 'since the day he arrived in the school.

'I was standing in the Maiden's Chamber and he drove up. I watched him get out of the car, and for a minute he just leaned against it and looked out to the sea. It was like he had been sent there – sent to me, really.'

She took a long drink from her wine, nearly emptying the glass. She immediately refilled it and didn't offer any to me.

'I ran down the stairs, like I just had to be there when he walked in. Because if I missed him arriving it would mean something. Anyway, he walked past me; he had this leather bag over his arm. And his hair, it was longer than it is now, scruffy, and then he turned back, just for a second, and looked at me.' She laughed, a light laugh.

She was somewhere else, clasping her hands in front of her as she spoke. Elated and triumphant in a place where I didn't exist. I took the bottle and poured some wine into my glass. I noticed my hands were shaking.

'And you know, you just know. Like everything is as it should be. The first conversation we ever had, it was in the summer house, he spoke about shame, about having failed in college.'

She looked up at me. Her eyes were full of hope.

'And it hit me, here,' she poked at her chest, 'like this hole opened up in me. And I had to fill it with him, with healing him, making him better. He is this great man and. . .' She was shaking her head and seemed to have run out of breath.

And superlatives, I thought meanly, and this thought surprised me. Nothing she had said since we first met had ever struck me as not agreeable, or not identical to my own world vision. In my head I saw my mother painting the thin walls of her crappy town house and eating a cheap takeaway with her new love. Their table covered in foil tins and plastic lids that they used as ashtrays.

'We haven't slept together, though, not yet.' She leaned forward and took my hand.

173

I nodded. Her hand was tight and uncomfortable on my wrist. She felt icy cold.

'I am waiting,' she said, her eyes big in the half-light, 'because we could have, I mean loads of times, but it's better if we wait.'

She sat back in her chair. She was like a child for whom disappointment was an alien concept.

'I didn't know if love would be like they said in the books. Like a sickness, a desperation even, like I can't live,' she said. 'But it is.'

I drank some wine, quickly. It made my mouth burn, as though it were full of acid.

'And of course the Helen thing, in case you're wondering, it's all fine. I confronted him last week and it's nothing. I mean, she is totally in love with him, has been writing him love notes. He showed them to me. I took one actually, I'll show it to you. She even wrote him a poem, can you imagine.' Her eyes were bright as she spoke and I wondered if she might be about to cry and not really with joy.

'But he feels nothing for her. He really regrets the painting too, he's going to destroy it. She just read too much into it. I mean, you know how he is, so charismatic,' she said, drinking a large gulp of wine and taking some cigarettes out of her jeans pocket.

She was rubbing her fingers together in a circular, agitated fashion and I wondered if they had lost feeling in the cold night. As she tried to light the cigarette her hands were shaking also. I leaned over to shield the lighter from the breeze. She took a deep drag. She looked pale in the half-light. Inside the house I could hear glasses being clinked, and there was laughter.

'Do your parents know you smoke?' I asked.

She laughed. 'I think that is the least of my worries, but actually yes, they do. My mother says there is no problem, if you moderate it and only do it every now and then. It keeps you slim. Same as eating food on sticks,' she added before laughing again. The sound was high-pitched and artificial.

I thought how the calm of the last few weeks was gone. How I had only seen the surface of things.

The door to the terrace opened then and we both turned, startled. A man with a cigar walked out. He did not look at us, just stood facing the garden, blowing large smoke rings and wiping his brow with a white handkerchief.

'We better go in,' she said, dropping the half-finished cigarette on to the ground and stepping on it.

As I stood up, she started to take off her necklace, an old-fashioned gold, heart-shaped locket.

'Here,' she said, handing it to me, 'it will be something to remember me by. You can put a photo in, or maybe we can get it engraved with our names. I won't forget how good you have been to me these last months.'

'Put it on me,' I said.

She gestured to me to turn and clipped it around my neck. It felt heavy and expensive. Something that belonged to another world.

'I'll never take it off,' I said, touching it gently.

I don't think she heard me, though.

'He's coming tonight. Well, he might be,' she said in a whisper.

I should have asked why he was coming and was that wise for him to be here, but I didn't. I was envious and fearful. He was taking her away.

Also, a very small part of me thought she was stupid. People in love are stupid. No one ever said it, or wanted to admit it, but it seemed like they were. Like that myth of the half-male, half-female creatures, cut in two and forever running around looking to be completed. A pointless chase because nothing would ever fit you right anyway. We are broken to begin with, our original sin.

'I didn't know what this term would be like, whether' – she lowered her voice – 'he still wanted me. You, you helped distract me from all that. You came at just the right time.'

A distraction. That's how she saw me. She had a way of hurting me. I felt like crying and rubbed my eyes trying to hide it from her. To pretend it was the cold.

And I wanted to say, *But Helen. He painted Helen. Not you. And he holds my arm sometimes.*

And don't do it. Of course. I wanted to tell her, *Don't do it. Stay with me.*

For what was it he had said in the summer house? Nothing is ever as it seems.

* * *

Victoria was accosted by guests as we walked in and I let her go and disappeared into the crowded and by now hot and smoke-filled room. I wandered back towards the hallway. I needed space to process what she had told me, that she would be leaving, they would be leaving. As I walked back on to the shiny tiles I could hear music again. And it was only then I realized it hadn't been playing in the room where the party was on. I wandered through another door off the hall, following the melody. It was Cole Porter, 'Night and Day'.

The narrow corridor off the hall was lined with photographs, family pictures. Trips to Disneyworld in Florida and Victoria standing *en famille* in front of the Eiffel Tower. There were degrees and awards too, words written in Latin so I did not know what they were for or why they had been awarded. I wondered how she could leave all this and her place within it behind and how it was to be afflicted with a dream. The things it made you do. But then I too was willing to leave my family behind. Sometimes you had to burn down everything behind you, a scorched-earth approach to life. Then you could start again. With no marks, or signs of who or what you had been before. And maybe he did love her, maybe they did have this union that was unstoppable.

They were rule breakers, not followers, both of them. And over time, maybe the scandal would die down and she could write home and everyone would know that it had been true love, and not a folly or a madness. And not illegal.

The music was getting louder.

And then she could come back maybe and visit. I would have my own place to live by then, with an elegant drawing room and varnished floorboards. And if she felt like she couldn't come home, I'd have the money to visit her so it wouldn't all be lost. We could lie on beaches and drink cocktails with umbrellas in them or visit ancient ruins buried among the sands. We'd wear white hats with veils, like the ones on the stern lady in the painting in the hall. And maybe sit atop a camel. And Mr Lavelle would have a tent and be dressed like Lawrence of Arabia. Everything we had wouldn't be lost. It would be different but the same.

She might not forget me.

I was not worthy of the kind of attention Victoria had aroused in Mr Lavelle. Or he had aroused in her. They were the kind of people that this type of love happened to. They had the leisure time for it. They were the sort of people who pulled the sky down, and burned things, and laughed, laughed when all around them cried.

I needed water and I needed to sit down. And to get away.

I felt tears again behind my eyes. I could not survive alone in that school without her, they would finish me. And I was jealous, deeply, darkly jealous, though I could not fully admit it. For it was manifesting as a restless energy and a sense of panic. Nothing ever happened to me. I was a person on the sidelines. This being part of something was going to end. She was leaving me.

And I realized I wanted to go home. It was the first time I had wanted that in a very long time. My narrow room, the posters of the Smiths on the wall that had replaced the earlier ones of Madonna. The pictures of endangered seals and Nelson Mandela. My small bookcase, the one I had reclaimed from a skip and painted white. My typewriter that didn't work, and my record player that did. And the view from my window, looking out at houses that were mirror images of my own, net curtains and chipped paint on the window frames. And the way the tree outside on the street seemed to be growing inwards, towards my window, and soon the branches would reach across and form a bridge. I could almost touch it.

A door was slightly open at the far end of the corridor. The music was coming from there. I could hear voices, low ones, on the other side. I paused before touching the round porcelain handle that had tiny red roses on it and looked back up the hallway. And something made me think I could see myself, like there had been a slight delay in reality and I could glimpse myself walking the corridor in the gloom, touching the pictures with my hand and thinking about love and about being left behind. A hiccup in time, a jump cut. But I didn't stop and go back to meet myself, I pushed open the door because that's what I had come here for.

And when I did so Mr Lavelle looked up. He was sitting in a leather armchair and at his feet sat Helen. And she didn't look sour as she turned her head to me, but instead passionate and majestic. Her dark red hair, alluring and abundant in the firelight, and her black, full skirt fanned out on the floor around her.

And something about him made me think of the Jesus in my children's Bible. A ray of sharp, white and gold light. Like he might blind you with the possibility of miracles.

And they both smiled at me, as if it was the most natural thing ever. To be there, together and alone.

As I backed out of the door, I thought I heard him calling my name.

The Journalist

Chapter Nineteen

Victoria's office was at the top of the building. The view was mostly sky, and it was dark now. The city lay below, lit up, bright orange and red. It was vibrant, fast and busy there. Alive. But where we stood there was nothing but silence. A monochrome cocoon of reinforced glass, a sleek long desk and a computer.

Victoria had finished her talk and walked me to her office. We didn't speak. She was wearing a black dress and around her neck a string of pearls. She fiddled with them as we stood in the crowded lift and avoided looking at me. After we got out, people in the corridor outside thanked her for the talk and looked forward to speaking to her later. She smiled and shook hands, a look of studied politeness on her face, taking business cards as they were offered to her. The graduate group turned away before her office and disappeared up a narrow staircase where the party on the roof was to be held.

Victoria lit a low lamp on her desk, gestured to the couch and went to a coffee machine in the corner and remained standing there with her back to me. There were no pictures on the wall of her office, nor on the desk. There were some large storage boxes in the corner of the room and it occurred to me she might be moving, leaving. The coffee table in front of the couch had business magazines, some newspapers and the carving of a woman's head. It looked African in style, shiny and black. I laid my bag down on the floor and took out my notebook as the coffee machine whirred into action. Then I thought maybe the sight of a notebook might put her off so I stored it away just before she walked towards me with a cup of coffee in her hand. She laid it on the table and sat down opposite me.

'You have been writing to me,' she said, 'about Louisa.'

I felt her voice catch slightly as she said the name and she looked down at her fingernails for a second. They were long, tapered and painted a dark red. There were no rings on her hands. There was a weariness in her body language. She looked like she needed to sleep, curl up and close her eyes. I had not expected this after Helen's rigid tension and air of menace. Nor indeed Victoria's own performance in front of the crowd earlier, where she had been strident, even amusing at times.

There was something tragic, haunted about her; it was there in the shadows under her eyes and the stiffness of her body.

I began by explaining why I was doing this, as I had done with Helen, though I was careful this time not to suggest anything too intimate in my desire for knowledge, nor any pity. These women didn't do pity. I did speak of having grown up near Louisa, of being always vaguely aware of her story.

She watched me closely when I said this, scanning my face. There was no looking over my shoulder or attempting to derail me with raised eyebrows or incredulous glances. Several times, though, she turned her neck from side to side, as if she might have a crick or pain in it. In another life I might have been doing a feature with her on the stress of modern life for women with high-flying careers. She was darker, though. I knew that, somehow.

When I stopped speaking she didn't say anything. She stayed looking at me, her eyes pale and shining in the low light, but I sensed her mind was elsewhere. There was a vacancy to her. The air in the room felt heavy around us. I heard a clock ticking. She turned her head suddenly, as if she heard something behind her. When she faced me again, she held her hand to her throat and stroked it slightly.

'Are you all right?' I asked as the silence between us became more awkward.

I tried to begin a conversation – 'I'm sorry, I know it must be. . .' – but then I paused, not wanting to tread too far, too quickly as I had done with Helen.

I wanted to ask her straight up, what happened to Louisa? You have all the answers, or more of them than anyone else. But I didn't say that, of course; there were rules to the dance. She demanded patience.

Victoria got up abruptly and went to get water from a jug on her desk. She offered me some but I declined.

'She haunts me,' she said, sitting back down, and for a second she put her hands up to her face, rubbing her eyes, and her voice was slightly muffled.

I nodded my head.

'She haunts me too,' I said. 'The photos of them.'

And the shadows on the street at home.

'And the policeman, the detective who worked on the case, he can't forget her either, and he's retired now,' I said. 'So many lives are affected when someone disappears. Her story, it deserves to be told, more fully, more authentically than it has been.'

I leaned forward towards her. If you were as close to her as all the reports said, you must respond to this, I thought.

'I feel it at night. When I am here sometimes – I work late a lot – but it's mostly when I am at home,' she said, looking around the room.

I wondered if she had heard me at all. I followed her gaze around the space.

'Things happen; I see things, remember random moments. Out of nowhere, like I'm back there. I can smell it too, the wild garlic that grew in the woods in spring, and the grass when it had been cut in front of the house, and the smoke from the bonfires. The village that was a few miles away; sometimes in the evening around Halloween they would light the fires and we could smell it. Even in our bedrooms, the windows were so draughty, everything got in. Even the smoke,' she said.

She had stood up again as she finished speaking and walked to the window. Her back was straight.

'Have you been to the school, visited it?' she asked, turning back to me.

I shook my head and told her I planned a trip there in the next few days.

'You have to see it,' she said. 'You can't understand anything really without seeing it. I can draw you a map, show you all the places to look, the things only we knew about,' she said and walked to her desk. 'Louisa told me she always loved books that had a map at the front of them. I had forgotten that.'

She spoke more to herself than to me.

'She thought it meant you would be entering another world, and you could follow the paths. I preferred when there were family trees at the start of a book, elaborate and complex. Like Tolstoy,' she said and laughed briefly. 'Everyone related in some way; it was always there. The clues, buried in the family tree,' she said, shuffling some paper on her desk.

I realized she was rambling, she must have been nervous. I longed to stretch for my notebook, but felt again that I should not.

'Oh there's no need to draw me a map, I have Google and everything I need. I mean, unless there is something in particular you think I should visit?' I said.

'When will you be going?' she asked.

'Probably early next week,' I said.

We looked at each other for a second, and something resembling understanding passed between us.

She sat back down on the couch, preoccupied rather than

defensive. I felt it was important that I kept her relaxed. Like when a deer emerges before you on a path in the forest; if you hold your breath, they might not run.

'I saw your article,' she said.

'Yes, I have another one going in next week. It's going to be more about Edward Lavelle this time. I have been rereading all the descriptions of him, and even found some people who studied with him, a friend of his named Xavier, willing to talk. It is getting quite a lot of interest from readers, the series.'

She looked pained at the mention of his name and I was sorry I had said anything about reader interest. She would think I was just another journalist, looking for sensation, which, as I kept having to remind myself, I wasn't.

'I always thought I would write a book,' she said, 'one that would matter and mean something. Everyone thought it, back then.'

I nodded and drank some coffee. It tasted sweet, foreign.

'It's funny really, or odd, I suppose, how things turn out,' she said, twirling a piece of her hair around her fingers. 'You wonder, what was the moment, the point that things tilted off, and you went another way. I would not have believed all this back then if you had told me,' she said, surveying the room around us. 'I did not seek any of this.'

I looked around us, quiet power and status in every corner of the place. Was this not what you expected? Was this not what you were raised for?

'Of course, I know, with my rational head on, it was the day Louisa didn't come back. No one was the same after, how could we be? But sometimes I'm not sure, and I think maybe it started even before that,' she said.

She had that vacant, faraway look again.

'What did they say about him, Mr Lavelle, the people you spoke to?' she asked, suddenly more alert and leaning forward in her seat.

'That he was this free spirit, a bit wild maybe but sort of unusual, and interesting, had this way of making people come out of themselves. They said he loved Temple House, really enjoyed teaching. But then I spoke to the detective and he talked about how people thought he had a dark side, kind of a fantasist, had an interest in women, much younger women. A desire for attention, adoration even.' For some reason, once I'd said this to her, I felt embarrassed.

She said nothing but stared slightly into space, distracted once more.

'Was that how you remember him?' I asked.

'No, not really.' Then, after a pause, she said, 'But also yes. I mean he was different, he was younger than the other teachers. You know, he was sort of like the greatest politician you could ever meet. I've met a few in this job. They have a hollowness to them, like they are not fully three-dimensional, and he was like that. The appearance was all fine, but when you touched it, or tried to, there was nothing there. He would just evaporate. I imagine celebrities are the same – maybe that would be a better analogy. Have you ever met anyone like that?'

'No, I don't think so. Well maybe, but not as extreme,' I said. 'Everyone holds a bit of themselves back.'

'I find now they don't much, don't you? Look at those people here tonight – they will be opening their hearts to each other up there.' She gestured to the roof. 'They have so little mystery to them. They seem to have no secrets. They don't even want to have any. We were different. He was different. There was more magic in not fully revealing.'

She was wrong, of course; everyone had secrets. You realized that when you tried to interview them.

'Did you try to get close to him, you and Louisa?' I asked, holding my breath.

She didn't answer. Somewhere outside in the corridor there was more laughter and the sound of glasses being moved or carried. Then she looked at her watch.

'I think perhaps, for a time, we thought we were,' she said. 'Close to him.'

She leaned over the coffee table and started rearranging the magazines, and then wiped the surface with her hand, as if checking for dust.

I complimented her on the sculpture of the woman's head on the table.

'I go to Africa every year or so,' she said. 'Morocco, mainly. I try and buy something, but mostly I keep them at home. I keep myself and the things that matter to me separate from here.'

She looked briefly over to the boxes in the corner.

'Do you remember the last night with Louisa?' I asked.

'I'm not sure now what are real memories and what is just my mind playing tricks,' she said.

'Did you ever believe they had run away together, or did you think something bad had happened?' I asked.

She sat more upright and I felt like her breathing became heavier, deeper.

'I don't know what happened. I thought I did, I thought they were going to leave but then, then I realized that wasn't it at all. But by then it was too late,' she said.

They were going to leave? I sat more upright in the chair. A hint of truth, insight emerging.

'Too late for what?' I asked.

She didn't answer for a few seconds.

'To explain, to make her understand. . .' she said.

I breathed in and folded my hands together, afraid they would give my urgent interest away. I was about to ask her more questions when she went on.

'You know, I never sense him. Isn't that odd? I was always waiting to see if there was anything, some sign, but there never was. I mean they went missing together, I saw both of them virtually every day, but it's only her I can ever feel. She is the only one. . .'

I remembered the detective said Victoria had a flair for the dramatic. But to me she seemed genuinely at loose ends, damaged. A loss so deep that no amount of time could heal. And there was regret, even guilt, somewhere at the heart of it all.

'Was there something special, private, between the three of you?' I said.

'I don't know now, really; that's the thing, isn't it, especially when you are a teenager, you tend to think you are the centre of the universe. Like everything moves for you, but you have such little power really, or power that you can direct in any useful way,' she said, seeming almost deliberately elusive.

'Do you remember the intensity of it,' she said, leaning forward slightly, 'the burden of being that age, everything still new, and you had to pretend to be jaded and not affected by it? I wish now I could go back, go back and say don't pretend, don't be embarrassed by it. It's only new once. What's that poem, the "hardest hue to hold?"'

I didn't really know what she was talking about. I needed facts from her.

'You were one of the last to see Louisa that night, before she disappeared in the village?' I asked.

'I'm not sure – possibly. But no, I wasn't in the village,' she said, falling back on the couch. 'It's all on file.'

She sat up suddenly then, and it felt like she had woken out of a dream. She checked her watch again.

'Yes, of course,' I said. 'I know it's getting late and I really appreciate your time tonight.'

She got up from the couch and walked back to the window.

'Do you write every day about her?' she asked me.

She seemed interested, genuinely.

I walked over to the window and stood beside her. Her face was reflected in the glass.

'I write most days,' I said.

She sighed then, as if envious.

'Do you feel like you are getting to know Louisa, him, both of them?' she asked.

'Yes, in a small way; it's kind of like cleaning an old painting or something, their faces start to emerge from behind the dust. Then other times I think it's more like fossil hunting; you know, getting in the dirt and digging. You don't know what it is you are looking for but you know it's there, somewhere,' I said, turning away from the window to look at her profile.

Looking at her reflection, I thought that she must have once been beautiful, everything in equal proportion, but the light had drained away and just a pale ghost of it was left on her features.

She turned to face me and was trembling slightly. She looked afraid, nervous.

'And him, what do you think of him?' she said.

'He sounds,' I began, then paused. 'I can imagine he was quite fascinating, once.'

She smiled then and shook her head gently. As if this was an old joke.

'Thank you again, for meeting me,' I said. 'I won't let you or Louisa down in the way I tell it. I want to give her back some dignity, that's all.'

'It's time,' she said, looking away and back to the window. 'It's just time now. She's been gone so long, losing patience.'

I thought it was an odd thing to say. She had closed her eyes as she spoke.

I started to walk to the door.

'Can I give you something of hers?' she said suddenly. 'I kept some things she wrote, pictures and stuff, and I meant to give them to her parents, but never did. I'm packing everything up now.' She indicated the boxes in the corner.

I gave her my address. She said she would have them sent to me.

'Are you leaving, moving somewhere?' I asked.

But she didn't answer.

'You are going next week, to the school?' she said, walking towards me, her face in shadow.

I nodded.

'Would I be able to come with you?' she asked.

'Of course, that would be, well, that would be amazing, it would make all the difference. I never would have expected that,' I said.

I had won. And for a second that was all that mattered. An excitement, anticipation of things to come. I felt myself smiling.

Then I remembered.

I saw Louisa's dad walking in the gate of his house. Always alone.

We arranged where we would meet for the trip to Temple House, and I took her mobile number and personal email details.

She walked me to the door of her office. A couple holding hands and carrying wine walked past us in the corridor. We watched them for a second; they looked happy and absorbed in each other. That was possibly what caught our eyes. Some people find their way to some kind of intimacy, and others don't.

'I'd like to show you the swimming hole,' she said as we shook hands. 'You won't find it unless I am with you.'

I didn't know what she referred to, nor its significance, but thanked her again and left for home.

Chapter Twenty

I didn't sleep after our meeting.

To me, Victoria, with her talk of memories and ghosts, had seemed lost. I don't know why this was a revelation to me. Possibly because Helen had been so resilient and defensive. I had presumed the Temple House girls were all the same, at least to some extent. But Victoria was different. Perhaps that's what Louisa had seen in her – a certain romance or Gothic element. Maybe my judgements were biased against them because I knew they had these comfortable lives.

Victoria seemed to be packaging up her life, moving, leaving. I knew catching someone in transition was often the best time to interview them, to get a fresh insight.

Reports of the disappearance at the time said they had been very close to each other, Victoria and Louisa. Lavelle must have been on the outside of their circle, even though they admired him. Had he tried to break them apart in some way, had he wanted one and not the other? Had that led him to steal away with Louisa in the night? Convince her she was in love, seduce her with his tales of art and travel?

I hadn't got any direct sense of Victoria's views of Lavelle. Her description of him as a hollow man was interesting. His elusiveness, the attempt to catch him that she referenced. These were phrases that suggested him not so much as a predator, but rather as the prey hunted by them. I had felt in both Helen's and Victoria's descriptions that there had been no sense of fear of him. I wondered, for a very brief moment, if everything we had assumed about the disappearance was wrong.

Early the next morning a brown parcel arrived by courier. It was tied with string, like something an ageing aunt would send you for your birthday. I made tea and sat down to open it.

On top was a note from Victoria, handwritten in black ink on heavy card that had her address embossed on it. She thanked me for our meeting and said she was looking forward to seeing me again next week.

Below that, there were three folders. The first contained photos, a mix of Polaroid pictures and some printed on glossy paper from a time when people stood in darkrooms working with chemicals.

There was Lavelle leaning against a car; the date written on the back was December 1990, along with 'Vintage Car Show, Temple House'. I had not seen this image of him before and decided to send it to the editor to run with the piece on him. Other images were of the school grounds, hockey matches and school concerts, photos filled with people I did not recognize. There was only one of Louisa. She was lying on the grass, a sweater rolled up like a pillow and her head turned to the side so you could only see one eye. Her dark stare was intense and unfriendly. The sun was shining, there was a flare-like light above her, possibly a fault in the printing, and I could see the blue sea off in the distance. The last picture was of an unusual glass cabinet, antique-looking, filled with items I could not quite make out. There was a small key in the cabinet door.

It was an odd assortment of random images, and apart from the new photos of Lavelle and Louisa, they were not much use.

The next folder was of Louisa's writing. There were two essays. The first was myth-like, describing two lovers who had been turned to stone statues. They stood in shadow under the tall trees and watched the world with sad eyes, never able to look directly at each other. Condemned to stand just off centre, only the vague sense of the other out of the corner of their stone eyes. It was a strange and eerie story. She wrote well, her voice strong and clear, with descriptions that, if not elaborate, were affecting. Her handwriting was squarish and certain, with no frills or embellishments.

The second essay was shorter, more like a speech that had been written quickly. It was titled 'Art Class – Cabinet of Curiosities Assignment, September 1990'.

I have chosen the skull as my symbol for this year in art class. I will outline my reasons for doing so below.

Skulls remind us we are weak. They show us the vanity of our thinking, in imagining we are different, unique. We fill our lives with trinkets, thoughts, lovers, art to distract us from the reality that lies underneath. The end that waits for us all. The skull is the manifestation not just of death, but the illusions we create around it. Our lives.

Often placed in still-life settings with rotting fruit and wilting flowers, the skull is a physical demonstration that nothing lasts. Our thoughts, wishes, hopes, intellect, they are temporary and finite. . . It is vanity to think otherwise. Artists have used the skull as a reminder to explore the bigger questions of life and not to be tempted to think that love will save you.

It sounded angry; the words had been coughed up on to the page.

The last part of the last sentence read: *The skull is the opposite of the heart.*

Apart from the essays, there was another page of quotes, ripped from a notebook. Phrases that must have meant something to her, copied from other books. I recognized some of them, including James Joyce, Sylvia Plath and J.D. Salinger, the usual suspects, and then one from Virginia Woolf: *Someone has to die in order that the rest of us should value life more.*

I stopped at this. The morbidity of being sixteen.

There was a tiny scrawl in her writing at the bottom of one page – *the fates can choose to come to the rescue of the hero.* Lavelle's name was beside it.

There was a copybook, yellowing slightly, with doodles and drawings that looked like they had been done at the back of the class. It included mock reviews of various albums and books.

It certainly gave me a sense of Louisa, her humour and love of irony, but again not much else. It was going to be helpful to have some of her original writing and it did make her seem more alive and three-dimensional.

The final folder was black and thinner than the others. I removed the elastic band around it. There was a charcoal drawing of a young woman with long hair, lying naked on a couch. There was no background to indicate where it had been drawn or when. She was not identifiable really; all you could see was her youth and beauty. It did not seem overly sexual, a sensitive rendering of the naked body. It was dated May 1990. Were there life-drawing classes in the school, held by Lavelle? The school, however, did not seem to have been a place where this kind of thing would have been allowed. Maybe he ran clandestine life-drawing classes after hours. I stared at the woman but nothing about her seemed familiar. She was anonymous.

I put the drawing carefully back in the folder and picked up the next small scrap of paper in the bottom of the file. It was a poem, not a particularly well-written one, but certainly intense in its feeling:

> You touch and I fade
> You breathe and I dissolve
> You speak and I am deaf
> You leave and I fall

I typed the words into Google to see if they came up as lyrics or some unknown poem but there were no matches. It must have been an original work, written more than twenty years ago to someone who was an object of fascination.

I rang my editor.

'I met Victoria, she sent me some things. I am not sure yet if they are relevant, but I just wanted to let you know,' I said.

'What did she send you?' he said.

'Photos, some essays of Louisa's, that kind of thing.'

A fly that had been trapped in the room was bashing itself against the window. I watched it as he spoke to me.

'What was she like?' he replied.

'She was odd, eccentric. Damaged maybe. I felt like she wanted to talk but just couldn't quite get there.'

'Does she think Louisa ran away with him?'

'She wouldn't get into their relationship and kind of fudged her responses on the subject when I asked,' I said. 'This visit was about building trust,' I added quickly. 'I didn't get everything I needed from her, but we are talking again.'

'Whatever works,' he said.

The image of Victoria as the deer in the woods came into my head once more. I thought about telling him we had planned to travel together to the school, but decided not to mention that yet. He might send a photographer with us and ruin any chance of her opening up.

'It's odd. Victoria kind of comes alive when Lavelle is mentioned, but when I talked about Louisa she seems, not afraid, but kind of unnerved,' I said.

'Maybe they weren't as close as everyone said they were,' he answered.

'No, there was something between them, I'm sure of that,' I said.

Picking over lives. Stringing incidences together and making meaning.

Finding a lesson in it all.

I put the phone down and went to the window, opening it gently. The fly flew out.

Chapter Twenty-One

I finished the draft of my article on Edward Lavelle and gave it to the intern to read before I sent it to my editor. She was taking ages over it, kept putting it down to look out the window and occasionally writing notes on the pages. I went to get a glass of water. A colleague was shredding some papers. I knew before he spoke he would say 'shredding the evidence'. Which he did. He didn't ask me about the Louisa story. I knew this meant I was doing well and everyone else knew it too.

The intern was finished when I got back to my desk.

'This is good,' she said.

I thanked her and took the pages.

'I mean, his friend Xavier, there'd be a book in him alone,' she said.

I laughed.

'Does he actually live in a castle?' she asked.

'No, more of a tower – not that I got to see it. I called him,' I answered.

'Still impressive, though,' she said. 'They seem like they are from a different world.'

I looked up at her; she had a tendency to sit on the edge of my desk. It was irritating.

'Faux bohemians are the words you are looking for, and entitled,' I said, starting to read through her scribbled notes.

'The teacher sounds like he was harmless,' she said, looking at her nails now.

They were always painted different colours, or had stickers on them.

'Not from what the detective said to me, and anyway Xavier was a friend, he might not have known what he got up to. He just heard Lavelle's version of events in the school. He probably wanted to appear like his life was a big success,' I said.

'We had a religion teacher like him,' she said, 'sort of wanted to hang with the kids type thing. We found it embarrassing, but then, he wasn't very good-looking.'

'I think Lavelle had charm, charisma, and that can make all the difference,' I said, sitting back in the chair. Made him dangerous, I thought.

'They were vulnerable in the school; there wasn't the language really to say no to someone like him back then,' I said.

She nodded.

I vaguely wanted her to leave now. She never picked up the signs. I wondered if she was suited to reporting. She heard her own voice above all others.

I thought about Victoria's view of Mr Lavelle. She had seemed wistful about him, the man who was there but also wasn't. He must have been compelling in some way, despite what Helen had said. I looked at the picture of him leaning against the car.

'Like a cult leader maybe, like Jim Jones or the Waco guy,' she said, still sitting on my desk.

'Yeah, exactly,' I replied, gazing at the picture. Power, influence, beauty.

My editor walked over. I told him I was proofing the piece and would have it to him that evening.

'We got a call from a researcher on a radio show, the one where people ring in and complain,' he said.

'A caller claims to have been abused in the school, by one of the teachers,' he said. 'Only had the courage to come out now, you know the story.'

The intern raised her eyebrows and started checking her phone.

I sat up.

'I'll ring the show, see if we can get their details,' I said. 'I'll ring the police too. The detective gave me a number for someone who might be helpful.'

'When are you making the trip to the school?' he said.

'Next week. I'll take photos when I'm there,' I said.

Don't send anyone with me.

He began to walk away.

'It was something to get to see Victoria. Well done,' he said over his shoulder.

'I'll write it up over the weekend,' I replied.

I went back to reading the notes the intern had made.

Are you sure the fact that he had grand ideas and was a bit precious about art means he was making stuff up and liked fantasizing. . .? You need to be careful, bit biased.

When Xavier said that Mr L thought everyone could be an artist, does that not seem kind of good, like a very New Age form of teaching but in a good way?

You seem to really like Louisa, is this just because she lived on your road? Maybe she was kind of arrogant and was trying to get his attention all the time, wanted to be special. She might have wanted him (though he should have said no).

Xavier says that Mr L loved teaching in the school, never gave any hint he was planning to leave. Interesting, non?

Her notes were actually helpful. She was possibly better than I gave her credit for.

I shouted, 'Thanks for these,' as she walked past later on. She looked surprised.

I opened the folder and looked at Louisa's essay on the skull.

Who was she, really?

Chapter Twenty-Two

It was raining as we drove along the coast road out to the school. Victoria sat silently for most of the journey, sharing a few pleasantries and nothing more. As we left the city behind and the road opened before us, I put the radio on in an attempt to keep things reasonably normal and sane. It was the phone-in show I had been in touch with; today callers were complaining about a local hospital. It was reassuring. We could have been any normal friends, sitting in the car, on our way for a day at the coast. Except it was March and the rain was falling heavily outside, with the windscreen wipers keeping a rhythmic and oddly melodic beat in time with the rain. And we weren't friends.

Victoria appeared not to be listening to the chatter but rather seemed to be looking at the countryside as we drove. I imagined it was a familiar journey, filled with memories. It was only as we slowed the car to turn off the motorway that she spoke, commenting on my choice of radio station, declaring, state-of-the-nation style, that it seemed as if people feel 'nothing works any more'. She sighed, then turned off the radio.

I thought about mentioning the caller last week who had rung in about abuse in the school. But I didn't. I hadn't been able to contact the person anyway.

We stopped for a coffee and to get petrol. Victoria sat on a stool that looked over the forecourt while I queued. She seemed out of place among the travelling salesmen and families on trips to visit relatives. I sensed that this was a kind of average life she did not engage with. A world where you stopped to shop and queue and eat greasy convenience food. She possibly wasn't as different from Helen as I might have thought. I placed the cups on the bench in front of us, she thanked me and remarked that all these motorway stops were new. Even the road itself had been re-made, widened and curved away from the sea and was not familiar to her. I asked her how long it had been since she visited the school, expecting she had gone back at some point, for some reason.

'Not since the day after Louisa disappeared,' she said, 'so twenty-five years ago this December.'

She ran her fingers over the lid of her takeaway cup as she spoke. I didn't know whether to believe her.

'How soon did it close after they went missing?' I asked.

'The following summer,' she said. 'After the investigation and all the headlines, enrolments dropped to nothing.'

'But you left earlier than that?' I asked.

'Yes,' she said. 'I left that Friday night, just before Christmas, and never went back.'

I told her I would be talking to Louisa's mum in the coming days. She nodded but did not respond. It would be in the next article, the one that would run after the piece on Lavelle. I explained it had been hard to get her to talk. Victoria remained silent. The rain had eased as we walked back to the car. As we got in she said that Louisa had been embarrassed by her parents, and had never really spoken about them.

As we strapped on our seatbelts she said, 'I think she wanted to get away from them, her parents. They seemed to mean very little to her.'

She then switched on the radio, turning it to a station that played classical music, and went back to staring out the window.

The topic of Louisa's parents was off limits for now and I silently agreed to obey her wishes.

The gates to the school were locked. I got out to see if they had just been shut rather than bolted but they didn't budge. They were wrought iron and rusting badly. I rubbed my hands on my jeans after touching them, leaving orange stains. Victoria got out from the car and said we could walk.

She led the way through the long grass, along a high stone wall that ran around the edge of the estate. It wasn't raining but the air was damp and misty and the grass was sopping against our legs. There was a vague smell of salt and seaweed in the air, though the sea was not yet in view. After a short time the wall became lower, with a small, broken wooden stile cut into it that we climbed over.

Victoria jumped from the wall ahead me and, after landing, stood still. I could not see her face, but felt again that heaviness in the air between us as she stood there looking up the narrow, tree-lined gravel driveway, the house not yet visible. We walked on in silence, only the crunch of the weed-filled gravel under our shoes. The drive was edged by thick overgrown grass; in some places there were clumps of daffodils peeping through. It was strangely beautiful. The drive veered off towards the coast, but Victoria shook her head and gestured for me to follow her. We walked through long grass, a shortcut that linked back to the drive. Tall yew trees stood each side of us. They reached over our heads, almost forming an arch, and the trunks were wide and looked like they had split in half, with a hollowness at their centre. Victoria stopped to look up.

'They have grown,' she said. 'They never used to meet in the middle. We were never allowed past the trees; they formed a sort of unspoken boundary, from all the mad, naked men that were hiding here.'

I laughed, then felt bad for doing so. She looked at me as we walked.

'We were plagued with flashers. Are you Catholic?' she asked.

'Raised to be,' I answered.

'What age are you?' she asked then.

There was something direct, a kind of boldness to her.

I ignored the question. She had no right to know my age.

She sighed then as if my silence explained it all. The difference of a decade or so.

We emerged from under the trees and the drive turned in a slow curve leading to the house. The cliffs and sea appeared off to our left, a sudden dispersal of the forest, like a gap opening up. It was windier, colder, as we left the shelter of the trees and for the first time I could hear the waves against the rocks. We passed a disused, net-less tennis court surrounded by a rusting high fence, standing almost on the edge of the cliffs. The gate to it was unlocked and swung back and forth in the wind. There were what must have been playing fields further away to the side of the house, now just empty and filled with weeds and an abandoned, waterless pond. The once white, low wall at its edge, now stained brown. In some parts there was graffiti that someone had then painted over in an attempt to conceal it.

'Is that the swimming hole?' I asked as we skirted the edges.

She shook her head and we walked on.

Temple House came into view around the next bend, somehow magnificent in its decrepitude and isolation. And for a minute I held my breath. Victoria stopped too. It looked like loneliness brought to life. It was red brick, three storeys tall with a round turret stuck on one end. The front windows were long and on one side faced out to the coast. Many of them were broken, panes smashed and, in some cases, missing glass entirely. Like

211

they had been blinded. There were 'Danger' and 'Hazard' signs lying in the grass near the broken and uneven front steps which swept up to what was once a grand entrance. Above the porch, over the closed front door, there was a large arched window with stained glass, some of which was also broken and in parts hanging delicately, precariously. Ivy covered much of the building.

I took a few photos on my phone. Victoria stood beside me. She seemed twitchy and uneasy.

'It looks as it should,' she said, 'just as I imagined it. With its soul hanging out, its rotten soul.'

I was surprised by the vehemence of her tone.

'It's to be demolished soon,' I said, looking up.

'It has been on the verge of being demolished for years now,' she said, 'yet it always seems to avoid it.'

There were birds nesting under the eaves of the roof. Every now and then one would swoop in over our heads and disappear into the cavity.

'Can't you feel it, the air?' she said. 'Louisa always said she was so cold here. It was the first thing she noticed. She used to pull the sleeves of her jumper down over her hands, they were always purple. It wasn't just cold she was feeling, but despair.'

She turned away from the house as she spoke and looked back over the driveway, the overgrown lawns and the tennis courts. The sea was grey in the distance.

'Even when it was painted up and supposed to be grand, the place was dead, dead inside,' she said.

I thought about the Church and how it had been dreamed away. The rules not rigid and permanent as everyone had thought, but ephemeral. A world that had drifted from us.

'Were they harsh, cruel, the nuns?' I asked.

In my head I saw black straps and crosses. Orphans and lost women. But it can't have been like that. It was 1990.

'It depends how you define cruelty,' she said. 'You know, Louisa used to say how they were nicest to the richest girls. They gave them the best rooms, they got the most praise, won all the awards, even when they were the thickest in the class. It really annoyed her. She said the nuns were snobs; they were the opposite, in fact, of what they were supposed to be. Enamoured with money, the gloss of it.'

I didn't respond. It didn't seem that surprising, really. I had once visited the Vatican, which to me appeared to be all about money and gloss.

'Louisa and the others, the other scholarship girls, they were a kind of experiment, you see. They were trying to find the best. . .' her voice trailed off. 'But you know, I think Louisa had, not a calling, but a certain fascination with them. The idea of living here as a bride of Christ, renouncing the flesh. Something about that appealed to her.

'There was beauty too, you see,' she said, her voice slow, hesitant, 'and a kind of magic.'

Wine that turned into blood.

'You saw them differently, the nuns?' I said.

'I remember anxiety about sin, reputation, failure, conformity. They didn't beat you, of course, or even shout that much. They didn't need to. They weakened you with mind games and nightmares about limbo, and hell. Saints who died agonizing deaths all for the love of God. And you were watched, all the time. If not by them, by the Holy Spirit,' she said.

She turned her head sharply as she said this, as if she heard something.

'It was a disaster of an education if you had any kind of an imagination or were superstitious. It just fuelled your belief in the unknown, made you see things that weren't there.' As she spoke, her eyes were looking from one side of the grounds to the other.

'And Lavelle, did he protect you from it?' I asked, watching her.

'He was the antidote.' She turned to face me. 'That's why we were all in love with him.'

Her words just lay there, in the damp air. Suspended by the light mist blowing in from the coast. Factual and unadorned. I pulled my scarf tighter around my neck.

He was no longer the hollow man.

We were getting somewhere. I wanted to press her, chase down her words, but I held back. She was setting the pace and I had to follow.

I took more photos and then we tried to open the front door. It was barred and bolted. I followed her around the side of the house. She pointed to various windows, including her own on the second floor. I asked where Louisa's room had been and she told me it was at the back of the house.

We walked through what must have been a walled garden of some sort, thick with weeds along a barely discernible winding path. An old-fashioned lawnmower leaned against the wall in the corner beside some buckets and a pitchfork. She walked on, slower this time, touching some of the long grasses with her hand. There was no birdsong here, only the call of white gulls high above our heads.

'Can you tell me about that last night?' I asked as we walked on towards a gate in the wall.

She stopped for a moment and turned back to face me.

'I am telling you,' she said. 'That's why we are here.'

There was irritation in her eyes. A hardness to her glance.

We walked on. Her back lean and straight. The air between us less companionable now.

The gate in the wall was rotten and although locked we were able to lean against it and push through. We were in full wilderness now; my jeans were wet around my ankles, the mist seemed to be heavier here, as if the walls of the garden had been shielding us from full exposure to the coast. Up ahead, nestled in the trees, was a wooden summer house, a rotunda, its white paint peeling. It looked like something out of a fairy tale, where a huntsman or woodcutter might have lived.

Her step was suddenly lighter and quicker.

'This was the art room, the summer house,' she said.

'It's beautiful,' I said as we got nearer, fishing out my phone again to take some photos.

And it was. It had a lost, faded glamour to it that made you think of tea parties and croquet on the lawn.

It was covered in a heavy green vine, and the door was almost completely hidden. Victoria pulled the branches aside and pushed on the door which opened easily.

The floor was carpeted with leaves and the room bare, except for an old stove covered in dust and dead flies. It was freezing inside, and damp, mouldy.

'We had all our classes here,' she said, turning slowly in the centre of the room.

Over our heads, the vine was sinewy and had completely covered the ceiling. It made you feel like you were underground, in a cave. The windows, which ran the whole way around the building, were grubby, though unlike those at the main house, these had not been smashed.

'It's odd to be back,' she said, 'though also not so. I dream about it. Here, this room, and the swimming hole.'

'What was it like. . . back then?' I said.

'There were couches, and the smell of cigarette smoke, we all used to sit here, and the cabinet of curiosities was in the corner. We each took an item from it and we got to paint it. It became your emblem for that year.'

There was a distant tone of faded excitement in her voice.

'Is that cabinet in one of the photos you sent me?' I asked.

She nodded.

'What was your emblem?' I asked.

'Oh I can't remember,' she said, now seeming disinterested in discussing it.

'You said before, about Mr Lavelle, that everyone was in love with him,' I said. 'Was Louisa? I mean, were they in love with each other?'

'He admired her,' she said. Her voice was tight, guarded. 'She was different from the rest of us, she had it harder. There was something more real to her, more definite.'

'An outsider,' I said.

'They were both outcasts. Him, by choice, I think, and her, well not so,' she said.

She walked to the windows and rubbed away some of the dirt.

'Did he have a relationship with her?' I asked. I couldn't help myself. I really wanted to say an inappropriate, abusive relationship but held back.

She looked vaguely affronted, and I noticed she hugged herself with her arms.

The tension was back again between us.

'No,' she said. 'Her relationship was with me, really. She, she got caught up and then she tried to save me and it all went wrong and. . .'

She slid slowly then down the dirty window and crouched on the floor. I walked over to her and leaned down.

She stayed looking at the floor.

'There was nothing between them that you knew of?' I said.

She wiped her eyes, still not looking up.

'It's just Helen said to me that Louisa and Lavelle were always together, that she thought they were having some kind of an affair, a relationship. . .' I said.

I could feel my own insistence rising.

Victoria lifted her head up to look at me. The sadness was gone. She reminded me almost of a child, a bold child who had been sent to her room and was wary of any offer of forgiveness. Sullen and sulky.

'Helen.' She said her name with a snarl.

I stood up again and moved away. Like I needed some distance, perspective on her.

'She was nothing, nothing to him ever,' she said. 'She didn't know anything about us.'

She had put her head down again and was tracing a shape with her fingers in the dirt.

'Victoria, I know this must be hard, coming back here, but. . .' I began, then stopped.

It was a weird place. Victoria seemed to be getting more distracted and strange the longer we stayed. For the first time I wished I hadn't come alone with her. I felt for my phone in my pocket. It was solid, reassuring.

She must have sensed my irritation and unease.

'I have to show you first,' she said, speaking slowly. 'We are not leaving yet.'

There was a deadness in her words. Like they were weighed down.

'Show me what?' I asked.

'What happened,' she said.

I felt close, really close now. And also afraid.

'Where?' I said.

'At the swimming hole,' she answered, 'on the last night.'

She was looking up at me. Her eyes a kind of challenge. I felt both curious and filled with dread.

I pulled her into a standing position and offered her some water from my bottle. She took a deep, long drink from it, and I gestured to her to keep it.

As we walked to the door she asked me, in what seemed apropos of nothing, if I had ever been in love.

The mood had changed again, like a breeze blowing in and out.

'Yes, I think so,' I said.

'If you only think so,' she said, 'then it's not the real thing.'

'That's quite presumptuous,' I replied, trying to sound lighter than I felt. 'How would you know?'

Then I thought of my life. And how, without meaning to, I had emptied it of people.

She just shrugged her shoulders.

We pulled the rotten and crumbling door shut behind us. It was soft and malleable in my hands. The kingdom of the art room was slowly returning to the earth.

'I chose a heart,' she said, stopping for a moment in front of me, 'as my object from the cabinet.'

Behind her the forest was a smudged, misty outline of branches, bare and sparse.

'A pickled heart,' she said, turning around to me.

It sounded gruesome and medieval.

'That was my emblem,' she said and her eyes were wide and alight.

She was impossible to pin down, an energy around her that was unpredictable and unsettling.

She walked on then towards the woods.

'What did Louisa choose?' I asked, moving quickly to keep up with her. I was finding it hard to keep the nerves out of my voice.

'A skull,' she said.

I stopped.

'And no one ever chose the skull,' she said, her words slow and measured as she walked on ahead of me, her lines rehearsed and pitch perfect. As if we were in a play.

I remembered the essay about the skull in the folder Victoria sent me. The heart and the skull. Entwined and connected.

What happens to one without the other?

I looked up to the sky. A large white bird soared above our heads, blown in off the coast, suspended, then released by the wind.

With a flicker of fear I followed her, deeper and deeper into the grey, watery woods.

Louisa

Chapter Twenty-Three

Victoria was not in school the Monday after the party. I was relieved, in a way.

I did not want to tell her I had seen Helen and Mr Lavelle together. I wonder about this now. It should have been the first thing I told her that night. Instead, I had left her house without saying even goodbye. I should have warned her, I should have said the words, I'm not sure he loves you. But I didn't.

My mother used to say that if you wait too long to make a decision, it tends to be made for you. I think this is probably true. You can be struck with a fatal passivity.

I walked the hallways that Monday as I always did when without her. Alone and at a distance from everyone. The girls around me rushed and chatted, books crashing to the floor in the overcrowded narrow corridors, answers to Christmas tests being scribbled on arms and secrets whispered in ears with cupped hands. The sense of holidays in the ether. But I moved slowly, as if time was of no consequence to me.

And I felt somehow older, taller even, than everyone around

me. And sadder too, a gloom in my heart. If what she said was true, Victoria and Mr Lavelle would be leaving after Christmas. I would be the orphan left behind.

From this distance, all these years later, I know it is possible to completely imagine the world. That there is your unreality and no other. We move in little isolated globes of our own making, and they are as real to us as anything we might touch or taste. Sometimes you wake for a moment and you realize it was not how you thought it was, but then the call of the imagined is usually stronger and you drift back. It is how you make sense of things. Stories and fairy tales. You are happier in the land of make-believe.

I think I may have misunderstood most things that happened to me. But I am never able to fully think of the enormity of what this might mean. There is no point anyway now.

Victoria did dream up her world; she was shameless about it. Though I could not fully admit this. I admired her too much. And there was always the possibility that Mr Lavelle and Helen were just as Victoria described. A one-sided infatuation that would play itself out. It would die on the steps of the school when Helen watched Victoria and him speed off in a cloud of dust.

I had art that afternoon. The bell rang, I changed my shoes and walked out into the walled garden that led to the summer house. It was windy and grey, the sky heavy with rain, and the garden was bare and sparse. I felt numb; half there, barely seen.

Sister Agnes, the science teacher, was in the garden. She was a large woman, white hair escaping from the side of her veil, her broad face red as she slowly leaned down to the ground. She was picking an upturned jar out of the soil. I felt a need to speak to her, someone, anyone.

'Trapping things, Sister?' I said as I walked past.

See me, hear me.

She looked up.

'Oh yes, you know the way it is. Dirt, always revealing itself,' she said.

I liked her. She was warmer than the others. Her eyes had life in them.

I tried to imagine her young, hopeful. Bags packed, a new life awaiting at the end of the long journey.

'Be careful, tread easy now,' she said as I walked on.

I was the first to arrive in the summer house. The door was open and the lights on, but it was empty. I put on the kettle and went to look at the cabinet of curiosities. Its sheer oddness and beauty never failed to ignite something in me. I tried to open the door but it was locked. I knew Mr Lavelle kept the tiny key on his belt. For some reason, looking at the cabinet that afternoon made me think of the tabernacle in the church. A tiny, adorned box, with its own gold curtains. A temple to mystery and curiosity. I looked at the heart in the cloudy jar and thought about Victoria's essay and the hearts she had taken to drawing on every surface, even her school bag. They were interlocking and blood red, sometimes with thorns cutting them open.

I made the tea in Victoria's cat mug and sat down on the overstuffed couch. I thought about this place and what it must be like to be with him, here alone. I wondered why Victoria hadn't had sex with him. I knew if it had been me and I felt about him as she did, I would have. Like the boy from my old school, the one who always wore a Les Misérables shirt. I had felt nothing with him, relieved, maybe. Like something else was done, achieved. A body explored, bought.

But I hadn't been in love. My own restless nights in the narrow school bed returned to me.

She was foolish to wait for Mr Lavelle; maybe that was why he had not discouraged Helen. He had become frustrated with the chaste and honourable Victoria and been distracted by Helen and her white skin. And yet it was Victoria who talked so dismissively of the nuns, and their virginal marriages with the Lord, the gold marriage bands with the Holy Spirit. While I thought something about their union was magnificent, a pure belief in the existence of a perfect other, a giving of yourself to the unknown.

She didn't make sense to me sometimes.

'There is no class today, Louisa.'

Mr Lavelle was standing at the door. He had some wood under his arm for the stove and looked vaguely puzzled by my being there.

'I posted a notice on the board,' he said, bending down to drop the logs beside the stove. A few of them tumbled across the floor.

'Oh, I didn't see it, I didn't know,' I answered, getting up from the couch and going to help him.

We stacked the stray logs. He smelled of earth and cold air.

'Where is Victoria? I haven't seen her today,' he asked, starting to light the fire.

'I don't know, she must be sick,' I said, gathering up my sketchpad.

'Did you enjoy the party at her house?' he asked, standing up and rubbing his hair. He walked to the kettle and flicked it on.

'Yes, I did.' I couldn't think of what to say. 'Her house is very grand.'

He smiled at me as he held the teabag in his hand. He looked tired, with large dark circles under his eyes.

'You are always so refreshing, Louisa, when you do speak,' he said. 'I gave Victoria some extra lessons, tutorials last summer, that's why her mother invited me along. I know it's always vaguely disconcerting to see a teacher outside of school. Civilian life and all that.'

He poured the boiled water from the kettle into the mug.

'Did you enjoy it?' I asked. 'The party?'

In my head I saw him on the leather armchair, Helen at his feet.

'In a way,' he answered, stirring the tea. 'These things are to be endured.'

I nodded. There was a weariness in his voice. He sat down on the chair.

'I guess it's not your world. And I am sure it can't have been easy these past months. It's its own universe here,' he said, looking at me.

'It's different, that's all. I don't try and fit in. That's not who I am. And Victoria has been great, showing me how to. . .' I stopped.

What had she been showing me? Irony, passion, hunger.

Love.

'Victoria, she. . . she gets very passionate, about people,' he said, 'when she believes in someone. It's happened before.'

Please don't talk about the other girl. Please.

'Last year. There was a girl she was close to but she had to leave the school,' he said.

The one from before.

He stood up, took a sip from the mug of tea; I could feel his eyes on me.

'Victoria was distraught, for a while,' he said.

'She is a very authentic and intense person,' I answered, still looking down at my sketchpad.

The empty, unturned pages. I felt embarrassed.

'Yes.' His voice was solemn and low. 'I do have a sense of that. And you, what is she to you?'

I looked up. He smiled at me, gently, eyebrows raised slightly. The sense of him pulling and prodding me to something other. To go further.

For an instant she was there with us, lounging like a cat on the couch again, like on that first day. The air in the room quivering, re-forming with unspoken expectation.

Possibility.

I thought of the reality of her leaving. Of her loving someone else, him.

'I can't live without her,' I said.

I surprised myself. Though I briefly felt relief saying it, announcing it, admitting it. The truth we never spoke. The feelings that drove my shame.

He touched one or two of the chess pieces, his head down. And he looked sad, older and sadder. I thought about Victoria saying how she felt she had to heal him. I hadn't understood that before, but watching him that afternoon I sort of did. His elusiveness had slipped into plain listlessness. There was something soft, almost a feline quality about him. He was a man, but not the kind that was very intimidating or forceful. He just wanted to play. I had never really thought about that before. He was beautiful, lyrical and weak.

He knew now that Victoria held my heart. And nothing would be the same between the three of us. I suddenly wanted to disappear. The desire to be recognized and seen was evaporating. I stood up to leave.

'Don't go,' he said. 'Do you play?'

He gestured to the board. His eyes were pleading.

'No,' I answered, shaking my head. 'I never learned.'

'Pity,' he said. 'Victoria does. She's very good, actually. A master, you might say, if she could only focus more.'

I began to back away from him, towards the door. The room smelled smoky and warm. It no longer felt like a refuge.

'I gave her some lessons. . . last year,' he went on, staring at the tiny king, queen and pawns on the table. 'There's always time. I might set up a chess club – you could join, maybe?' he said, looking up.

'Aren't you, won't you be leav. . .' I let the words fade away.

He leaned forward in his chair, resting the mug on the stone floor. It spilled slightly as he did so; a damp patch began to spread out around it. I watched it slowly inching across the ground.

'I'm not going anywhere, Louisa. Everything I want is here. . .' he said, holding his hands out to encompass the room. 'You too, I think. Everything you want is here. With Victoria. . .' When he finished, he looked at me closely.

I didn't answer but looked away to the fire. The flames starting to ignite. Stuttering and spitting into life.

'Yes,' I said, turning back to face him. 'Yes. Everything I want is here.'

I heard my words. Not elaborate or rich, like Victoria's, any more.

I walked out the door. A mist had descended; the trees at the edge of the forest had turned to shadows and vapour. A place to get lost. To run away. To hide from who you were.

If I could speak to her now, that girl in the twilight, what would I tell her?

It is possible to fall in love with the first person who sees you.

And it can turn you to stone.

I was getting ready for bed when Alice came into the room that night.

I was hanging up my uniform. She pulled the curtains, I always forgot to do this, and then she sat on the edge of her bed. I knew she had been at one of the meetings for the school concert.

I ignored her for a minute, which was not unusual. As I climbed into bed she was still sitting on the edge of hers.

'Are you okay?' I asked, grabbing my book.

She turned to me.

'I have just seen something,' she said.

The room was shadowy now, with just my small light on. I couldn't clearly make out her expression.

'A love letter and a poem. All typed up and everything. To Mr Lavelle, from someone in the school,' she said.

'It's probably a joke,' I replied, putting the book back on the bedside locker and pulling the covers more closely around me.

She didn't answer.

'How did you get it anyway?' I asked.

'It was in Helen's locker,' she said, rubbing her eyes.

This was not what I expected to hear.

'How odd,' I said. 'And Helen showed it to you?'

'And to the other prefects. Yes, of course. Helen has nothing to hide. She was worried someone was starting a poison-pen campaign against us. Lots of people are jealous of us prefects, our positions and our relationships with the teachers,' she said. 'Helen was warning us to be vigilant, someone is obviously trying to get us into trouble.' She lay down on her bed.

'Of course, yes,' I said quickly.

I had to find out what was in the letter, what could be in it. I felt a throb of curiosity and fear in my stomach.

'What did it say, the letter?' I asked.

'That they are in love and going to run away,' she said. 'Also something about a painting, a drawing.'

I sank further under the covers.

'Sister Ignatius was sent a copy too. Called Helen in this evening,' she said.

The throb had turned to a pain.

'There is going to be a major scene of some kind, mark my words,' she said.

For a second I saw Victoria in my head, posting anonymous letters from her sickbed, playing games. But then I dismissed the thought. She would never be stupid enough to bring this level of attention on Mr Lavelle. And why would Helen tell the other prefects? Why draw attention to it?

'What will they do – the nuns, I mean?' I asked.

'Well, last year there was this man who used to hide naked in the trees down by the gate, a flasher,' she said, lowering her voice.

I laughed nervously.

'It's not funny, he was this complete weirdo, and he was arrested in the end. Anyway, when the nuns found out he was there we had mass every morning at seven thirty for two straight weeks, the long version, and then they had this retreat in the school, with this priest, where we had to talk about passions and not giving in to them. It was excruciating. And no food for the whole day also. A twenty-four-hour fast. I was too tired and hungry to get any study done by the end of it.'

Passions and not giving in to them.

'It will be so much worse this time,' she said, shaking her head.

Alice started getting ready for bed and I turned on to my other side.

'Why did the school get the students to do penance when it was some sick man who was. . .?' I asked.

'Because, well, because it's a warning,' she said.

A warning of what? That people are fundamentally bad and without control? That they want to do dark things to you in the shadows? And, somehow, you are in the end responsible?

'We're going to meet later, the prefects, about the letter. I thought I'd better tell you in case you heard me leave after lights out,' she said. 'We have to wait till everyone has gone to bed.'

A midnight conflab in the draughty Hall. Like witches around a cauldron. And Helen, leading the charge, chief amongst hypocrites.

'What can you do now – I mean, if Sister Ignatius has seen the letter and the poem?' I said, staring at the cracks on the wall beside me.

'Well, Helen says it's important we stick together, get our story straight and obviously find out who wrote it and is pretending to be Helen,' she said. 'It really is slanderous.'

'I think you mean libellous,' I said. 'When it's written down, it's libellous.'

I ran my fingers over the uneven wall. The air in the room was damp and the walls had moisture on them.

'Yes, right,' she said.

'Is Helen upset?' I asked.

I imagined the creeping redness on her white neck. The alarm in her pale eyes.

'No, of course not. It's not from her so she feels very strongly that she will be vindicated. She made it clear to Sister Ignatius that someone was trying to tar her reputation. She also had some things to say about Mr Lavelle to Sister,' she said.

'What things?' I said.

There was something ominous in how Alice had said his name.

'Look, I'm not sure, but you know what he's like. . . And Helen has been working with him a lot lately with the anniversary stuff.

I think he has made her feel uncomfortable. I don't know.'

She no longer wanted to confide in me. Her voice had become more distant.

'Does Sister Ignatius believe Helen?' I said.

'Yes, of course,' Alice replied. 'Well, Helen thinks so.'

Maybe not.

I reached to turn off the light when I heard her climb into her bed.

I found it hard to go to sleep. I was waiting for Alice to make her move and disappear off to the Hall. The clock read ten, then half past, but still she stayed where she was. The wind picked up outside, the lights in the hallway went off. A door closed somewhere deep in the house and the black phone in the hall outside the office rang, stopping almost as quickly as it started. And I thought about the letter, what it might have said and whether it was Victoria who wrote it.

Eventually I must have fallen asleep, for I dreamed. It was of Victoria and this was not unusual, most of my dreams featured her. In this one she was dressed like a pilgrim, a white bonnet on her head. In the distance, on the far-off hills, there were bonfires.

And the sky was lit up, angry and raging.

Chapter Twenty-Four

If only our lives were like a book and you could stop and ponder the ideas raised for a moment, turn the pages back and read again. But this time more carefully.

It would make all the difference.

Alice was standing over me and the room was dark. Black, blind, dark. She had her torch in her hand and was shining it not quite in my face, but just above my head, on the wall. I sat up, rubbing my eyes, and looked at the alarm clock on my bedside locker. It read 3.45 a.m.

'I need you to come with me,' I heard her say.

She sounded far away and I wondered for an instant if I was still dreaming. The icy temperature in the room suggested not, as did the slow click of the pipes that ran around the ceiling. The school's archaic and eerie heating system.

'What's going on? It's the middle of the night,' I mumbled, sitting up more fully.

The cold air of the room a shock after the warmth of sleep.

'We need you to come,' she said. 'I'm sorry but they won't wait.'

A point of no return.

'Who won't wait? I'm not getting up now. We'll get caught,' I answered.

'You have to come. It will be worse tomorrow if you don't, I promise you,' she said, and her voice was not unkind, but worried.

I wished I could have made out the expression on her face, even though I had read somewhere people's voices betray them more. If you want to tell if someone is lying, phone them and ask them the question that requires the truth. It was something about tone and not seeing their eyes. Which it seemed were not windows to the soul. And what was Alice's tone? Anxious. My mind was still in that place between sleep and wakefulness, the one where you are supposed to have visions and somehow see things as they really are.

It must be Victoria, I thought, as sleep slipped away; they have found out about her and Mr Lavelle and maybe it was her letter and poem after all. I was awake now.

I climbed out of bed and dragged on my dressing gown, stumbling over my shoes as I did so. It was so cold in the room I could see my breath. I grabbed my scarf off the back of the door as we left.

The corridor was silent and lit only by the pale neon light above the door that led to a balcony at the back of the house. Alice had switched off the torch and led the way. We approached Victoria's room and for a moment I wondered if she would stop there. I thought perhaps Victoria had returned to the school late. And I felt, for some reason, that she would know how to handle this and it would all make a strange kind of sense. We would laugh about it later. But we passed by her door.

We went down the stairs carefully; the carpet was torn in places and the stairs creaked. At the turn in the Maiden's Chamber, moonlight was streaming through the stained-glass window, making a red and blue pattern on the floor. It was strangely magical, peaceful even, and I felt like I wanted to stay there a minute. To sink to my knees and trace the outline of the pattern on the floor. The statue of Mary stood on a ledge on the wall. Her eyes were downcast.

Alice did not turn towards the Hall as I expected. She went towards the back of the house and the door that led to the walled garden. She opened it gently and we walked outside. The sky was clear and the air cold and fresh, an easterly wind blowing in off the sea. The moon was bright, lighting the path that wound through the now-bare flower and vegetable beds. A fox ran out in the path ahead of us.

I saw the tension in Alice's back ease as we walked on silently, as if the oppressive house with its shadows had weighed her down. Bats flew above us, small and darting towards the woods over the high wall. There was the sound of water running as we neared the gate; someone had left the outside tap on. I walked to the wall and turned it off; the ground was soggy. The bucket underneath the tap was overflowing. I could see the moon reflected in the water. Alice stopped for a second. She had got a stone in her shoe and cursed quietly under her breath as she tried to remove it. I turned back and looked towards the house. The fox had returned and stood on the path staring at us. Intruders in his night.

As we walked on, the summer house, a dim light shining from its windows, came into view.

The door was open. Alice stood aside and gestured for me to go in. The room was lit by candles and I saw again how romantic a place it was. A refuge in an enchanted forest. And I wished I could have visited here one summer night, just the three of us – me, Victoria and Mr Lavelle. We would have talked, and no one would have fallen in love with anyone else.

Helen was sitting in his chair, by the stove. She had one of the throws around her shoulders and somehow it only added to the sense of majesty about her. There were no other prefects. I turned back to the door but Alice shook her head and shut it without joining us.

'What is going on, Helen?' I said.

I could hear my voice and it didn't sound right.

'In a way, you should be honoured, Louisa. It's not everyone who gets to come here after dark.'

I didn't answer and I didn't sit down. I felt safer standing.

'But then maybe I am completely wrong and you do get to come here after dark. Or maybe you visit him in the village?' She fiddled with her bracelet as she spoke and didn't look at me, but past me.

'What are you talking about?' I said loudly.

'Quiet, Louisa,' she said. 'I thought Alice explained that we found your letter and poem to him? The one that talks about how it felt when he put his mouth to your chest – the flowering of something, I believe? Not exactly a subtle metaphor. We would have expected better from the English ace.'

She gestured to the table, where a piece of paper lay.

I felt like walking over and destroying it. I didn't want to read it. There was something bad, toxic, within the words.

Helen got up then and walked to the cabinet of curiosities and trailed her fingers slowly across the protruding glass. It was glinting, the candles reflected in it. I thought again about why she told the other prefects of the letter; she could have used her powers of persuasion and just papered over the cracks with Sister Ignatius. She was loved. They believed the things she said.

'More Mills and Boon than – who is it you like these days? Virginia Woolf, is it?' she said, turning briefly to face me.

'I didn't write him any letter or any poem,' I said. 'And I have never been here at night or anywhere else with him.'

'Did he get you to choose an item?' she said, touching the cabinet again.

'Are we here to compare art classes?' I said as the door behind me opened in the breeze, and I jumped slightly at the sound.

Helen didn't seem to notice.

'In a way, yes,' she answered, opening the cabinet. It was unlocked and I wondered why and how she had a key.

The trees, black shadows, moved in the wind. I closed the door. Alice, who for some reason I thought might be standing guard outside, was nowhere in sight.

When I turned back, Helen had reached in and taken out one of the cloudy jars.

'You know what's in here?' she asked, holding it up to me across the room.

It was Victoria's heart.

'He told me it was a human heart,' she said, 'all shrivelled up and beating no more.'

She looked lost in thought for a moment, staring at the jar in her hand. And I wondered what else he might have said to her about hearts and how they live, and die. And who gets to hold them.

And how she maybe believed him once.

'Helen, as much as I find this thrilling, it's almost four in the morning and we shouldn't be here,' I answered. 'I don't know anything about a letter or a poem.'

She laid the jar carefully back in the cabinet and closed the door before turning back to me.

'Louisa, we've all seen how you are with him these last few months. The way he watches you. I mean, I can see how flattering it is. I do understand how hard it must have been to resist. I'm sure you wouldn't really have met anyone like him before. But it's crossed a line and we are all going to have to pay for it now, which is why it's become my business.'

Was she jealous of the way he was with us? Did she mean to punish him or just me?

'I think you must have confused me, Helen, with you. You seemed really cosy with him the other night at Victoria's house,' I said. 'Quite touching.'

She said nothing for a second, her face in half shadow. The door of the cabinet slipped open behind her and hung ajar.

'I felt like I was interrupting – how would I describe it? Something quite intimate,' I said.

'As head girl, I have meetings with the teachers. It comes with the role,' she said. 'It's not exactly unusual and hardly cause for alarm or indeed suspicion.'

I laughed. She looked indignant, her eyes darting and wary.

'Role, that's a really interesting way of putting it. Like role model, or maybe just model,' I said.

Her face did not move. The gaze still now.

'Because isn't there some kind of a painting of you, here, actually?' I pointed to the couch.

'You don't know what you are talking about,' she said, shaking her head slowly. 'I have tried to warn you against messing with me, with this school, with the way we run things. But you just can't seem to take it in, can you?'

She moved away from the cabinet and walked slowly towards me, her arms folded tightly across her chest.

'There is no painting of me. There is no Mr Lavelle and me. What there is, is a cheap slut from the wrong end of town who thinks she can make her way in the world by hanging out with rich kids and sleeping with the first man who shows any interest in her.'

Her voice was defensive, with a hint of nerves. The letter represented as much a danger to her as it did to Victoria or me.

We were face to face. Her eyes looked black and closed off in the dim light of the room. I felt like it was a dream again, and she was something from a tale, a story of warning and menace. Of alchemy. Why did we meet? All the small, tiny decisions taken long ago that lead us to where we are. My ambition, the desire to do better, the sense of my calling.

'We know you have a good head for facts, Louisa, so you need to repeat that back to me,' she said. 'This is your last and only chance.'

As she spoke, the door to the summer house blew open again, more violently this time, and a draught blew out two of the candles above the stove. We were in almost complete darkness, only the moonlight stayed constant and bright. The breeze was ice-cold on my legs. Helen wrapped the throw more tightly around her shoulders, her eyes never moving from me. The cabinet was in shadow now, only an outline in the dark room.

'You talk such rubbish, Helen. I am not taking the blame for your own – what should we call them – indiscretions,' I said. 'I mean, what would all the nuns think of you if they knew? The girl most likely to succeed. . . but at what exactly?'

Find your voice, I said to myself. This is not a dream. Spit out your anger.

But she got there first.

'I don't know what Victoria, let alone Mr Lavelle, sees in you. You are nothing, nothing here. One word of your lies about me and they will show you the door. You will be back to the crappy world you came from. No one will believe you if you dare try to pin this letter and poem on me.'

She stood still, staring at me.

'What there is, is a letter typed by you which at this moment is sitting on the desk in Sister Ignatius's room. She is going to come down on all of us like a ton of bricks tomorrow morning and Mr Lavelle could be fired or suspended. Admit that you wrote it, tell her you are sorry, get on your knees and possibly you will survive,' she said.

Mr Lavelle fired. The words were stark.

I saw myself on my knees, but it was not in front of Sister Ignatius. It was Victoria I sank before. I was admitting everything to her, waiting for her hand to fall on my head and let me confess my feelings.

'They were ready to be disappointed; you were an unknown quantity when they let you and the rest of them in, a *social experiment*.'

The depth of her dislike of me and all I represented was clear in her tone, a frozen sense of distaste.

Reputations, reputations. What are they made of? I know now they are the lies we tell ourselves and everyone else. One person has many faces. And voices. Is there any truth about any of us? It's all a game. Charades with shadows and words.

Only the brave ever lift the veil. And face the consequences.

'Helen, this isn't even that good a school. There are plenty of other schools. And I will tell them what a weird, fucked-up, living-in-the-1950s hole this is. Where we spend more time saying decades of the rosary and getting our lines straight than actually getting an education. Of course, what makes it really priceless is that amid all the penance and piety, the head girl gets naked for her teacher. All in the name of art. I will make sure everyone remembers your name, and when you meet them at a random college party, you'll know why they all want to get you a drink,' I said.

She picked up the piece of paper and shoved it into my hand. It was folded-over, heavy, thick paper.

I struggled to read it in the low light. It was typed, the rows of words close together.

```
My eye never leaves you. I see you when you
aren't even here. I trace your journeys and
imagine I am there, beside you. I didn't know
I was lonely, until I met you. Everything
changed when you came. I am not the way I was
and I can't go back. You unlocked my heart.
That night, when you knelt in front of me, in
```

```
your room. I have not been the same since.
    I count down the days till we leave. It
will be a new life, together. They cannot,
they won't blame you for it, when they know
what we mean to each other. . .
```

It was from Victoria. I didn't have to finish it. She could have at least tried to make it sound like something Helen would write. What was she trying to do?

I put it back on the table.

'I have no idea who wrote this,' I said. 'Where is the poem?'

'In my locker,' she said. 'It's more of the same, morbid and pathetic. As if I would ever write this.'

She picked up the keys that lay on the table.

'If it's not from you, is it Victoria's?' she said, looking at me.

The bitchiness was gone; it was the first proper question of the whole conversation. She knew as well as I did.

I shook my head. There was no place for truth between us.

My poor, stupid Victoria.

Helen looked briefly up to the ceiling, as if composing herself.

'I feel nothing but pity for you, Louisa. None of those schools you mentioned would even look at you now, because you can imagine the kind of reference you are going to get if there is any notion that you are planning to run off with a teacher. I called you here to try and give you a warning, but I will let you sink now. And I am going to enjoy it and so will everyone else here.' She paused. 'Even Victoria, deep down, because she will get over you, just like Mr Lavelle will. Everyone will survive, except you.'

She spoke with power and assurance. Her place in the world not precarious, like mine.

'It was in your locker, Helen,' I said. 'Explain that.'

'It was placed there by you, and if not you, Victoria,' she said. 'You are both trying to ruin my reputation, and you won't get away with it. I matter.'

She had mattered. With Mr Lavelle. And Victoria hated her for this.

Helen started to blow out the remaining few candles. The only thin light came from the still-bright moon. The air cold, the door swinging back and forth in the breeze. And if you happened to be passing through the dark woods and saw us in that moment you might have thought we were ghosts. You might have pressed your face to the glass, curious to know what we were and what mysteries we might have held in our hearts, for what would bring two souls here in the middle of the night, but a passion of some sort.

But you would have been wrong. It wasn't passion that brought us together but lies. And everything really comes back to that.

'I'm not afraid of you, Helen,' I said.

I was, though. And she knew it.

I went out ahead of her. I could hear her locking the door of the summer house behind me and I thought about the cabinet, she hadn't shut the cabinet. I was shivering as I walked back to the gate into the garden. I walked fast, breathlessly fast, tripping over branches and stones as I went. My throat felt like it was burning. It was an elaborate performance, like everything in this school. The words had literally burned my throat. I had done the best I could. I was not afraid. I would defend myself and protect Victoria. And Mr Lavelle.

I didn't yet see that sometimes there are forces stronger than you. It is an empirical fact, not a moral failing.

Chapter Twenty-Five

I woke the morning after the fight with Helen in the summer house still feeling like I would survive the storm. Foolish, maybe. The room was in semi-darkness, the curtains closed.

I could hear Alice starting to shift in her bed and the bell ringing in the hall warning us that breakfast would be served in fifteen minutes. I hoped Victoria would be back so I could explain to her the strangeness of it all, though I feared for her.

Alice rose first. I expected she would say something to me about the summer house but she dressed in silence. I lay on my side, offering her privacy as I always did and thinking about what I would say to her. I was about to speak when she left the room, the door closing gently behind her. I sat up in bed.

She often waited for me.

I was one of the last to head for the stairs, the final bell ringing. Victoria's door was shut tight. As I reached the entrance hall I noticed Mr Lavelle through the glass, standing on the porch steps, as he always did at this time, cup of coffee in hand. It was reassuring to see him there. His back lean and straight, facing the sea. And I broke the rules and did not go to the dining hall but instead opened the front door and stood beside him.

He didn't turn his head. The air was cold and fresh; the sea in the distance lay still and had a glassy, grey colour like the sky. I thought I could smell smoke on the air from somewhere far off. Someone burning leaves and wood.

The peace was broken by a group of men working in the drive; they were setting up stalls and stands, dragging poles and containers over the gravel, getting ready for the Christmas fair. A photographer with a large camera was putting up a tripod. They looked like emissaries from the real world, their chat and laughter breaking the atmosphere of ice and gloom that hung around the building.

Mr Lavelle took a sip from his cup and then half-turned to look at me.

'So you know then,' he said. 'She has summoned fire.'

I swallowed and felt ill. I reached out to steady myself on the railing at the side of the steps.

My hand was white against the rusted black paint.

'I had a visit last night, from Sister Ignatius,' he said.

His voice was tight and hard in a way that wasn't usual. Like he was pretending to be mature now.

'It's serious,' he said. 'Quite serious, in its own way.' He looked up to the sky.

I followed his gaze. White seabirds were flying high above our heads and the sky was a faint pink colour. Shepherd's warning.

He didn't sound angry, more confused. Dismayed.

'Helen is going to say I wrote it, or maybe Victoria, and it's not true, we didn't,' I said, facing him.

He turned more completely then to stare at me. He looked puzzled.

'Isn't it from Victoria?' he said. 'I'm sure you have read it.'

I shrugged my shoulders, pretending to know little. I could feel a faint tic or twitch in my eye. I put my hand over it to stop it. He watched me.

'I saw them last night, the letter, the poem. Sister showed me,' he said, taking a drink from his cup. 'It sounds like Victoria.'

How could she do this to him? If she loved him, why would she try to create this drama? He must have rejected her, told her he wouldn't run away with her. A change of mind, of heart. I felt faint hope that I wouldn't lose her after all.

'There is going to be a meeting of the Board of Governors today,' he said. 'I will be summoned to explain how a student could develop feelings like this and whether I encouraged it.'

The workmen were laughing, huddled beside one of the cars.

'Who are the governors?' I asked, watching them.

'Priests, parents. Helen's and Victoria's, I believe,' he said.

'I'm sorry,' I said, bowing my head. I could not think of anything else to say.

'Why are you sorry?' he said. 'It's not your fault. I have received letters and poems before, from both of them.' He paused, staring wearily at the steps. 'But in some kind of cosmic justice, this letter, the one I was shown last night, is not even one of those. It's made up, to get me into trouble.'

'Are you afraid?' I asked.

He laughed half-heartedly. 'Are you?' he said, looking back at me.

I shook my head, lying.

He looked beautiful, almost transparent in the grey light, even though his eyes had shadows under them and his face was thin with worry. Worry that he was trying to conceal from me. The smell of smoke that had been faint earlier was stronger suddenly. The damp, still air holding it.

'It's only a stupid letter and a poem anyway,' I said. It was cold on the porch. I could feel the chill enter my bones through the thin jumper. 'I mean, how bad can it get? It doesn't mean anything.'

'But then maybe it does mean something. Words do, they are weapons.' He watched the men as he spoke. They had started to smoke as they went about their work. 'If you choose to use them as such.'

He took his cigarettes from his pocket and lit one. I followed the click and hiss of the lighter and then a pause to inhale.

'You know that words are weapons,' he said. 'Isn't that what we do? The three of us, the sophists.'

He laughed again, but not in any joyous way.

Another car drove up, a deep rust colour. The driver parked it at an angle near the yew trees but didn't get out.

Mr Lavelle flicked the ash from his cigarette into his cup rather than on to the steps.

There was the sound of something metal falling on gravel; one of the tent poles had come loose.

'Some people are insecure; their love is built on the fear of loss. They are defensive of it. It becomes anxious and they end up destroying things,' he said.

I knew he was speaking of Victoria. Her anxiety and jealousy of Helen; she had let it take over.

'You know she loves you, then,' I said.

I held my breath briefly after I spoke the words.

He nodded, not looking at me but staring out to sea. He placed his cup down on the ledge at the top of the steps and took another drag on the cigarette.

'How could I not?' he said.

'And you, do you want her? Do you love her?' I asked.

'In my own way, but not as she would like,' he said, looking at me then. 'Not, perhaps, the way you do.'

His words fell like stones, dashing me on their descent.

I sank to the wet steps and put my head in my hands. He reached down and touched my shoulder. I felt the weight of it. I wanted to cry but there were no tears. My desire to be seen for who I really was, that was another of my illusions. They were right to shun me.

'We cannot choose who we love,' he said, taking his hand away then.

My breaths were loud, shallow and rattled in my ears.

Can we choose who we love? Maybe not, and all of it is decided before, long before.

'It's not just about her. There are some other things too, and I might have done them differently,' he said.

'What things?' I said, looking up at him.

My eyes felt red and stinging. Like I hadn't slept for months.

As he spoke I thought of Helen. Seeking revenge for past indiscretions.

'Well, I can't say. It seems the nuns thought they wanted me here, but now I don't think they do. They are not ready for me, and what I bring,' he said, exhaling smoke.

The school, a universe of the pure, that none of us fitted in to.

He stood silently for a moment, his eyes staring into the distance. Then suddenly his energy flared up again. 'It's going to come to an end; everything they teach, talk about, it won't last. They can't hold it back for much longer. The dusk of the gods.' He threw his cigarette on the ground and twisted his foot onto it.

I wasn't sure what he meant, but I knew today felt like the end of something. It was there in the bare trees and the pink sky. The wet, moist air getting into us and putting out the light.

A bell was ringing inside, keeping time segmented, cut-up.

Victoria. How her heart would be broken. I would need to tell her that sometimes you dream, and it's not real. Nothing is as it seems. He wasn't the one you were meant to be with.

'I am sort of to blame,' he said. 'It was easy to misunderstand. I forget I am your teacher, not. . .' He stopped and shrugged his shoulders.

And he spoke the truth. I could see again his knee touching hers, and then the way he had looked at me as we left the forest that first afternoon, and also the gloating Helen sitting silently at his feet. And I thought, shouldn't you know better? Didn't he know that we Temple House girls lived for these things, a glance that might stop the world?

He liked to think he was a force for liberation, someone who would blow the cobwebs from our thoughts and free us from the straitjacket of our narrow and constricted teachings. He wanted to make us not afraid of who we were and the alchemy that lay within. He was offering us sermons and miracles. He embodied the bohemian who walked among the uptight daughters of the professional classes.

But somehow things had got muddled up. The playing went too far. He had been careless with hearts that were still forming. Everyone had read more into it than was there.

And he was also naive. He thought he was loved for his mind, but in fact it was his face.

'I think you are great, a great teacher,' I said, getting to my feet.

He smiled at me. About us the light had subsided again. He touched my arm the way he often did. The way that he shouldn't. This time I knew there was pity more than admiration in it.

'It might be best if I do move on, after all this is settled, explained,' he said.

And for a second I understood how you might want to kiss him. He was made of magic and light, and it was impossible to catch him without reaching out and grabbing hold. There was nothing romantic about it. There was just the body. I did not want him to leave and sometimes the body speaks clearer than the mind. He was the nearest I could get to Victoria.

'And be brave: you might have to let her go,' he said, looking at me.

That was impossible.

We were meant to be together. Everything was happening because she and I had met. The world was falling down because I loved her. It was an interruption of the normal way of things. People fought wars for love, died on crosses for it. I understood that now. Nothing else mattered.

The door opened behind us. It was Sister Frances, her face a mask of disapproval.

She didn't speak to either of us, but her hand was cold and hard on my shoulder as she directed me back inside.

Chapter Twenty-Six

I saw neither Helen nor Victoria that day. They had evaporated.

Art class was cancelled. As was library study.

No one mentioned the letter or the poem.

There was chapel at six o'clock. A priest was waiting at the door; he was new. He had a narrow face, grey hair, and eyes that were too staring. He was biting his lip, slowly, over and over, and I thought I saw a spot of blood, a tiny cut on the surface. Sister Ignatius stood on his right-hand side. The thin band of her wedding ring glinted. We walked past them, heads down, and took our seats in the pew. Sister Ignatius sat behind me. I could feel her presence, much as I had felt the empty spirit of the dead nun that first night in the school.

The sky was an inky, dark blue behind the stained-glass window over the altar. The candles flickered and wavered as the door closed behind us. We said a decade of the rosary, our voices fell and rose in the semi-dark. I thought about having to let Victoria go.

And I couldn't do it.

Mr Lavelle did not want her, and she would need me more than ever. I was her saviour. She was the one who had failed to read the warnings of the prophets. I raised my head to look at the angels on the ceiling, just shadows in the dark, the ecstasy on their faces no longer visible.

The room was filled with the deep aroma of musk and sweetness. The priest swung the censer over our heads. Clouds of incense so as to purify.

It would be over soon. That's what it signalled. All sins can be forgiven and nothing lasts for ever.

Somebody coughed.

And I heard the voice of Mr Lavelle whisper in my ear, reminding me that long ago, people had laughed and played cards here. Games of chance. And they had thought not of their sins.

Then silence again, our heads bowed, our knees sore and turning red. The marks of devotion.

Sister Ignatius led me not back to the school, but instead through the archway and the door in the wall that led to the nuns' quarters. The floor changed underfoot from polished parquet to a thick, soft carpet. The type you left footprints on. Sister Ignatius seemed tiny in front of me. It was endlessly surprising to recognize how small a person she was, and how you forgot it so quickly when she spoke. She was a giant then. Her thin navy cardigan pulled tight across her narrow shoulder blades. Dry bones and sinew. Powerful in her slow and measured stride.

A cleaning woman in her green housecoat and a brush in her hand passed us in the gloom. She stood aside as we walked by. I noticed one of her eyes was milky white. Victoria had once said they only employed people who were wounded, deaf, mute.

We entered a large dining room, a long mahogany table in the centre with a brass chandelier overhead. A fire was lit in the corner. The priest from the chapel sat at one end, another man in the middle. Sister Ignatius directed me to take a chair. There were teacups on the table and some plates that had leftover sandwiches on them. The air smelled of stale food and stewed tea.

The priest began to speak about their grave concerns. About what had come to their attention. A correspondence between a student and teacher that was inappropriate. They had spoken already to Mr Lavelle. It was not the first time concerns had been raised about him. Other matters, trifling ones that now seemed more serious. He got too close to some students. He had lots of new ideas about things.

The new priest looked hungry but alert and awake, leaning over the table, hands tapping the wood. He was ravenous for detail.

He talked on. My eyes wandered to the window and the sky now black. I felt that I would be leaving very soon and the school would bother me no more. I had a strange sense of grandeur, of access to higher things. Like a peace had descended and I knew exactly what it was I had to do, the calling. The ending. I thought about Mr Lavelle on the steps that morning. And how he knew everything, all of our secrets.

The sophists.

Words provided the escape, *they* were the thing that marked us out. We could dissect, cut them, patch them up together. They were our strange gift. The thing we mastered. I could save both of them.

I dragged my gaze back to the table. The room was getting hotter, I pulled at the collar of my shirt. The fire was sparking and spitting orange and red in the corner of my eye.

The man in the suit said it was an alarming situation. And one that could not be allowed to continue. There would be consequences, and not just for those students involved with Mr Lavelle but for all of us. His eyes darted from one end of the table to the other, but never once rested on me.

Sister Ignatius took notes. The Holy Book of Observations, as Victoria and I had christened it. When the man stopped she raised her head and asked if I had anything to say on the matter. Her face was composed and impossible to read. And something about the directness of her question, the getting to the point of it all, was to be admired.

I thought for a second of how I should have asked to speak to my parents. But they were not wise people whose opinion I valued. So I didn't.

In my mind I saw Victoria. Her dreams, smashed like bits of coloured glass around her. Little things that she might have collected, and shown to me. All sliding off her lap and broken now. Mr Lavelle wasn't the one in love with her.

He wasn't the one who wanted to run away with her.

He wasn't the one who wanted to touch her. Hold her.

And I said: 'I wrote the letter and the poem. It was a joke, just something to pass the time. I do that kind of thing, to be funny, to. . . to have something to do. And I am very sorry for it. Mr Lavelle knew nothing about it and did not in any way encourage my attentions.'

I sort of smiled as I spoke, as if to say: look at me. The stupid teenager. One whose every thought, no matter how dumb, becomes an emotion.

Sister Ignatius paused and stared at me. Her gaze steady.

The priest bit his lip again and leaned back in his chair. Satisfied.

The man in the middle pulled at his tie and breathed out loudly.

I sat forward and continued: 'He is very warm and open. He believes in us, wants the best for us, and it can make you think something which you shouldn't. It's not him, despite what you may have heard, and I don't know what that might be.' I turned my head to look at each of them in turn. 'But in case you have heard anything, it's not true either. I'm. . . I'm sure of that.'

The air in the room was dry. I felt my voice disappearing, like it was slipping down my throat. There was no water on the table.

'It's possible to be foolish,' I said, 'and to see things that are not there. He is the best teacher here and it was just a crush, nothing more.'

The smile again. Pay no attention to me. I know not what I do.

Do I regret what I said? I don't know really, even now. When I have nothing to do but think about it. When so much time has passed, and seasons have changed and people have grown older. And all our mysteries should be resolved by now.

I thought words were my ally and could be sculpted into stories, shaped into things that people could understand. Because even if a story is not true, it can serve a purpose. Like the miracles the nuns taught us about day after day: the dying and the crippled who can rise from their beds, the man who walked on water, the turning of water into wine. The mystery of Eve and the serpent in the garden. They didn't happen, never happened, but it didn't mean they weren't beautiful ways of looking at the world and explaining things. About the way we are and the things we do.

And I loved Victoria. I could never tell her this so I lied for her instead. It was the only way to keep her.

Sister Ignatius spoke again: 'You are quite sure, that you wrote this letter?'

I nodded.

'You are not in any way trying to protect someone, someone else?' she said.

She pulled in her lips; they were like a thin line. She touched the cross around her neck as she spoke.

I shook my head again.

Helen, Victoria, Mr Lavelle. Saving all of them.

A vocation without meaning.

The priest led me out of the room.

We returned to the chapel where I kneeled in the pew while he entered the confession box. Sister Frances stood at the altar, barely discernible in the half-light, just a silhouette, placing the chalice on the altar and finding the correct page of the Bible to leave open for morning prayers. I wondered what she thought of me, sitting there in the dark, or did she even think of me at all? Maybe God dominated her thoughts and I was just one of the lost, anonymous sheep. Nothing special about me. He might choose to save me, he might not.

After a minute I went into the confession box. I knelt in the dark, hard space and waited for the iron grille to open and his narrow face with the bleeding lip to appear.

Bless me, Father, for I have sinned.

Chapter Twenty-Seven

It was after 10 p.m. when I returned to my room. Alice was asleep, a book lay open beside her, torch on the floor. I turned on the lamp beside my bed, covering it with one of my shirts to keep the light low. Sitting on the edge of the bed I started to write a note to Victoria. I would leave it in her room in the morning.

I stared at the blank page for what felt like hours, the empty blue lines merging and separating. I rubbed my eyes.

> You touch and I fade
> You breathe and I dissolve
> You speak and I am deaf
> You leave and I fall

My pen scratched against the page. I was exhausted, my thoughts jumbled; feelings, secrets, desires leaking out on to the page. The pen was slipping from my hands, the blue ink stained the edge of the white bedsheet. I rubbed it with my fingers and only made it worse. I lay back against the pillow.

They would send me away. I would never see her again. I wrote my address and phone number down for Victoria. Just in case.

The fog horn sounded down the coast, deep and low. My eyes were closing.

I climbed under the covers, not bothering to undress. And when I dreamed it wasn't of Victoria. It was of a forest in the mist, on the edge of a cliff. I was high up above it looking down, the waves crashing beneath me.

Helen was back. She was sitting in the middle of the sixth years' table as usual. She nodded to the girl beside her as I laid my tray down. Then she ate her toast slowly without taking her eyes off me. Like a medieval queen at court.

A murmur ran around the room as I took my seat. I was ravenously hungry and thirsty, like I had run a race in the night. I could feel their stares. Glances like tiny arrows of disdain.

There was no art class listed on the timetable on the wall outside the Hall. No Mr Lavelle on the steps with his coffee either, just the toing and froing of men setting up the fair and parking old-fashioned cars on the gravel driveway.

I spotted Alice going up the stairs and ran after her, asking if she knew where Mr Lavelle was. She shook her head before continuing up the stairs. I was about to follow her when she turned back, a look of pity on her face as she stared down at me.

'They have asked him to leave. Helen told me,' she said.

'Because of the letter?' I asked.

'Yes, but other things too,' she whispered. 'Victoria's parents have been in touch with the school. I think they are going to make a complaint. And Helen, her parents did too. They said he was not, as a teacher, not. . .' Her words drifted off.

I felt weak and leaned against the banister. It had been for nothing. I had lied and it would serve no purpose. I had lied so Mr Lavelle could keep his job, and so Victoria would not be sent away for wanting him.

'Why did you do it?' she said, shaking her head. 'It's one thing to write a letter to him, but to try and blame it on Helen. . .'

Students pushed past us. Alice glanced at them as if vaguely embarrassed.

I couldn't answer. There was too much, but also too little to say. Figments, phantoms, dreams, visions. Love was all of these things and none of them real. An act of imagination.

'It wasn't wise,' she said, frowning.

She left then and I knew I could not ask her any more about it. The Maidens swayed past me, all knee-socked, crisp, blonde perfection. One of them pretended to hold her nose as they moved around me and they all laughed. They had been chosen to do tours of the schools later that day. The day the organizers of the festivities and their wives were to come and gape at the girls with their brushed golden hair and black velvet hairbands. The girls on the hill.

I skipped French class. It was possible to not be missed that day as various students had been assigned different tasks to get ready for the visitors, so there was an air of confusion and the rigid roll call would not be adhered to. I walked to the summer house, leaving the school through the front porch to avoid any teachers. Many of the tents and stalls for the fete were still only half built. A woman in a long blue dress was twirling a hoop, two small children played beside her. They stopped talking as I passed and stared. They were sucking giant red lollipops. A man with snowy white hair and a trombone was sitting beside the gate to the walled garden. Despite the grey of the morning he was wearing sunglasses. He tapped his foot as I passed. His shoes were shiny and black.

I thought about Victoria as I walked through the garden. When we were apart, at weekends, I had taken to living as if she was watching me. I read books that I knew she would approve of, took out French films from the video store that she had mentioned in passing, bought a paler shade of foundation. I lived as if her eyes were on me, as if I had to make her proud, make her faith in me justified. I had to be perfect. Worthy.

She watched over me. Time and space were no barriers. She could see me now.

I pushed open the door to the summer house. Helen was cleaning out some of the cupboards filled with art supplies.

Beside her the door to the cabinet of curiosities stood open.

I felt my breath catch in my chest.

'You did it then, Louisa. You took my advice,' she said, looking up and appearing not in the least bit surprised to see me there.

She went back to emptying the shelves, placing crayons, charcoal and pencils in some large brown boxes. It was a surprisingly menial task for her. She was looking for something – possibly the picture of her?

'Yes,' I said. 'I did, for Victoria and Mr Lavelle, because it's not true what everyone is saying about him.'

'Isn't it? It hardly made things better for him, admitting you wrote those things,' she said, looking up briefly again.

She got up off her knees, wiped her hands on her skirt, and walked over to the window, the one that faced the forest and the path that led to the swimming hole.

'I was protecting him,' I said.

And Victoria.

'From whom?' she said, her back to me.

'You,' I said. 'You wanted to damage him, get rid of him.'

'Oh please,' she answered, shaking her head and a smirk on her lips. 'He is his own worst enemy. You all are. I didn't write the letter.'

Victoria. I could feel her there in the room. The sense of her. Watching me.

'What happened at the party, at Victoria's the other night?' I said.

'After you left, Mr Lavelle spoke to her, tried to explain that her feelings for him had gone too far. She couldn't take it. We overheard them arguing in the garden and Victoria's father came out. I don't know, but I imagine she then made up some kind of story about him.' She turned to face me. 'That's why she hasn't been in this week.'

'If you knew all this, if you were so sure about it the other night, why didn't you tell me?' I said.

'But you knew she wrote it,' she said, shrugging her shoulders slightly. 'You made a choice to lie for her. Collateral damage.'

I sank down on to the chair near the stove. A scene at the party. The public humiliation of Victoria. I could feel her shame. It would make her do foolish things.

'The person you need to talk to is Victoria. She tried to set me and Mr Lavelle up. You should find her and ask her why,' she said, walking to the couch and sitting down.

She looked calm and controlled, the uniform perfectly straight and laundered, her hair tied in a bun high on her head. Any sense of the nerves from the other night gone.

Dominion restored.

There was noise outside; some of the younger classes were in the walled garden. I could hear shouts and Sister Agnes calling for attention.

'You might also ask her why she told you nothing of this. Despite your closeness,' Helen said, her eyebrows arched. 'Don't feel bad, though. You were just convenient to Victoria, the audience she always needs for her drama. This year's model.'

She was cruel. People are when defending their world.

She looked at me, crossing her arms. 'You know it's a habit of hers, don't you?'

She continued before I could get any words out.

The story of the other friend.

'Her last friend had to leave also. They were planning to run away together, bags packed and everything when they were caught on the driveway at midnight. It was almost amusing.' She smirked again, looking down briefly at her watch. 'So unfortunate, to get so tangled up with her, and him.'

Her voice hard when he was mentioned.

I tried to imagine Victoria at midnight on the dark driveway, frustrated, thwarted. Her plans shredded. It made me want to protect her even more. Everyone conspiring against her. We didn't belong here. There was another future, another place for us.

And below this selflessness, I felt something else. The familiar stain of rejection. I was the only one she never planned to run away with.

'I believe in loyalty, Helen, and in standing by people we lo— care for and admire,' I said. 'Mr Lavelle is a great teacher and Victoria is my friend.'

I tried once more to ape her majesty, slow my words down, control my hands, not stutter or sweat.

'I had an aunt once who was really full of energy,' she said, 'always volunteering for things and doing classes in the evening.

Everyone admired her. Then one day she just collapsed and had
to go to hospital.'

I thought to myself, Victoria is here. She sees it all, she will
come for me.

'And they found out she had this condition. I don't know
what it was. Anyway, it turned out everything about her, all
the energy, the running around, had actually been part of the
condition and not her personality or character at all. Can you
imagine?' She looked at me. 'Everything she is, everything we
understand her to be, is an illness.'

She stood up then and walked over to the cabinet, shutting
the door gently.

'Do you see where I am going with this?' she said as the door
clicked shut.

I didn't respond.

'Because it's the way you should see Victoria. It's all an act, to
conceal the craziness in her,' she said. 'And I should know, we've
been forced to play together since we were children. I have had
to endure her for far longer than anyone else here. She imagined
Mr Lavelle was in love with her.'

Mr Lavelle's words came back to me. When he had silently
moved the chess pieces around on the board and talked of her
mastery. Victoria as sphinx.

'He made her think there was something between them. He
didn't mean to, but he did,' I said. 'She made a mistake, he made
a mistake.'

271

'So he is guilty, to some degree?' she said.

Agree with me. He uses girls like us.

'It's just the way he is. . .' I couldn't think how to explain it.

'I did try and warn you,' she responded, walking over to my chair.

'No you didn't, you tried to pin the whole letter on me,' I said, looking up at her.

'I wanted to see what you knew, I wanted to see. . .' She paused. 'I wanted to see what you would do. It was a test of your loyalty, and your supposed intellect.'

'But you couldn't know I would say I wrote it?' I said.

'No, if you hadn't admitted it, I would have said it was from Victoria. But I had a feeling you would take the blame for her,' she said. 'Look, if anyone was going to be the one to get him out of the school it was you. You were straight out of central casting, the one he would seduce, the cheap slut. You did everything you were supposed to.' She was smiling again.

I jumped up from the chair; she stepped back.

She didn't rule me, or any of us.

'You don't know anything, Helen,' I said, 'you don't know anything about me or Victoria.'

'Don't I?' she said. 'Victoria is one of us. You are the one that has never been quite bright enough to see that.'

I was shaking. I could walk to the cabinet, take out the knife, plunge it deep into her heart. That is something that Victoria would understand, Mr Lavelle too. It would be beyond Helen to know passion, how to sacrifice yourself for someone else.

'It's not a sin to love someone, to want them. . .' I could feel tears and I couldn't let myself cry in front of her.

Because she had won. She had seen and understood everything.

'I pity you, really,' Helen said, walking back to the window.

'Does everyone think I sent the letter to him?' I asked, trying to calm my breathing and looking up at the vine that reached over our heads.

She nodded.

'Do people know about Victoria, her parents making a complaint?' I said.

'No, only the prefects, and the nuns will work around it. He's not the first unusual teacher they have had to move on.'

'What are the other things he is supposed to have done?' I asked.

She looked vaguely irritated then and walked away from the window and back to the cupboards and trays that were strewn on the floor. She kicked one with her foot and a paintbrush rolled out.

'Is it about you and him? Did Victoria tell her parents about that too?' I asked, my voice raised.

Her back was to me. I could see her tense up.

'There is no him and me; he is a diversion from the boredom here, nothing more,' she said, her voice quiet. 'I'm not mad.'

Keep the outside positive and shiny and you can get away with anything.

'There is no proof anyway,' she said, turning back to look

at me. 'Ask Victoria what she told her parents. She will be here tonight to pack up.'

I could see her sitting in front of him on the floor at the party. The intimacy of it.

'Where is she going?' I asked, panic in my voice.

'Her parents need to bury her somewhere else for a while, see if she can avoid another unfortunate entanglement in the next place,' she said. 'Her mother has been on the phone to mine all week, in despair at how her precious, perfect daughter could have been so badly used by this cad of a man. And we all have to play along, nod our heads and see her as a victim.'

On the phone all week.

'Besides, Sister Ignatius has had enough. Diplomacy and connections will only take you so far. Victoria is more trouble than she is worth.'

I thought about the line of Virginia Woolf's that I had transcribed in my diary, the one about someone having to die so others could value life more.

Helen bent down to the floor, putting the stray brush back in the tray.

'Where do you think he will go?' I asked, standing up, legs weak.

I could hear the bell in the school.

'Abroad. Africa, probably,' she said. 'The school will give him recommendations. He is sort of a gypsy, not suited to teaching; thinks he is, of course. He barely even covers the correct curriculum here. It won't matter so much over there.'

'But you, you and him. . .?' I said.

And the letters he told me you sent him. And the picture.

We stared at each other in silence for a second.

And for a moment all the stories of him were back, the aesthetics of his existence and how they had captivated Victoria and me. And I thought of Helen lying on the couch for him.

'What if I tell people, tell them that it was Victoria? That she made it all up: the complaint, the letter, the poem?' I said.

'You wouldn't do that to her,' she said.

And she was right. I couldn't do that to her.

'And besides, he is guilty of something; we just don't know quite what. Victoria has probably exaggerated, but we know he did nothing to dissuade her. He enjoys it,' she said.

There was revenge in her voice. She too had misread him. He had drawn her naked on the couch. And she regretted it all now.

I walked to the door and as I did the cabinet of curiosities caught my eye once more.

'He won't leave this behind,' I said. 'He will come back for his things and the collector's things. They meant something.'

I tried to sound defiant. To remind her that mystery existed. And with it hope.

She looked at the cabinet briefly.

'They never belonged to him,' she said.

And it seemed like all we stood for dissolved in the acid of her words.

Chapter Twenty-Eight

It was after 4 p.m., almost dark, when I spotted the car parked at the side of the house. Victoria's parents were here. I ran to her room, expecting to see her packing up, but she was not there and there was no sign of anything gone. Maybe Helen was wrong. Victoria wouldn't be leaving. The storm would pass.

I sat on her bed. There were books piled up on the side table – *Wuthering Heights*, *Moby-Dick*, *Pride and Prejudice* among them. Hardback, expensive versions, deep red in colour with gold embossed lettering on the spines, the pages turned down in places. Gifts to her, bestowed at birthday parties, in exclusive hotels, with the tinkling of pianos in the background. Rooms with sea views.

I left my poem under the pillow. She would understand when she read it.

I found the girl who shared with her; she was studying in the library. She didn't know where Victoria was. I walked to the summer house for what seemed like the millionth time. The lights were off. I opened the door, imagining she would be there in the gloom. But she wasn't. All of Mr Lavelle's things were gone. The throws and rugs packed away, the art books and paints stored neatly in boxes. It felt like a place that had been deserted for years. A folly constructed and abandoned at the edge of the woods. The vine hung down heavy over my head, brown and dry. The cabinet was locked tight. The collector's menagerie sealed. I touched the curved glass, tracing its protruding outline.

The sense of an ending again, but this time I felt not hope but anxiety, a falling downward.

I walked back through the walled garden, passing a group of the festival organizers and the Maidens. There was the smell of thick perfume, hairspray and aftershave as I squeezed past them on the path. They had dressed in their Sunday best to see us. A man with a cigar stood back to look at me as I went past. He was fat, rolls of flesh spilling over his collar. 'Cheer up,' he said and a few people laughed.

At the front of the house, the scene resembled something from a dream. There were balloons attached to stands, men leaning over cars doing the last of the polishing in the low light. A woman was lugging a crate of teacups out of the back of a white van. The school dinner ladies stood in a line on the steps leading up to the school, their green housecoats blowing gently around their knees. One of the nuns stood in the Maiden's Chamber above the door, surveying all. Just an outline of black against the red and blue window.

Other men were standing around a white convertible sports car, smoking and laughing and looking at the darkening sky, hoping for a dry day tomorrow. I saw the gulls overhead and felt like telling them: it will rain, rain on your parade. That's how it will be remembered. See how cheerful you feel about that.

There was the smell of burning leaves in the damp air again.

I tried to focus my thoughts, bring them back from the edge. Where would Victoria be? Did she know the letter had been found and that I was now the supposed author? That Mr Lavelle was leaving, banished? Helen had seen to it. I had to let her know I had tried to fix things. Mine was the act demanded of love.

I saw her again as she had been that first time in the summer house. The curled-up body, the glance that had asked me to prove myself. It had been there from the beginning. I didn't want to be her. I wanted to be with her. For ever. We shared a fate, and she must see that. There was an inevitability to us. A finishing of each other's story.

It was time to tell her.

A black bike was leaning against the side wall of the school. It was unlocked.

She would go to him.

To his cottage in the village.

She would rank her loves, like they told us Saint Augustine had preached. For when we sin it is only because our loves have become disordered.

And Mr Lavelle's name was before mine.

I had to tell her to erase it. Because it would be better that way.

I knew the road to the village from the journey to and from the school. It was dark now and the bike had no light. I cycled along the narrow lanes, past the dusky hedgerows, startling the occasional rabbit and fox with the fury of the bike and its squeaking chain.

I found his cottage easily. It was as Victoria had described, a gate lodge just on the edge of the village. A long driveway was behind it, leading to what must have been a big house. A light, covered in cobwebs, was lit over the front door. His car was nowhere in sight. I leaned the bike up against the wall and rang the bell. I thought I heard a noise inside but no one came to the door. The front windows were not lit up so I climbed over a low wall and went around the side. The back door was swinging open, a faint light reflected from within on to the grass outside, which was long and wet against my legs. A small bowl was beside the door. If he had a dog, he had never mentioned it.

'He feeds the foxes,' she said.

She gave me a fright. A disembodied voice in the gloom.

Victoria had been sitting unseen on a bench at the end of the garden, and now emerged from the shadows into the patch of light. She was wearing her uniform. I remember for some reason that gave me hope. Maybe she was staying.

And joy rose in me. Like it always did. And a mild forgetting, as if each time I saw her it was the first moment all over again.

'He's been told not to, but he still does it.' She walked slowly towards me. 'And isn't that just like something he would do?'

'Victoria, this week without you, it's been a nightmare,' I said, reaching out for her.

She stepped back, almost imperceptibly. I ignored it and reached out to hug her. She did not respond with any warmth. She felt cold, thin, like me. Like we were both empty, as if the truth of our unspoken love had left a gap, like the dead nun in the chapel.

'Can we go inside?' I said, feeling a sense of enormous relief to be with her. To have found her.

She nodded, watching me in the dark.

The kitchen was tiny, the lights were off, and the small light there was came from a log fire. The fireplace was large and covered in black soot; it stretched almost the length of the wall. The kitchen was tidy, no unwashed dishes or food in sight. There were hooks on the back of the door but nothing hung there. There were some books on the windowsill and a folder of papers on the table but nothing else to suggest who the occupant was, or indeed if there was one.

'He's not here,' she said, sitting on the chair by the fire, her legs hooked up under her in the shape of a Z.

'I was looking for you,' I said, sitting down at her feet.

I warmed my hands against the heat of the fire.

'Were you?' she said, staring at the flames.

'Yes, I told you this week has been. . .' I began, then leaned my head against the side of her chair.

I felt exhausted suddenly, like I might sleep.

She lit a cigarette.

'He's gone away, you know.' Her voice was quiet and low.

'They made him,' I said, turning to look up at her.

One side of her face was in darkness. She stayed looking straight ahead at the fire.

'They found out, the letter and the poem. . .' I could not bring myself to say it. I turned back to look at the fire. My eyes wanting to close.

'Oh that,' she said, stretching herself in the chair. 'That was just a joke.'

She leaned forward then and flicked some ash into the fire.

Of all the things I thought she would say, that was not what I expected. There was a lightness in her voice I recognized. It was the one we used when telling one another amusing stories about the downfall of others. The words rising slightly at the end.

'Why did you send it?' I said, watching the flames, my face growing hot.

'He needed to see I was serious, that there was no way back,' she said.

She was inhaling. I could hear the catch in her voice.

'Back from what?' I said.

The fire was hypnotic. I could see edges and cliffs, waves of orange and burning light. I remembered drying my hair in front of the fire at home when I was young and my mother telling me to count all the faces I could see in the flames.

'Our future, all our plans,' she said.

She moved in the chair, turned towards the window more fully, and her face when I looked again was in shadow.

'Last week at the party, he just wouldn't hear me properly, he didn't seem to understand, so I needed him to see there was no way back. If everyone knew about us. . .' She sounded confused, perplexed somehow.

'Did you fight?' I said.

'No, just. . . he wasn't sure about running away together,' she said. 'He was worried about the consequences, for me, not him.' She leaned down towards me and whispered in my ear, 'He always puts me first.'

Her breath was warm and smelled of smoke.

She sat back in the chair. I watched her with new eyes, looking for signs. Naively, I thought that maybe there was still a way of deciphering who she truly was.

'Why did you send it to Helen and Sister Ignatius and not just to him?' I asked.

Saying those words was an effort. I had to force them.

She shrugged her shoulders. 'To show Helen he is mine,' she said. 'I was sick of her.'

'But you knew Helen would protect herself, would blame him, us?' I said, moving my back away from the chair and looking up at her, to see her more clearly.

The fire was hot behind me.

She didn't respond, closing her eyes briefly. I felt she had been infected with fatigue also, the role too demanding now for both of us. Irony had drained our energy.

'Where has he gone?' I asked, staring at her.

'He rang me last night, he couldn't really talk. I think there were people here and it was late. But he said he would be going abroad and would write to me when he got settled, would send for me,' she said.

She was awake again. Her eyes wide open in the firelight.

I couldn't play along any more. It had all become too real. She had to stop loving him. I gripped her chair, summoning the energy to call her back. To call myself back.

'Victoria, he told me he wasn't going to run away with you, that you. . . you imagined it,' I said, moving closer again, kneeling in front of her.

She sat up slightly and started picking the fabric fraying at the corner of the armrest. My words were in the air around us.

She breathed in slowly, eyes not meeting mine but resting somewhere on the dark wall above the fireplace. She held the cigarette away from her.

'Helen said your parents made a complaint about him. The letter you sent, it's caused all kinds of shit, can't you see that?'

I touched her hand where it lay on the armrest of the chair.

She withdrew it and looked down at me. Her eyes were wide, the light from the fire reflected in them.

'I did not expect you, of all people, to speak to me like that; you know what we have, what we mean to each other,' she said. 'I would expect this of Helen, or my parents, but not you.'

She threw the last of the cigarette into the fire.

'I am worried about you. I just want to protect you, that's why. . .' I stopped and put my head down.

'Why what?' she said.

'Sister Ignatius asked me about the letter and the poem. I didn't want you to get into trouble so I said I wrote them, that it was a crush, just a crush I had, and he hadn't done anything wrong. I was worried that you were both going to be caught. . .'

She didn't speak for a moment, just went back to staring at the fire.

'You said you wrote it to protect me,' she said quietly.

'Yes, and him,' I said, an ember of hope burning in me.

She looked at me, alert, when I mentioned him.

Please, please understand.

'But I wanted it to be found,' she said. 'I wanted everyone to know. I wanted them to know that he wanted me and they couldn't have him, that Helen couldn't have him.'

This was not what she was supposed to say. She spoke as if it was a game. That lives weren't going to be changed.

'Do you love him?' she said, looking at me.

I felt stunned momentarily. I could not think of an answer to this. She didn't know me at all. It was astonishing and couldn't be true.

I shook my head vigorously. Again, she reminded me of a child, like she had on the stairs weeks ago, when she had asked me who my favourite author was. It was sort of a jolting lack of self-consciousness, or consideration for context.

'No, of course not,' I said. 'It's not him I love, it's. . .'

The words wouldn't come.

'Why did you ask him if we were running away then? Did you want him to stay? Do you want him for yourself?' Her voice was harsh.

She got up suddenly, nearly kicking me in her haste, and picked up a poker at the edge of the fireplace and began stoking the fire. Some sparks spat out on to the rug and she stepped on them, twisting her foot into the material. I moved back from the fire and sat on the chair opposite.

'You are really important to him, Victoria, but I don't think he meant to encourage you, to make you think that he was going to leave everything and run away with you,' I said.

She turned, her back to the fire, putting her face in shadow again.

'He was lying to you, Louisa, can't you even tell? Don't you know anything about him?' she said. 'He didn't want you to get into trouble, to have to lie for us, that's why he said that to you. Now he's gone, left everything. Isn't that evidence enough?

He's gone to set things up, get them ready. We are going to Morocco.'

She looked to the window then. As if another country lay out there in the dark of the garden.

'He's gone, Victoria, because he is in trouble; they are suspicious of him and don't want any scandal. They fired him,' I said.

It felt like our script had gone astray. We were reading different lines, the roles diverging.

She walked over to me, grabbed my arm and pulled me out of the kitchen and into the dark hall. She pushed open another door off the narrow hallway. Lit only by moonlight, it was a bedroom, a large, sheetless brass bed in the centre of the room. As my eyes got used to the dark I could make out a tall mahogany wardrobe against one of the walls, the door hanging open and all the clothes gone.

'I have been here, with him. In that bed,' she said, pointing at it.

I didn't want to hear. I felt a pain in my head and things slipping away, dissolving again.

'Maybe we should go, get back to school. Your parents are waiting for you,' I said, 'and I believe you, of course I do. I was only trying to protect you and him, that's why I said I wrote it. I knew, I knew you would need this time to lie low. And even when he said you weren't going to run away together, I thought he was probably just pretending.'

I lied and knew there was an air of desperation coming off me. But I was afraid of her there, in the moonlit room. I could feel a sickness in her. Did she not even remember telling me they hadn't been together? That she was waiting?

'You were never a good liar,' she said, pacing around the room. 'You keep contradicting yourself: you believe me, you don't; you believe Helen, then you don't. I don't know how I could have trusted you; I thought you were different.'

She looked disdainfully at me, the way Helen did. I was small and insignificant.

'This week has just been like this weird parallel world, where nothing seems like it should be. Two of the most important people to me have just disappeared and I've realized something, something important that. . .' I stopped.

We stared at each other for a moment.

Say it, tell her.

She sat then on the side of the bed for a second before lying down across it. And the moment was gone. And it was hopeless anyway. Her anger was a barrier to me.

'Don't you want to ask me about it?' she said, looking up at the ceiling. 'What it felt like, to be with him.'

The pain in my head travelled downwards, inflaming my neck and resting finally on my chest.

'The first time, I cried. I felt like I had given him something, something that was never going to come back and I would never be the same again,' she said.

He was there then, beside us. A spirit of passion and possibility. Enticing us. I could smell the smoke and the peat of the summer house. The glow of him.

I bowed my head.

'But after that, it was me who wanted more. We even did it at the swimming hole, in the grass, just before term began. . .'

I raised my eyes then, remembered the walk that first week, the three of us, and how she had said she hadn't been there in ages.

'If you loved him, why did you write the note?' I said.

The fact, the truth that could not be played away. Maybe it might anchor her, bring her back.

'Because, I told you, he was getting nervous about me, and whether I might back out. He wanted to save me from any trouble, or scandal. Just like you, really,' she said. 'I had to make him see. There needed to be something, something to show him the extent of my feelings. I wanted him to know that I would burn everything down. That I was willing to do that, that nothing matters except him.'

She sat up then. And she looked curious. Her eyes wide, the brows raised.

'You know, the two of you are kind of alike. He thinks so, he thinks you are lost. And he's lost. He told me he thinks about you, worries about you,' she said. 'It nearly made me angry, like I was about Helen, but then I realized, it's just who he is, he can't help opening up to people. He can see into their souls. I believe that now. He would never love someone like you.'

I could not be loved. And there was a part of me that agreed with her. That always agreed with her. I hung my head again.

'It will all work out, though, you know,' she said. 'It always does, you can't run from your fate. He is going to send for me, and we will forget all of this ever happened. Forget you, even. Because it was fate, the day in the hallway when he walked in.' She looked up at me then, noticed me backing out the door.

There is a chance that a feeling once felt will never leave you. Hearts are stronger than minds.

'We need to go back,' I said.

She was not herself and it scared me. The silence, the melancholy that I had pretended, imagined was something else. I saw it now. A part of her kept slipping away, drifting; she couldn't control it. She was a fantasy. And I felt like I had that evening in her house, like I could see us from somewhere else, a jump cut in reality. A moment so important that it escapes out and away from the normal flow of time.

She got up from the bed and followed me back to the kitchen. I would never tell. I could never tell her.

My love was a false and dark thing. Of dreams and the night.

I left the house and walked to the front of the cottage. I wasn't sure if she would follow me, but she did. The folder that had been on the table was under her arm. The light was still burning over the front door. I thought about going back in to switch it off but I didn't want to return. It had felt dead in there.

I cycled slowly, her weight heavy in front of me, partially blocking my view of the dark road back to Temple House.

There was almost no wind, just the vague smell of smoke in the distance. There was no mist. The road ahead was clear.

We said very little. My heart was on fire. She had given hers away.

Chapter Twenty-Nine

As I walked through the dark woods to the summer house on my last night there, I thought about not being loved. I regret that now. I could have done better. My life, short as it was, deserved better reflection and consideration than that. There had been more to it, I think.

If I had known that it would be the last night, what might I have done? Run far away from Temple House, demanded a different fate?

Might I have told my parents that their not loving each other did matter? We had once been a family.

Or should I have simply lain on the wet grass, looked up at the stars, lit a cigarette, and marvelled at the mystery of it all? At how it made no sense and then just did. At how there were rules to existence, principles underlying things, but you never saw them, or understood what they meant until it was too late.

And ranked my loves. I might have done that. The list that had no people on it whatsoever, for they were too disappointing. And loving them was simply too painful.

I knew, as I cycled away from his cottage, that I was back to the beginning, becoming the person I was before. The one who was never seen. It was there in the silence of the black trees and sky around us. The familiar, a reversion. The unseen once again. And I felt something hard settle inside me; something that had been fluid before was now solid. And it would never change again.

We arrived back at the school close to 6 p.m. The grounds were empty of all the visitors and the line of stalls and cars resembled something from a ghost fair. A few flags and white sheets on the tables were blowing in the light breeze. It looked like a place where the fun had suddenly stopped.

The lights were burning in the windows and we could hear the choir practising for their performance at the concert the next day. Victoria's parents' car was still parked at the side of the house.

Once off the bike, she looked tired and drained, the bravado and confidence of the cottage weakened slightly.

Maybe reality had emerged for her too on the ride home in the dark. The real world, of rules and consequences. But I doubted it.

I leaned the bike back up from where I had taken it earlier.

'You need to go in, Victoria. It will only be worse if you don't,' I said.

I could hear my voice, weak and spent, as if it was coming from far away.

Where was irony now when we needed her most? All shields were gone, all masks removed. No protection.

'You don't know how it feels to want something you can't have,' she shouted at me.

And I knew that the understanding I thought we shared was just another of my illusions. Another of the things I made up to get through the day. And I felt sure I would never be close to anyone again. Intimacy was a dream.

'Victoria, I am in trouble too, I need to go in,' I said. 'They are probably looking for me. I need to just face it and get it over with.'

The stoic me. The tenacious, sane me.

'Fine,' she said, 'but when you hear about me, find out what I do to myself, you will be sorry. You won't be able to live with yourself.'

I felt like grabbing her, shaking her. I wanted to wake her up.

'I did it for you,' I said. 'I got myself into trouble, for you. You wanted loyalty, you wanted us the same. I did that, I tried to become you. Can't you even see that?'

I knew she wasn't listening, not because she was cruel but because she just couldn't hear me, or anyone. She cared for no one but herself and Mr Lavelle.

She too was selfish in her love.

She said nothing but walked off into the dark, in that haughty way she had. Her shoulders straight and I'm sure her eyebrows raised. I watched her back for a second, disappearing off towards the gloom of the playing fields and the coastal path that eventually wound round to the summer house.

I opened the heavy front door of the school, which was still unlocked.

The smell of lemon. One of the cleaning ladies was in the hallway, kneeling on the floor. She didn't look up as I walked in. The choir were singing 'The Lord is my Shepherd'. We would be expected in church soon.

As I stood there, the silent woman continued cleaning almost at my feet.

If something about me was an error that could not be fixed, why was I staying?

All Victoria's talk of running away, when all along it was me.

I was the one who was supposed to leave.

I walked down the steps of the school and took the shortcut through the walled garden rather than follow Victoria directly. I was careful to stay in the shadows, avoiding any lit windows, as I did so. I didn't think I was looking for her. But I suppose I was, really.

The summer house had a small lamp on inside but when I looked in the door there was no one there. I always ended up here: the place you could walk away from but never escape. You would always return to its door. Like a limitless maze. The cabinet was locked and forlorn. I thought about breaking the glass and taking my skull. I had earned it.

I took some throws down from the shelf and began making a bed on the couch. I would call my parents from the phone box in the village in the morning. They would understand eventually. I could move to the town house with my mother, start in a new school. I would downgrade my aspirations, make them neat, not take up too much space with them. The lesson learned. I took off the locket Victoria had given me and laid it on the small table.

The door opened. It was Mr Lavelle. He was wrapped in a long grey coat, like something from an old army store.

'Louisa,' he said. 'I came to get some things, to find something, but. . .'

He looked around the room, a vaguely bewildered expression on his face.

'Are you looking for the picture? The picture you did of Helen? If so, she was here already. She beat you to it,' I said.

He looked startled; his eyes were large and liquid in the low light.

It was the hardness in me speaking. I needed to be cruel to someone.

'Louisa, please don't be angry,' he said, stepping towards me.

'Do you enjoy making people love you?' I said. 'Pretending they are special when it's all a game, not real?'

I was talking to him but also to Victoria.

He sat down on the couch then and held his head in his hands.

'I didn't do anything. I have spent the last two hours explaining this to. . .' His voice failed. 'I told you I didn't feel that way about her, you know that,' he said, looking up at me.

'Why are you even here?' I said, sitting beside him.

'I had a last meeting. I'll be leaving tonight. And I won't be teaching here again,' he said. 'I tried to explain the letter was not from you, that it was from Victoria and that she has been pursuing me, but I don't think they believe me. It's such a mess. I just wanted to. . . make you, all of you, think well of me. I needed this job.' He shook his head, and looked at the floor again.

He seemed pathetic to me then. Where was the castle and the yacht, the poetry?

He raised his head; there was fear in his eyes. 'They are monsters here,' he said.

There were monsters in all of us.

We said nothing for a minute. He turned to look at the empty grate of the stove. I looked at his profile. The movie star in the wrong show.

'Are you camping out?' he said softly, trying to smile, his gaze moving back to the couch and the throws.

I nodded.

'Where will you go?' I asked, leaning my head back.

'I'm not sure – far away,' he said.

He took my hand. 'It's a child's hand,' he said. 'So small.'

We were barely grown. Victoria and I.

'Thank you for trying to say it wasn't from me, the letter,' I said.

The tiredness I had felt in the cottage was back. He stayed holding my hand, staring at the stove. Where the fire should have been.

'You know she loves you, really loves you, Victoria,' I said.

Maybe I thought it would make him feel better.

'Yes,' he said.

He turned to look at me and for once I could meet his eyes.

We heard a noise at the door, felt the breeze enter the room and looked over. It was Victoria. She seemed dazed. He dropped my hand and stood up immediately.

'What are you doing here?' she said, her face red and raw.

He didn't respond but just stayed staring at her.

She turned slightly to look at me. And I thought of how it was the opposite of that first day. All recognition gone. We were strangers.

I got up and moved towards her.

I noticed her glance to the bed made up on the couch.

She stepped out the door then, into the darkness. She was shouting angry words at some mystery assailant into the night. We could hear her.

Mr Lavelle stayed still a moment.

'You need to follow her, find her, help her,' I said loudly, looking at him.

Be the hero, that's what she wanted from him. And it was how he always wanted to be seen.

He looked vaguely surprised at the suggestion.

'She could hurt herself!' I said, gesturing to the door.

He still didn't move.

'She's not well, she's confused,' I said, staring at him.

He nodded then. 'No, she isn't well.' He pulled the collar of his coat up.

'And what do you think might have made her that way?' I said.

He looked down for a second, at the floor, before returning my gaze.

'Come with me to find her,' I said, more desperate now.

'She needs to learn to live without me, she needs time to get better,' he said.

'Yes, I know, but she's not able to. Help me get her back to school and to her parents. Then you can disappear,' I said.

I will pick up the pieces, I felt like saying. After you have tired of it all and run away, I will mind her. Despite everything.

'I didn't. . . nothing happened between us,' he said. 'You do believe me?'

The pleading to want us to love him.

Fear when he realized we did.

'I don't know any more,' I said.

And I didn't know. Anything.

He shrugged his shoulders and I thought it meant he agreed so I walked past him out into the night.

She had gone into the woods that led to the top of the cliff. I could hear her shouting in the distance, fading in and out. I ran after her and for a few seconds I didn't look back. I just presumed he was behind me. It was only after I was well into the middle of the woods that I turned around, out of breath, and realized he hadn't come. No sound. There was no one there.

I walked on, slipping every now and then on the damp pine needles or tripping over a branch. I was in a dream world of shadows and fear, where behind every rock or bush there waited something desperate to take me. I thought of the collector, the one who owned the cabinet, and how he was supposed to have hanged himself in the woods. I imagined his body, decayed and rotting, dangling from one of the branches that touched my face. I would not have done it for anyone else, run into the woods in the dark. Only for her.

Her anger was my guide and I imagined her words left a trail of sharp pieces of glass on the forest floor. They would cut me if I wasn't careful.

When I reached the other side of the woods and emerged out on the cliff, she was nowhere in sight. I felt such relief to be away from the trees and the shadows that for a moment I just stared out to the sea, the sky clear, a sprinkling of stars. It was much colder here, as always; the moon pale and only partly visible. A waxing crescent.

I could not see or hear her but knew where she had gone. The swimming hole. Because that was the day when everything had seemed perfect. I remembered the sun as we walked through the woods that afternoon, and the air of celestial magnificence. The luxury and glamour of it, like a dream now. And the story that I wrote about it. The statues in the wood. Condemned to stand side by side, never able to see the other.

I pushed my way through the gorse bushes, scratching my arms, and found the path; the 'Hazard' sign buried under the leaves grazed my ankle and cut it. I reached down and could feel blood. There was no pain, though. My breath was heavy and it was difficult to hold my balance. The ground was slippy, large stones poking out from the undergrowth. The steps must be here soon, I thought. Everything felt sharp and rough.

I would bring her back, and it would all be over soon. I would tell her there was no shame in loving someone who didn't love you. I should know. Some people were not meant to be together. They weren't good for each other. They cancelled each other out. And everything that once was good became twisted.

I made my way down the broken steps, edging slowly to where I knew she must be. Sitting there in the dark, the sea far below. I thought about her friend, the one from before, the one she was going to run away with. I wasn't good enough. I hadn't been enough. There was something about me that made people not want me.

I made it to the bottom of the steps and lowered myself to the narrow shelf of cliff where I knew the swimming hole was. All rotting and rusted in the moonlight.

Victoria was a lean shadow facing out to the sea. The sky seemed bigger here, on the ledge. An expanse of black velvet shot through with stars.

The sea was a low, rhythmic hush in the dark below us. She turned.

'I thought he would come,' she said, shivering. 'I thought he would follow me.'

She didn't seem surprised that it was me.

'He can't; he wanted to, but I made him go. He has to leave the school.'

She turned away and went back to looking at the sea. I walked over to her. The edge of the cliff a foot or so in front of us. And for a second I thought she was a ghost, like she had gone already and I was just seeing her shadow.

'You made him go,' she said under her breath.

'Come back with me, Victoria,' I said.

And I meant it.

'To what?' she said. 'There is nothing left. It's happened before.'

'It mightn't be like that,' I whispered. 'Just a new school, a new start, away from him. He confused things, he played around, and it wasn't fair. He should have known better.'

She looked at me then. She was mesmerizing again. The girl whose imagination had been too vivid. Her body was shaking more visibly now, her arms crossed, holding her together.

'Why didn't he want me?' she said.

I wanted to say: I forgive you almost anything. And you don't need him. He is just a bit player and our lives are bigger than that. We can still go to Morocco and smoke thin cigarettes on a veranda and you will write a book about living without love or favour and I can paint pictures of the desert, and something else, something new, will take the place of this pain. And we will put the shame behind us.

And he doesn't matter.

I do.

It was what I wanted to tell her that first day, in the summer house.

That I never felt anything but whole when she was near.

She was shivering and pale. A part of her gone, and the cold getting in.

Her eyes were huge and filled with moonlight.

I saw her raise her arm and I thought to myself she will hold me now. She is so cold and I will warm her.

And in the future we will be ironic about it all.

When we have lives that are different.

We will remember this night, and think how foolish we once were.

I moved closer to her. I wanted her then. I would always want her, and it wasn't her mind, but all of her. She made me better.

She didn't take a breath or turn away, but just looked at me like she had never seen me before. Like I was a vision of something she didn't particularly want to see.

'You wanted him all along,' she whispered, her breath uneven in the cold air.

It was spoken like it was a truth she had long understood.

And then she struck me, hard and fast, across the cheek.

I saw her look at me with something resembling pleasure, as if someone else had to feel her pain.

I lost my balance and fell. And she didn't try and catch me.

I fell backwards into the night and on to the rocks on the ledge that was half hidden below. There was light, sharp and harsh. And noise, like a rush of voices in my ear.

My head hurt and then it didn't any more.

She stayed looking at me.

She spoke to the stars of my jealousy. And how some people could just never be happy for anyone else. It was not in their nature. She stretched her hands out into the dark, and they were not pleading for forgiveness but for him to return. But there was no one there and she knew it. He would never answer her call.

The universe was empty.

Except for me.

Then she kicked dirt over the ledge on to my body and walked away, back to the dark woods.

The Journalist

Chapter Thirty

I stopped the car around the corner from her office. We had barely spoken the whole way back. Victoria cried for most of the time. I didn't attempt to comfort her or ask any more questions. I kept looking straight ahead, the road the only thing that mattered. My phone lay between us in the car like a conscience, flickering to life every now and then.

She sat there for a minute when we got back to the city, her hand on the door, eventually opening it. We didn't say goodbye. I watched her walk away, her back slightly hunched against the rain, through the grey, wet street to her office, her home of steel and glass. A rubbish bin was overflowing on the path, and she had to weave her way past decaying sandwiches and rotten vegetables. A large black crow was perched on the roof of the shop as she passed, looking down at the spoils. It was strangely fitting. I felt no relief.

I let her go. I might have dragged her to a police station. I didn't. Shock, fear, a sense of unwanted responsibility maybe prevented me. I had shouted I would be calling the authorities.

It was the first thing I had said when she led me to the edge of the cliff. And she had looked relieved, almost grateful that the decision was no longer hers. Yet I didn't call. Minutes passed, the evening darkened, and I just sat there. The instinct to watch, to document the lives of others, stronger in me perhaps than anything else. I would call them later that night or early tomorrow. I trusted Victoria, and I knew she wanted it over. We would both face it all tomorrow.

I scrolled through the pictures of the school I had taken earlier. The empty house, and the cliffside where Louisa had lain, broken and alone all these years.

The orphan.

I opened the article on my laptop that was due to run the next day on Lavelle. I typed a new ending, one that would not reveal all yet, but toned down any sense of the pair having run away. Subtly erasing the notion that teacher and student ever had an inappropriate relationship, or that he had killed her. It was ambiguous and not my best work, but it would do. I wrote then a short line under it, saying the series would be concluding in the following days.

The heading should read – Louisa died for someone else's passion, another person's greed. But I don't get to write the headings. I emailed the revisions to my editor.

I looked at the photo that was going to run with it, the one that Victoria had sent me, the one of Lavelle leaning against the car. I wondered where he had gone and why he had never come back to say he had seen them that night in the summer house. It could have made all the difference. Victoria might have been implicated then. They could have found the body.

Strange and elusive, a hollow man after all.

I stayed sitting in the car, and rang my mum. She was making dinner for herself; there was the clash of pots and a kettle whistling. I asked her if I could come over, stay the night. She said nothing for a minute and I could see her, standing in her tiny kitchen, staring at the rain on the windows, worrying. I knew she would then, having caught sight of herself in the glass, stand more upright, shoulders back, before saying in a soft voice: 'Of course, that would be lovely. I will make up the bed.'

I needed to go home.

When I arrived at my mother's house there was a note on the fridge. It was her bridge night and she would be back later. I was exhausted and went to bed.

I dreamed of Louisa. She was standing in the hallway outside Victoria's office and people, lots of them, were crowding past her and up the steps that led to the roof garden. She looked tiny compared to them, and pale, and she was wearing that T-shirt, the one that said 'Enjoy the Silence'. She was mouthing words at me but I could hear nothing. After trying and failing to tell me something, she took a last look at me, then bowed her head and followed the others up the narrow steps.

I woke and it was 3 a.m. I thought about texting Victoria, even grabbed my phone and started typing. I was worried she would say I had made it all up or that she would run away. But then I decided against it. Nothing could be done until later and so I tried to find sleep again. But it was useless, I turned from side to side. Images of Louisa and the school coming and going in my head. I would ring Victoria early, then alert the police.

I sat up in bed and looked around my room. It had not changed much since I had left at nineteen. The white dressing table with the pink curtains covering the legs, giving it a look of some modesty. I had inherited it from a cousin and used to hide my journals under the curtains. Spanish dolls in elaborate, colourful dresses were lined up on the table part of it, still in their boxes, and perfume bottles, empty now, the scent long since evaporated. And some nail polish, bright candy colours.

The things you leave behind. The things that don't fit you any more. That you run away from.

I went to the window, pulled open the curtains and looked across the street to Louisa's house. There was a light on over the front door. New people lived there now.

I went downstairs and made warm milk with a generous helping of whiskey in it. I opened my laptop and started to describe the journey to Temple House with Victoria, the emptiness and the sense of desolation as we climbed down the steps to the swimming hole. The smell of decaying undergrowth, the slippery rocks and the rotting, strange sight of the pool, rusting and with leaves and creepers growing over it. A mausoleum to something, something from long before. A fantasy that had gone wrong.

I described Victoria, leading me to the edge of the cliff and saying, 'She is there because he always seemed to understand her.' And it made her cry with rage. And how she told me that she had left the skull from the cabinet and a heart-shaped locket on the ledge, and then she got on her hands and knees in the dirt looking for them but there was nothing to find. And I had to turn away then.

And how she kept saying, *Louisa follows me everywhere.*

I didn't hear my mother enter the room until she was beside me. I was far away. She had her thin red dressing gown around her and sat down at the table. Her face in the low blue light was lined and drawn. I spoke first.

'I found her,' I said.

She looked alarmed, and rubbed her forehead with her hand before placing it on her chin the way that she did when she was worried.

'I found her,' I said again.

'She's not lost any more then,' she said, reaching out to touch my arm, and she did a sign of the cross.

'No, she's not,' I said.

'Can you tell me what happened?' she whispered.

'Victoria, it was Victoria. Her friend. . .' I said.

She breathed in sharply.

'And the teacher?'

'No one knows,' I said.

'Louisa's mother,' she said then and bowed her head, 'her father.'

I saw him: shabby clothes, overweight, dragging the bins in.

And me afraid of his sadness and what it meant.

That things that shouldn't happen sometimes did.

My mother and I didn't speak much after that.

I looked at my watch: five thirty. I would ring Victoria soon.

She was expecting me.

Epilogue

The Orphan

How did my story unfold? I have had ample time to think about this. My life is like a book, one that is read too early when you are not quite ready for the ideas it contains and you put it back on a shelf. All that remains is some sense of a theme. And a promise to yourself that you will try to read it again, some other time.

Occasionally, I think my story was about shame and what it makes you do, both to others and to yourself. Then at other times I think it is about love and how it is a sickness. That love is a taking over of your being by something alien, someone else. It is a death of the person you were before. You do things you otherwise might not. You are not yourself.

Or maybe that is obsession, a love unuttered. I can't really tell which is which any more. Maybe there is no difference.

I knew immediately I wouldn't be coming back. I woke and saw the trees above my head at the top of the cliff; they were not bare and dark as they had been that December night but instead were full and luxuriant, with the fresh, almost luminous green of very early summer. The colour of hope, the colour that in the past had been a herald, falsely promising that this time my life would be different.

The ground felt like it had melted and there was tall grass, a breeze blowing around me, and every now and then it would caress my hands and legs. I heard the waves against the rocks, and a bird, I think a cormorant, let out a mournful cry somewhere high above me. I remember thinking I finally wasn't cold, and I had been cold from the day I had started at the school.

I felt instead just right. It was a perfect moment of idleness.
I could feel a fly on my arm, and the low hum of some bees. The
earth underneath me was soft, deep and dark, and it was caving
in slightly with my weight – not in a way that should alarm me,
though. It was welcoming and, like Alice in Wonderland, I was
being invited to fall into a new world where nothing seemed
quite as it was any more. But I wasn't scared. I owned it all, and
this new world was there to be moulded and shaped. I might
remember things, or not. I might create a completely different
history, tell a different story.

And I did that for a long time, until I couldn't any more.

There was no part of lying there that I wanted to change.
I think that's how I really knew I was gone. There was no
restlessness, no desire, no need or want. Just me lying in the tall
grass. I didn't notice my blood, of course, or the odd angle of my
head and how I was broken, every part of me. I didn't see any of
that. I'm sure that might have upset me or indeed someone else
if they stumbled on to me. I might not have looked so peaceful
then. But no one ever did find me.

It stayed summer, gentle and warm, and it never got dark.
I wondered about all the people who had died before me. I
imagined them as a long and endless chain of bodies and I
was holding their hands, the latest addition, and others would
soon come to join me. We could have wound around the earth
many times; there were more of us than the living. A not so
mortal coil. But I couldn't see any of them. I was just in the

grass. There was no God, unless he was peace and sunshine. And I could actually believe in that. It made more sense than all the prayers and the penance, the words of which I no longer remembered.

Memories came in and out of my head. They were neither good nor bad. Rolling down the hill in the field at the back of my parents' house. The drive up to the school on that first September day; the black wrought-iron gates and the crunch of the gravel under the tyres, the beginning of the end.

I made some things up too. It is Mr Lavelle who is with me in the forest that night. He came back. And we don't walk to the edge of the cliff and he doesn't strike me and I don't fall. Instead he takes my hand and we fly like birds over the sea, high and distant, up to the moon. And I forgive his frailty and his words. And then I don't. And I am on my own again.

If I am honest I see it as a life of nothings. Very little happened to me. My life had been small. There was nothing to even regret. It had all unfolded as it was supposed to. And the search for meaning had ended here, in a place where even the concept of meaning could not be imagined.

It seemed to me that perhaps living was the dream, the unreal fantasy. Or a long suicide, maybe, like Mr Lavelle had said. Something that would end. With some small highlights, things that were real. Like falling in love, although even that lasted only a short time. And it counted for little when you realized you were really part of eternity. Wind, light, air, sun, darkness, love, envy, and also hate. Death was the central story. Life was small in comparison. And in their own way, the nuns had probably tried to teach us that, but it had come out all wrong, twisted. They should have said, accept death, the endless nothingness of it, and then everything will be possible.

Sometimes I would see Victoria as she was on the first day. Just a girl in love with irony and looking to be noticed. Like I had been. But then she grows a head like the devil and I have to turn away. Because she took things from me.

I loved her but I never understood her.

Victoria was right about one thing: there are ghosts. I came to understand that the dead have one choice left when it comes to the living; they can offer them absence or presence. And the world becomes divided between the people who are haunted and those who are not. It's never their choice, it's ours. You can pray in a church all you want, or summon the spirits in a graveyard at midnight – it will make no difference. You have either been chosen to witness the return or not.

I left my parents to their grief and their guilt. I gave them my most complete absence and never went back to see how they coped. I set them free. To build something new, be something else. They didn't have to see me in the shadows. And I knew nothing of what became of them.

To Victoria and Mr Lavelle I gave presence. And without moving from the grass I let my mind find them whenever and wherever I wanted.

Mr Lavelle in sunshine, wavering heat. A white shirt and his hand shading his face as he looks into the upturned eyes of a girl. He talks of illusion and an oasis. At night he can't sleep in the hothouse of his white room, and instead he drinks and writes letters. Letters he never posts. And he watches the fan over his head and thinks about telling the police that he saw me that night, but then he is afraid and that takes over.

It doesn't last long, his sojourn in the desert. He reads poetry to people who can't understand him, he tells them he is a painter, that he is chasing the light. Then he touches an arm and messes things up. He dies on a dusty road, a glance that went too far. They buried him outside the village.

I was almost sorry for him then.

Victoria I watched for twenty-five years. She was moving in a world that became less and less familiar to me. She was my ghost and I, over time, became hers.

I watched her reading in the corner of the library in her new school, her chin in her hand, occasionally staring out the window; the school she went to after the doctors gave her pills. Or sitting at the back of a large amphitheatre with a man in a suit at the podium. She has piles of books in front of her and there is a boy beside her, tall and fair, a bit like Mr Lavelle. Every now and then, he writes something on her notebook and she smiles. I watched her on a train; I did not recognize the countryside that passed by the window. She was sunburnt and drinking beer from a plastic cup. There was laughter.

Once she was in a beautiful cream lace dress, standing at the top of the stairs of her house. I think she wanted to cry but she bit her lip instead. I wanted to touch her veil, pull it back, in case it would help her see me, her broken, dead friend. She wrote me a letter that day and placed it in the jewellery box that she kept under her bed. The box that has my essays and photos in it. I don't know what her letter said, I just heard her say my name out loud before locking the box. And she was scared, scared the way I had been that night, on the rocks in the dark. The night that I fell.

She gets older and thinner. She stands at street lights in busy cities, she stares out the window of her office at the tail lights of the traffic in the morning, when it is still dark. She eats dinner with people she doesn't like; women with downcast eyes paint her nails and when she gets her hair done she stares at herself in the mirror. The face that went to waste. She stands in front of people in dark suits and tells them what to think about something. They clap politely and take notes.

She sits on a shaded terrace with a white hat on. Like the woman in the portrait that hung in her hallway. The light is blinding. A dark head bends and leaves food on the table in front of her. She is in Morocco, and she is waiting for him. But he never comes. Because he never really existed. Not as she wanted him to, anyway.

And night falls, and she is always alone.

She can't sleep and drinks wine in her kitchen. Her head is bowed under spotlights and everything is shiny chrome and grey around her. She tries to be like everyone else but fails. She asks for forgiveness. And I can't give it.

She speaks of a journalist who wants to talk to her, talk about us. A journalist who has thought about me and seeks something of the truth, who wants to unearth our story, dig me up. Victoria cries out in the dark, saying this time she will. She will speak, she will atone and take the penance. It has been long enough. You can run from the consequence of your fate, run far even, but it will never cease its pursuit of you. You will falter, and it will be there, at your side, when you do. In weakness you will reach out, like a blind man in the dark.

I have seen her turn her head at twilight on the street, convinced there is someone there, or just before she switches on the light in her hall. Some part of her sensing me, just out of sight. She is never quite quick enough to catch me. And I'm never clear if this is her tragedy, or mine.

I think now my fear of being forgotten, of being eminently unmemorable, is what drove almost everything in our relationship. It was my weakness, my fatal flaw, and it turns out it was the strongest thing about me. The only thing about which I ever showed any resilience. Even now I want her to remember me. To be haunted. I push the limits of my watchfulness, invade her life to see if I can interrupt her, as she did me. It is both an act of hate and of love.

Then she came back to the school. After all this time. I see her staring at the front steps, looking up. It is all boarded up and there are yellow 'Danger' signs, weeds in the garden and the yew trees have grown so close they are touching. The stained-glass windows of the Maiden's Chamber are smashed. I wonder where all the students and the nuns went, the photos on the corridor to the church, all the girls caught in a moment in time. I imagine the pictures still hang there, covered in dust and forgotten in the empty house. And the cabinet of curiosities. I see the vine that grew around the door thick and strong, covering the empty glass case that had once looked as if it came from Versailles. And it covers nearly all the summer house now. Choking any of the ghosts that might remain there.

Victoria did not come alone; there is a younger woman with her. Together they walk past the empty tennis courts and take the path to the woods, and then to the cliffs, which is covered in briars, overgrown now and never used. They pass under trees and over rocks, they hold back brambles and low-hanging branches. They stop and look lost for a while; the woman sits on a rock and holds her head in her hands and Victoria looks out to sea. Then they find the last of the broken steps, barely visible, that lead to the swimming hole. And the woman looks pale and turns away from the sea and the sky.

They are coming to find me.

As I wait for them to climb down, I know it means all that is past will now have to be revisited again. I will have to go back, observe no more but instead retrace my steps and the path that led me here.

Victoria will need to face it too. No redemption. It is time for the fall. The scales need to balance. She is nearing the end. And it is right that it comes.

I choose this fate for her.

I open my eyes for what feels like the first time, again, just before she stands on the spot where she hit me. The waves crash below against the rocks and the sky is deep blue with clouds above my head. They are fluffy and white, like something a child would draw, and they race by, speeded up. In some ways time has passed and in other ways it hasn't. Yesterday lives on, an endless circular loop of remembering and forgetting. There is no line into the future for me, and not for her any longer.

I think how it is ironic that there should be darkness and light, even now. When she is old and her heart is sick. She has resolved so little, and is haunted by things that are no more. One love that never existed and another that did.

And now there is nothing left of me. Just dust and some teeth, inside a skull.

A fragment. Something for the cabinet of curiosities.

Acknowledgements

I'd like to thank Ivan Mulcahy, MMB Creative, for his belief and encouragement.

Aoife Casby for her sensitive early reading and patient, insightful advice.

The kind and wise at Corvus, in particular Sara O'Keeffc and Poppy Mostyn-Owen.

Family, friends and colleagues who should have doubted but never seemed to.

Ger, Ava and Charlotte for understanding I had to write this and making sacrifices so that I could.

And Ciaran Carty for publishing my first short story.